Cauvery Madhavan was born and educated in India and worked as a copywriter in her hometown of Madras. She moved to Ireland in 1987, arriving on St. Valentine's Day, and has been in love with the country ever since. Cauvery is a regular contributor to the *Evening Herald* and lives with her husband and three children in the beautiful county of Kildare.

THE UNCOUPLING

This is a dark and comic account of the disintegration of a marriage . . . Balu and Janaki Shankar are a typical, traditional, South Indian couple in their late fifties who have been married for thirty-three years in reasonable harmony. On their first ever trip to Britain their son is too busy to show them around and so books his parents on a sixteen-day coach tour of Europe. A two-night stop in Amsterdam leaves Balu struggling with an appetite for newly discovered sexual possibilities — with his wife Janaki. And as the coach hurtles around Europe, the Shankars' marriage disintegrates . . .

CAUVERY MADHAVAN

THE UNCOUPLING

Complete and Unabridged

ULVERSCROFT
Leicester

First published in Great Britain in 2003 by
BlackAmber Books Limited
London

First Large Print Edition
published 2003
by arrangement with
BlackAmber Books Limited
London

British Library CIP Data

Madhavan, Cauvery
  The uncoupling.—Large print ed.—
Ulverscroft large print series: general fiction
1. Married people—Fiction
2. Bus travel—Europe—Fiction
3. East Indians—Europe—Fiction
4. Large type books
I. Title
823.9'2 [F]

ISBN 1–8439–5099–5

Published by
F. A. Thorpe (Publishing)
Anstey, Leicestershire

Set by Words & Graphics Ltd.
Anstey, Leicestershire
Printed and bound in Great Britain by
T. J. International Ltd., Padstow, Cornwall

This book is printed on acid-free paper

For my father

Men can be men only if women are unambiguously women.

Deborah Cameron in
Feminism and Linguistic Theory

Acknowledgements

My immense gratitude to Jan Deitch, my editor, for her astute guidance and gentle wisdom, to my publisher for keeping faith with me, and to Alannah Hopkins for her very sound words of advice before I started on this book.

Heartfelt thanks are due to my mother, Bollu, to my friend Marie Carberry and to Jim Hodgetts for their help, insights and critical appraisal. My warm appreciation also goes to Siobhan Mullet, John Fitzpatrick and Aruna Mathur for all their efforts on my behalf, and to Sue Booth Forbes, for always being there — my sounding board at the end of the phone.

As for you, Prakesh my dearest, and Sagari, Rohan, Maya — may your patience go on and on.

Prologue

Rupinder Singh examined the two Indian passports. She had guessed right. They had arrived from *idli-dosa* land. Last in the weary queue that stood facing her, the Madrasi couple had for the past half hour served as her markers, the queue having been cordoned off behind them. With every slow and considered stamping of the passport in her hand, with every emotionless waving on of the owners, with every unspoken *'Next!'* that she ordered by merely looking up, Rupinder could see them doing the shuffle, getting closer and closer, nudging their hand baggage over the carpet tiles with the sides of their shoes. Their eventual arrival at her desk marked the imminent end of her shift as an Immigration Officer at Heathrow Airport.

Before she opened their passports, Rupinder glanced quickly along the row of a dozen or more immigration desks that stood steadfast and uncompromising, like the Thames Barrier, between the rising tide coming off the planes and London and beyond. John was nowhere in sight, his desk occupied by someone else. John Smith, who

1

had asked her out. Asked her *in*, actually.

He was going to cook her a curry.

'Do you like it hot?' he had asked.

She had nodded uneasily, remembering her father's reaction from the night before.

'John Smith? What sort of a *pheeka* name is that? Too ordinary. Too bland. Like boiled beef, not spicy enough.'

Rupinder had ignored her father. He was taking his amateur interest in reading faces a bit too far. He was now theorising about people's names! And anyway, what would he know about beef?

Now with a mental shake of her head, she turned back to examining the pair of passports in her hand. Rupinder prided herself on being conscientious, thorough. Mr and Mrs Shankar stared back at her woodenly from their photographs, their chins tipped upwards no doubt at the request of the photographer, who at the very last second would have asked them each to sit straight, smile and please look up. They look different in person, Rupinder thought as she eyed them in the flesh across the chest-high counter.

The prominent bands of grey that ran through Mr Shankar's side-parted and neatly slicked-back hair seemed to have been nearly lost to the camera in the dazzling coming

2

together of brilliantine and flash. Though his lower lip was fleshy and drew one's attention immediately, he was on the whole a pleasant enough looking man. Mrs Shankar looked younger than in her photograph and despite her obvious tiredness, slightly crushed and dishevelled sari and the several strands of hair that had escaped from the loose bun at the nape of her neck, she radiated a quiet dignity which could very nearly be passed off as beauty. Curiously enough, she looked vaguely familiar. She reminded Rupinder of someone she hadn't seen for a long time — maybe an aunty-*ji* in distant Punjab, or was it closer to home? Did she look like an ex-schoolmate's mother or one of the ladies who worked with Rupinder's father Mr Singh at the Drop-in Centre? Rupinder looked down, her eyes lingering a while on Mrs Shankar's photograph. However, it was clear the lady had never travelled out of India before; the passport was newly issued and the pages crisp and clean with no record of her ever having arrived anywhere.

When she looked up again, Mr Balu Shankar was smiling weakly back at her. 'The visa is on page six.'

Mrs Janaki Shankar shifted awkwardly from one foot to the other.

'Her visa, that is my wife's visa, is on her page five.'

'The purpose of your visit, sir?'

'Our son is driving down from Norwich to pick us up. The purpose? The purpose is enjoyment, tourism and family reunion. It will be cold but we will manage. Socks, gloves and balaclava — we have brought it all. Our daughter-in-law has already purchased thermal underwear for us. We will manage.'

Rupinder flicked through the pages of Mr Balu Shankar's passport. These South Indians with their *aiyaiy-yo* accent were all the same. Yunjoyment, yunderwear and so bloody yover-confident just because they spoke English.

'How long do you plan to stay, sir?'

'Returning end October.'

Yend Yoctober. Rupinder smiled as she carefully stamped and then briskly initialled the passports. She waited patiently while Mr Balu Shankar checked both passports, pausing briefly on each of the pages that she had stamped, and then slipped them into the inside pocket of his rather limp blazer, buttoning them in firmly. Seconds later he patted his chest to double-check the passports were still there. Finally, with hand baggage slung on their shoulders, Mr and Mrs Shankar turned and walked away and then,

4

barely a few steps on, looking up at the multitude of signs and instructions that hung from the ceiling, they hesitated.

'Yelevator,' Rupinder said to them as she stepped out of her booth and straightened her skirt. She pointed left. 'It will take you to baggage reclaim.'

Yand then to customs yand then yonwards to yarrival, she thought grinning as she walked away in the other direction, digging in her pocket for the small piece of tissue in which she had, this morning, so hurriedly wrapped a plump green cardamom and a clove. She slowed down for a moment to carefully pick the two spices out of the folds of the disintegrating tissue and then slipped them in between her lips. In seconds her mouth was awash with the fragrance of crushed cardamom seeds and her breath tinged with the sharp freshness of the clove. Rupinder quickened her step again. It was time to find John Smith.

1

Janaki lingered upstairs, tipping her head to one side and then the other, vigorously rubbing her damp hair between the folds of the large towel. For all its fluffiness it wasn't absorbent at all, not like the thin cotton *mundus* she had at home. It was difficult to believe she was here, a mother-in-law in her son's house. She could hear them downstairs, father and son talking. She frowned in concentration as she combed back her hair and then, peering into the small mirror that she had placed on the windowsill, she deftly gave herself a centre parting with a couple of quick flicks of her wrist. She began to work the knots out of her waist-length hair section by section, running the pink plastic comb through the tangles, her eyes closed in a vain attempt to shut out the self-inflicted discomfort.

Balu had been adamant about bringing the stainless steel folding mirror. There were certain things he just would not travel without and Janaki had never been inclined to argue with him about his particular idiosyncrasies. He had insisted on packing nearly a week ahead and, in his usual fashion, he had sat cross-legged on the floor, in front of the opened suitcases, determined as always to be orderly in his method and economical with the limited space. From this position, he was able to mutely claim a helpless inability to fetch anything, while at the same time vociferously exercising his veto over things that she handed to him, disallowing what he thought was too heavy or totally useless, but eagerly finding room for what he considered were essentials. As he packed, Janaki passed on to him, one after the other, his concertina-style Tamil-English *Year at a Glance Calendar* which he insisted would keep him informed about goings-on in Madras, his wooden-handled folding umbrella, his telescopic walking stick for use against dogs and his ultra-slim retractable torch.

And then, fully anticipating what her husband was going to do and say next, she had immediately busied herself around their bedroom. As he held the umbrella at arm's length and ceremoniously clicked a button to unfurl it with a flourish, she folded the selection of drip-dry shirts and Terylene trousers that he had picked for the journey and left at various points in the room — on the bedstead, hooked onto door knobs, cupboard handles and window latches, and even draped on the domed wooden cover of her precious Singer sewing machine.

'Japanese mechanism so it will never fail. I knew that when I bought it eight years ago. Didn't I tell you then that it was the ultimate in compact umbrellas? Fail-safe and user-proof. User-proof I tell you, Janu, is the most important feature. How many people would be careful like us? Still, this model would have lasted with anybody, yes anybody. Bar that old oaf. How many umbrellas has he ruined? As many as you have ever given him. Oaf, ace oaf, number one oaf. Now don't say anything, Janu, because I know already what you are going to say. Just look at this, look at the way it glides back so smoothly. Mind you, there is no friction at all, just super smooth movement back to the folded position. I bought the ultimate umbrella.' He placed it in the suitcase, shifting it this way and that till it sat snug amongst his cotton vests.

Janaki had given him a couple of shirts at that point but he laid them on the bed behind him and looked at her intently. 'So, have you arranged for him to sell the milk? Will the old fool know what he owes you at the end of the six weeks? Just cut it from his salary if he tries any tricks. Oh, don't say anything. I can see by the look on your face that you are going to try to lecture me.'

Janaki was frowning. Why did Balu have to say such things? 'I wish you wouldn't call Patta names. He is nearly seventy years old, maybe even seventy-five. And you know well that he doesn't fool me for a minute. I just let him get away with a *rupee* here and a *rupee* there. Poor man. He has nothing to give in return but his blessings. Think of him as a *hundi* in a temple. The more you donate, the more you and yours will get.'

Balu had drawn his breath back in exasperation. 'You bring God unfairly into the conversation and then expect a reply?'

But it was a good-natured withdrawal and they had continued to work companionably with Janaki folding clothes, wrapping his shoes and her *chappals* in sheets of newspaper and handing them to him. He had been extra careful packing the folding mirror, pulling the balaclava over it first and then wrapping the scarf snugly around it.

Now, as she combed her hair and peered into the mirror once again, she was glad that he had packed it. She had been reluctant to leave the shower, lingering long past the need, huddled within its steamy confines, not even wanting to put a hand out into the cold beyond the radius of the hot water to replace the soap on its rack. When she pushed back the shower curtain, she had found the mirror

10

completely fogged up and her attempts to wipe it had only made matters worse. Now it was smeared with trails of soggy little bobbles — the remains of toilet paper that had disintegrated as she had wiped back and forth — and her reflection, though visible, was very fuzzy. Yes, the folding mirror was going to be very useful every morning.

Janaki reached for the maroon leather pouch on the bed and unzipped it. She could smell the newness of the plastic lining immediately. Like this pouch, all the complimentary gifts from the Golden Life Chit Fund had that same fresh plastic smell and she had over the years smelt them all. Years ago, before Balu had become the Manager of the Adayar branch, he had been in the habit of surprising her once in a while with a stealthily purloined sample of the latest consignment of giveaways that had been delivered to the branch.

'They owe me one,' he would justify as he handed it to her. 'Why only reward customers? Reward staff as well is what I say.'

He would make small impatient noises as he waited for her to first take the item out of its box and then carefully open the plastic or paper wrapping. But he would nevertheless leave it to her to do, as she was far more dexterous, and when they had together

11

examined and taken in deep breaths of the smell of newness from the desk set, key chain, calendar or imitation leather wallet, she would meticulously go through the whole process in reverse, sealing the item back into its box. It would then be placed on top of his wardrobe, joining a cache of other complimentaries that would be dished out, on a need only basis, to people of importance.

The telephone linesmen who were normally difficult to appease, were strangely partial to diaries, while the man at the ration shop had almost begun to think it was his birthright to receive from Balu the yearly wallet, with a crisp five-*rupee* note in the new replacement to ensure he had an auspicious start to his earnings. Any desk sets, calculators or staplers were saved for the more difficult and cranky of their son's schoolteachers, while oddments like shoe-horns, Thermos flasks or magnifying glasses would always be appreciatively accepted by the unexpected relative visiting from the village. Balu would never hide the fact that these were complimentaries brought from work, but when it came to relatives he couldn't resist adding, 'I had kept this for an occasion, but how could I let you return empty-handed?'

Of course, all that was years ago. Now her

husband Balu was the Manager and he could ring up the Stores Assistant in Head Office and ask for the double compartment leather pouch, usually reserved strictly for Ten-Year Fixed Deposit customers, to be sent for his personal use to the Adayar branch. In fact, the occasion being what it was — their first journey abroad — Balu had asked for two and he had given his wife the maroon one. Janaki rummaged around in the new pouch for the tiny tin of homemade black kohl, twisted the cap off and place the tin on the windowsill. She picked up the mirror, holding it to her face and then, dipping just the very tip of the index finger of her right hand into the kohl, she gently pulled down her lower eyelid with her middle finger and ran the black paste expertly along the rim. She kept her eye closed for a few seconds and then repeated the process with the other eye, finishing by casually wiping the little bit of excess kohl still on her finger off on her hair. Her hair was still very damp and as she ran her fingers briskly and repeatedly through it, separating the thinning strands, it struck her that she had not, unlike Balu, had the same inclination to quickly shower and change and rush downstairs.

Putting the mirror back on the windowsill, she caught a glance of the sheen of sweat that had appeared without any warning on her upper lip and around her brow. It was almost as if her body was beginning to exude back the heat it had absorbed during her prolonged shower. She dabbed at it with the back of her hand and then sat down heavily on the bed. It was unnerving not to have anything to do. Even as she had showered she twice found herself straining to hear the pressure cooker, trying to count the number of whistles it had let off. Thinking of that fleeting lapse into her Madras routine made Janaki smile. The momentousness of her very first journey abroad could not obliterate a habit acquired over a lifetime. Balu liked his *parapu* cooked just so — soft but not mushy, the grains of lentil had to still be distinct, not boiled into a thick paste — and regardless of what else she made, he had to have his *parapu* every day, at the start of every meal, along with *ghee* dribbled into the well that he would make in the small mound of rice. Counting the whistles from the pressure cooker was vital. Four whistles and it would be just right, but anything over five meant that she would have to relegate the lentils to make into something else. The fourth whistle was a signal to call out to Muthu in the kitchen. Muthu, the servant maid, was not to be trusted entirely and was known to have once let at least eight whistles go before turning off the cooker.

Why did I have to think of that unpleasant day now, thought Janaki, sighing as she got up and shook loose the folds of the silk sari that lay on the bed. As she tucked the ends of the sari into her petticoat, draping and pleating the five metres of silk with a practised hand, she could almost picture the panic on the old man Patta's face that day, as she had alighted from the auto rickshaw. He got to the point straight away.

'Eight whistles, Amma. She let it go for eight whistles.' Once that initial bit of information had been divulged, like a problem shrugged off, his face assumed its normal blank façade and he shuffled back to the shade of the verandah where he squatted on his haunches and carried on with his mid-morning enterprise.

Janaki knew that he had more to say and that Patta had affected a retreat in order to draw her to the furthest corner of the verandah of her house where Muthu would not hear him, a corner that he had begun increasingly to consider his own. There, surrounded by his hoard of the previous day's used milk sachets, painstakingly collected from almost every household in the neighbourhood, a pair of scissors, a dirty rag and a large pock-marked and pitted aluminium basin filled with brackish water from the garden tap, the old man waited, dramatically holding his peace, while Janaki haggled over the fare with the rickshaw driver.

Patta was a part-time servant with no fixed remit, an errand-boy when she needed one, her inefficient gardener and an unofficial watchman for the house when he had nothing else to do. He got more respect than most servants for he was old, older than her father would have been, had he stayed alive. Janaki could never quite remember when Patta had progressed from his spot under the young mango tree outside the gate to the relative comfort of the verandah nor even whether it had happened on one day or if it had been a slow stage-by-stage incursion. Not that he lived on the verandah of course — Balu would never have allowed that. For Patta it was nothing more than a dry platform on which he could get on with his small enterprise, a refuge from the stray dogs that used to plague him under the mango tree, drawn by the smell that clung to the sachets, eager to bury their noses in the plastic half-litre bags and lick off any remaining drops of milk.

On the verandah however, Patta could take his time cutting the sachets open fully, rinsing them inside out in the basin and then wiping them dry. When he had finished counting the bags he would cut a thin sliver of a plastic ribbon off one of them and then, rolling up the bags tightly, he used the plastic to truss up the bundle securely. At the end of every week Patta sold the plastic bags to the proprietor of the Ganesh Refuse Mart who sat comfortably on the floor of his shop, in front of an enormous weighing scale, amidst neat piles of empty bottles sorted by size and colour, tin cans, plastic cartons, old magazines, newspapers and assorted bits of copper, lead and iron ware. Patta would count aloud in unison with the proprietor, who clenched the plastic bags between his toes and flicked the sachets between a finger and thumb, occasionally stopping to moisten the latter liberally against his tongue when the going got slow.

The first time Janaki had realised that Patta was getting paid one *paise* less per sachet than the Ganesh Refuse Mart's regular rate she was very indignant. Balu had insisted that she must not get involved.

'What do we know about the wholesale rates for plastic? Recycling is a complicated business. We are world leaders, we Indians recycle everything.'

He had continued, slapping the table with

gusto, 'Even our own selves. Of course, Janu, cheats prevail even in the cremation grounds. They have been known to half cremate bodies, dousing the flames when the family have left, using the same pyre for two to three bodies in succession, and when the poor unsuspecting relatives come to collect the ashes, what they get in the pot is a mixed fry. A nation of cheats — one cannot even die in peace. As for that old man of yours, rates are rates and we must not upset the natural balance of these things. Tomorrow if the *bania* at the Refuse Mart takes offence at our interference and stops buying our old papers and bottles, you will have to pay to take it by rickshaw to the fellow next to your sister's house!'

An hour later, when Balu returned from his regular evening constitutional Janaki heard him call out to her from the gate.

'I made certain enquiries. Just for your satisfaction, mind you. The *bania* lets Patta sleep in front of the shop at night. It is well lit, out of the elements, and there is enough dry concrete for the old man to stretch out in comfort. I tell you, Janu, these *banias* — business is in their blood. Would we ever think of deducting rent in such a subtle fashion? This is what I was trying to explain to you earlier. It is best not to disturb the natural balance of things.'

Why all these old memories now, Janaki wondered, shaking her head. She thought again about Muthu, who thirty-six hours earlier had been dramatic in her goodbye, swaying slightly, about to wail, holding back only because she had spotted Balu coming through the door.

'Amma, don't forget us,' she said, holding the crumpled end of her sari against her face.

'Enough of your drama, Muthu, we are gone only for a few weeks.' Balu was brusque with her, the way he had been ever since the incident nearly six years ago with the *parapu* and the eight whistles of the pressure cooker. Even after that length of time he would not trust her entirely.

He had been angry even with Janaki. 'Today she was flirting with that good-for-nothing who works for the neighbours and she forgot the *parapu*. Tomorrow if she forgets her good sense, where will she be? Where will *we* be? We are responsible for her, Janu. What will I tell her father if that rascal next door gets the only thing he is after? The trouble is the poor have no morals — no morals, is what I say.'

Janaki's own anger at Muthu had some-what diminished after the immediate and severe dressing down she had given the servant girl. Watching Balu bristle she regretted telling him the day's events as soon as he came home. She was angry with herself — she should have known better; she should have waited for a few days, told him the whole story but in parts. Instead, she was now going to have to stand by while his anger took its course, meandering along slowly at first, rapidly gathering momentum as he pointed out one aspect of the problem and then another, and finally going over the edge, thundering down, out of control.

He had called out to Muthu himself, questioned her angrily as she stood in the doorway, lectured her on the unspeakable dangers of being misled by the young lout of a manservant next door, warned her that he would be writing to her father and by now consumed with fury, had directed the tearful girl to look at Janaki.

'Do you see the worry you have caused Amma? It is written on her face. She who has looked after you as her own, trusted you as her own.' Balu had paused dramatically and walked to stand beside Janaki. 'Come and fall at her feet and beg forgiveness like you would of your own mother.'

Muthu had needed no encouragement. Sobbing and eager to show her remorse and just wanting it to be all over, she had prostrated herself in front of Janaki, clutching at her ankles.

'Amma, Amma.'

Even now, years later, simply thinking back on that moment upset Janaki. It was a display of absolute power followed by an act of total subservience, and she had felt distinctly uncomfortable about it. It didn't matter that Balu had not demanded that sort of servility for himself but rather, had channelled it pointedly in her direction, making Janaki the reluctant object of the deference.

Her sari draped to her satisfaction, and the pleats precise, Janaki placed her leather pouch next to the folding mirror on the windowsill and then hung her towel on the already cold radiator. How quiet and still it was in her son's house! There had been many, many days in the thirty-three years of her marriage that she had yearned for this kind of peace, dreamt of having nothing to do, nobody to give instructions to and no one to take instructions from. Now that the moment had arrived, it didn't feel like anything special and she was unable to get rid of that niggling feeling of urgency, of having tasks to finish before Balu came home.

How well my husband knows me, she thought to herself, smiling as she walked out of the bedroom and headed down the stairs. Balu's pride was obvious to everyone when he claimed that his wife would never learn to relax.

★ ★ ★

Balu was not a superstitious man but, unlike most people, he could spot an omen when he saw one and this, he was sure, was most certainly an auspicious one. The last time he had seen Janaki come down a flight of stairs wearing a sari very nearly the same colour as this one, her still damp hair knotted in an identical fashion, the ends gathered up and loosely tied into a ball, had been the very first time he had seen her. He remembered well the feeling of self-satisfaction that had come over him, the sense of accomplishment, of a job well done, a piece of good fortune well-tracked and unearthed.

2

If Balu had to start at the very beginning, he could trace his thirty-three-year-old marriage back to his very carefully worded matrimonial advertisement in *The Hindu* newspaper, the advertisement itself being the culmination of a fortnight's effort of trying to fit into forty words his requirements in a wife. He had initially allocated thirty words to the task, leaving the remaining ten words for a brief résumé of himself. But he had found himself overwhelmed by the choice of adjectives, and unable to shake off 'fair and beautiful', yet unwilling to follow the standard formulas of the *Brides Wanted* section, he decided to first work on describing himself.

He started with 'broadminded' and 'understanding', writing the words one below the other with calligraphic flourishes. He thought of 'young' and 'handsome' but this time, jotted the words lightly on the margin of the foolscap sheet that he had placed on the laminated clipboard that he balanced on his lap. He had bought the dozen sheets of foolscap and the laminated clipboard on impulse after having left the offices of *The*

Hindu, having made tentative enquiries about the cost of a classified matrimonial. The clipboard and the foolscap seemed a part of the natural progression that he should make after putting forward an enquiry of that nature.

Balu had been hailed by the half a dozen or so scribes sitting in the shade of the *neem* trees, on the pavement outside the newspaper office. Business was brisk and yet they stopped what they were doing to call out to him from behind their low wooden desks, where they sat surrounded by their own clipboards, rough and fair paper sheets, blotting paper, ink-bottles and fountain pens, the tools of their trade.

'You want job application, impressive bio-datas?' they called out.

'Birth, death and marriage notices? Shorter is cheaper!' They beckoned him with their pens.

'House for rent? Premises for sale? Within ten words!'

'Private tuitions offered or wanted? Guaranteed response!'

'Special rates for palmists, astrologers, numerologists!'

Balu ignored them all and they fell silent one by one as he walked away down the road towards the bus stop. The scribes went back to their flowery but economical compositions on behalf of the not so literate clients who squatted opposite them, in front of the weather-worn and ink-stained desks.

I am honour bound to do this entirely by myself, Balu thought as he waited for the bus. The chosen forty words, for that was all he could afford, would initiate his quest for a partner in marriage and to actually pay someone to be part of this decision making would, he felt, defile the process at the very start. But he couldn't resist the clipboards that hung festooned, omen-like, over the entrance of the 'Sita Stationery and Fancy Goods Store' right behind the bus stop. Sitting in the bus on the way home, he pulled out his purchase and ran his hands appreciatively over the laminated picture of the Taj Mahal that was repeated on both sides of the board. The clip and its spring were satisfyingly stainless steel and the foolscap that lay in the brown paper bag was crisp, clean and white.

Balu had never thought that working on the wording of his advertisement would take so long. But he was unwilling to go back to the newspaper office to place it for publication till he was totally satisfied with every single word. He was not as concerned with the actual words and what they meant, it was the implications that lay behind individual words that caused him to agonise. He had gone over the limit of ten words that he had allocated to himself, finding he needed the assistance of three or four more to arrive at a near-satisfactory self-profile.

Words were placed in margins and then brought out for trial runs. After some thought Balu decided that 'sober with traditional values' was more important as a wifely requirement than as an essential husbandly virtue, and the phrase was relegated for use in the latter half of the advertisement. He toyed with 'well-placed' and 'salaried', finally putting them next to each other, where they stayed one complementing the other. Some words like 'wheatish complexioned', 'healthy' and 'enlightened attitude' remained on the sidelines. Some like 'cosmopolitan' were crossed out soon after they were written. Balu had the uneasy feeling that 'cosmopolitan' carried with it some rather ambiguous implications — beef-eating, card-playing and divorced being the few that sprang to mind. No, 'cosmopolitan' he decided would certainly put off a lot of prospective alliances.

Amongst the pledges that he proudly put down were 'early, decent marriage' (though he did debate substituting decent with 'simple') and 'no demands'. He underlined 'no demands' several times, wondering if he would have to pay extra to have the two words printed in bold. He was aware that there was a danger that a 'no demands' promise would be interpreted as a signal that there was possibly something physically wrong with the prospective groom. A leg lost to polio, a glass eye or worse — impotence, for why else would a man forsake a dowry? Balu hastily added 'no impairments' to his profile list. In this eager yet indecisive limbo he remained for a whole week, torn between words and their meanings and possible interpretations. His pocket dictionary, which he had barely used during his college days, was now well thumbed, having accompanied him to work and back.

In the week that followed his first visit to *The Hindu* offices, Balu had initiated some casual enquiries at work. He had asked Perumal, the other apprentice accounts clerk, with whom he normally whiled away the lunch-hour, what sort of woman he would want to marry. Perumal, who had cultivated a reputation for himself amongst the girls in the typing pool, a reputation based purely on the brazenness of the lingering looks that he would cast in their direction as he dropped and picked up documents and files, didn't have to think before he answered.

'A girl who will look after my parents, obey them, respect them.'

'Why? Considering you don't!' laughed Balu, stirring his milky coffee and then pouring some into the saucer to let it cool a bit.

'You know I never smoke in my father's presence. Or drink.'

'That's what I mean — where's the respect? Disobedience is disrespectful.'

Perumal folded the last limp piece of the *dosa* on his plate into two and proceeded to wipe the plate clean of any chutney and *sambar* that remained. Then with his mouth full he looked Balu in the eye, shaking his head as he spoke.

'What would you know? When you have no father, where is the opportunity for disobedience? You probably never find the need to assert yourself.'

'Okay, so you want an obedient girl, but is that all?'

'What's this about? You don't even have a sister to marry off. In fact, because you don't have a sister I'll tell you what else I want.' He paused to light a cigarette. 'She must have mangoes, ripe round ones, and she should be shameless.' He paused again, concentrating on folding and refolding the strip of silver foil from the top of the cigarette box till he had

28

improvised a shiny toothpick. 'I don't think I am asking for too much. What do you say?' He suddenly leant forward across the table, the toothpick dangling from the corner of his mouth. It fell into Balu's saucer of coffee as Perumal whispered loudly, 'It's you, isn't it? You are looking for a girl, a wife.' He paused to fish the toothpick out of the saucer, flicked the coffee off it and stuck it back into the corner of his mouth. 'You are right, you know, not to leave it to your mother. Mothers and sons don't look for the same things in a wife. Believe me, your mother won't be looking at the size of the girl's mangoes. Not unless,' and he began to snigger, 'not unless the girl's father has an orchard.'

I have no one to blame but myself, thought Balu as he tried to blot out the lewd advice being handed to him. 'Is nothing sacred to you?' he complained. 'It is a wife I'm looking for, not a whore.'

As they walked back to the decrepit grey building that housed the offices of the accountancy firm to which they were apprenticed, Perumal broke the awkward and quite unfamiliar silence between them.

'Don't take offence. Have you been looking long?'

'Haven't even started.'

'Will you advertise or consult a broker?'

'I'm leaving it entirely to my mother,' lied Balu with a shrug, angry and not wanting to discuss the matter with Perumal for the moment.

So it was with a degree of reluctance that Balu broached the subject with Mr Nath, his section supervisor. Mr Nath had begun with a series of gentle belches, saying by way of explanation that his wife was an exceptionally good cook.

'She is in the family way again and these days my tiffin is full of strange items. She likes me to guess what the ingredients are. Keeps her happy if I get it right. So, Balu! You are thinking of marriage? The girl is not important, the family is. A good family breeds good girls. Make sure she has plenty of sisters. Women find sisters are most useful. If a wife has no sisters you will be burdened with all her problems and yet Balu, and yet, mark my words, you have to make sure that your wife's sisters' problems don't become yours. Keeping a reasonable distance from the wife's family, remaining the complete master despite the temptations to be otherwise — it is not easy.' He looked thoughtful as he belched apologetically again. 'You must better your prospects, sit for the Public Service exam, for instance. In any case, it looks better on your marriage bio-data. Tell the broker to say that you are sitting for the Banking Services exam as well. That always impresses the girl's side.'

That evening, Balu retrieved 'well-respected family' from the margins of the foolscap and incorporated it into his list along with another quality 'accomplished' that he had spotted in a caption under a photograph in the weekend edition of *The Hindu*. 'The employees of South India Engineering congratulate their Chairman on the marriage of his eldest son to the accomplished daughter of the Managing Director of the Ramco Group.' He liked the idea of sharing a common bond with the eldest son of a doyen of industry.

The evening before he was to place the advertisement, he showed the neatly copied out thirty words to his mother. He rarely interrupted her fervent daylong prayers that had become very nearly her only occupation after the sudden death of her husband. Her low, murmured incantations reverberated mournfully through the small house, a constant reminder to the deities of her misfortune, lest they should forget and want to burden her with anything else. When his widowed mother immersed herself in her devotional dialogue with a plethora of gods and goddesses, Balu, then still in school, discovered a new freedom.

With the maternal eye suddenly cast in another direction, he found himself master of his own time and thoughts. His mother did not entirely abandon her duties to him, for he continued to be fed and clothed in more or less the same fashion. She remained content with his average academic performance and unquestioning when he chose to do accountancy at the suggestion of his headmaster. It did not surprise Balu that, when he gave her the news about getting his first job as an apprentice clerk, she had hurried away without a word to him, instead rushing immediately to offer additional grateful prayers to her growing collection of papier-mâché idols and framed religious calendar prints. Her withdrawal of interest from all but the very basic aspects of his life had meant he had, for the last twelve years since the death of his father, been left largely to his own devices.

'Read it to me,' Balu's mother had said, pushing the paper back into his hands before adding, 'What is it about? Have you been promoted? I have been praying for you.'

'It's the advertisement for the matrimonial column. I want you to read it yourself, tell me what you think.'

'What about your two uncles? They should be informed.'

Balu was squatting on his haunches next to his mother, a shoulder resting against the doorframe of the built-in shelves in her room. He had only recently, at his mother's request, whitewashed the four thick cement shelves that housed the more important of her deities. The rest of the divine pantheon were accommodated around the doorframe, hung on the walls and arranged on two low stools on either side of the doors.

'Read it, Amma. If I am to marry, I will choose the bride myself. My uncles will want to approach the matter via a broker and I have told you I will not have my future decided by a broker. Now read it, Amma, and tell me what you think.'

He watched as his mother read the few lines and then folded and refolded the paper till it was a small, fat square. She seemed to hesitate for a moment as she scanned the array of powerful facilitators in front of her, before placing the paper in the lap of a small ten-armed terracotta Devi.

'Let us ask the goddess what she thinks. She will tell us all we need to know.'

Balu sighed. He was used to his mother's methods and his opinion of the divine judgements that she garnered was influenced by how much they went along with what he had in mind. He watched as a lotus petal, dislodged by his paper from the goddess's flower-laden lap, fluttered to the floor. He waited for his mother to pick up on the signal that the goddess had sent.

'She has spoken, Balu, and you have her blessings. Tomorrow is an auspicious day. Go to the newspaper office tomorrow. I will stop by your uncles' houses on the way to the temple. We will have to keep them informed at all stages, whether you like it or not. Offended relatives can wreak havoc on marriage arrangements.'

★ ★ ★

A week later Balu cycled to his younger uncle's house with a copy of the newspaper under his arm. While his uncles' wives first enquired about his mother and then made sly remarks about his hairstyle and the cut of his trousers, Balu's older uncle read aloud from the newspaper.

'Salaried groom, broadminded, good prospects, Hindu, 26, 171cm, slim, no impairments, clean habits, seeks healthy, homely, accomplished bride 20–24, sober with traditional values, from well-respected family. Caste no bar. No horoscope, no demands. Early, simple marriage. Send bio-data, photo (returnable).'

Balu sipped his coffee slowly and listened to them analyse each word. This was the way many thousands of others would be reading his advertisement: many prospective fathers-in-law would be marvelling at this rarity — the groom with no impairments who promised he would make no demands. Their wives, just like his uncles' wives, would initially be very suspicious. They would wonder what revelations his horoscope contained. There would be speculation that perhaps it had been predicted that the bride's father would die soon after the marriage, or an unfortunate positioning of the planets at the time of Balu's birth would ensure a barren union.

Balu's older uncle folded the paper and handed it back to him. 'This modern type of wording will not get any replies, you know.'

The younger uncle, who had been shelling and eating peanuts, tossing the shells in the direction of the small garden, coughed pointedly and waited for his own wife to pay him some attention. 'Why ask for a simple marriage? It is a celebration after all.'

'If we had approached the broker on your behalf, the one on North Temple Street, he would have suggested some progressive families. The problem is that girls from such families have upstarts for brothers. Negotiations can be difficult from the very start.'

Balu's aunts were cleaning platefuls of rice, systematically picking out stones and husks, sending them over the rims of the stainless steel plates with well-practised flicks. Small knowing smiles played on their faces, though as always, Balu was never quite sure whether they agreed or disagreed with what their husbands had to say. They looked up at him in unison.

'Prayers can overcome all difficulty.'

'Your mother's devotion will do the needful for you.'

Balu's uncles were not mollified. The mention of their sister nearly always caused irritation. Balu's mother was a freak. A widow who was dependent on no one and who therefore had no one to answer to. Their pity for her was sometimes tinged with envy, for it seemed to them obscene that she should have, by her widowhood, done better than them, for the compensation from the factory for the accidental death of her husband, put together with the company's benevolent fund for Balu's education and the payout from the life insurance meant she was comfortably off with no financial worries. What a luxury! To be able to sit and pray the whole day long, all year round! Their sister's piety more often than not caused them to sharply flick their heads and snort discreetly. As for their sister's son, they both agreed that he was typical of a fatherless boy, opinionated and with a mind of his own. It had come as no surprise to them that Balu had wanted to arrange his own marriage and that he had started the proceedings without consulting them, his own maternal uncles.

When Balu left, unperturbed by their attempts to chastise him for his failure to follow the proper order of things, they turned on their wives, needling them about this and that in sheer frustration, peeved that they were both once again unable to do what they had wanted to do all these years, and that was to give Balu a good clip about his ears.

By the end of the week, Balu was beginning to wonder nervously if his uncles had been right. Maybe the wording of the advertisement was indeed too forward, and his first visit to the newspaper offices confirmed his fears. There were no replies for him. He asked the clerk to double-check if he had the right box number.

'Matrimonial, is it? First insertion? Check your box again next week. People take time over these things. Rushed replies are not a good sign.'

So he was delighted when the same clerk

handed him four envelopes the next week. 'You may still receive a couple more. Check again.'

Balu placed the envelopes in a little cloth bag he had brought for the purpose, and hooking the bag onto the handlebar, he cycled all the way to the grounds of the Theosophical Society. On the way it occurred to him that four replies was a poor rate of return, given the daily circulation figures for *The Hindu*, which were in the hundreds of thousands. However, he was still in good spirits as he settled under the shade of one of the enormous banyans for which the Society's grounds were so famous. Balu found it hard to concentrate, skimming eagerly through the four replies, growing despondent when he realised that not one of them had any potential.

Two letters were similar in their content. They appealed to his stated broadmindedness, requesting him to consider the widow whose photo was enclosed. One widow had no encumbrances, the other a quiet child aged two who, he was assured, was well brought up. He wondered about the other two replies, had they not read his words? How could a working woman ever be homely? It annoyed him that the respondents, the families of the prospective brides, had chosen to ignore his specific requirements and had, in effect, wasted his time. These useless replies forced him to consider the wisdom of having used the word 'broad-minded'. If widows and working women were being foisted on him because of that word he was glad that he had dropped 'cosmopolitan'.

Balu cursed his uncles for their black tongues and stayed under the tree, his thoughts drifting between his next course of action and the fact that he could not afford another classified ad for a couple of weeks, until salary day. The evening was warm, the air under the tree still and the dappled light on the dusty ground and on the gnarled exposed roots of the majestic banyan was beginning to fade into shadows. He closed his eyes, tired with disappointment, and soon dozed off, lulled into an hour-long sleep by intoxicating dreams of marriage and happiness. He was woken by a dull crack of the watchman's *lathi* on the tree trunk in the close vicinity of his head. The *lathi* remained raised and Balu realised he was being observed with disgust.

'Who are you waiting for? The grounds are closed. Fellows like you give this place a bad name. Can't you find yourself a woman instead? Pervert!'

★　★　★

39

Balu waited two weeks before going back to the newspaper offices. He had confided the details of the four replies to Mr Nath, who had without hesitation advised him to wait.

'For what, sir?'

'Just wait. Pass the time and time will pass. This is my favourite advice at the moment. I am trying it on my wife. Now that she is in her eighth month she is always complaining about her ungainly size.'

Balu had waited, because there was nothing else he could do. At the next visit, the clerk at the newspaper office didn't show any signs of recognition as he went off with the box number scrawled on the palm of his hand. He returned with four large bundles of letters.

'Have you not brought a bag? There are more than a hundred letters here. If we give a bag to each one of our advertisers we will have to register as a charity.'

Balu folded his handkerchief diagonally, trussed up the four bundles together and, securing the parcel on his cycle's carrier, headed home triumphantly. Time and again while waiting at traffic lights and at the railway crossing, he turned around to check if the parcel was still secure, touching it and making small adjustments to the way it was held under the spring-backed clip. He showed the letters to his mother who seemed genuinely shocked but also very pleased that so many should have replied to her son's matrimonial call.

'I will pray while you read the replies,' she told him. 'Then you can show me the ones you think will be suitable.'

Earlier, on his way home, Balu had decided he would approach the matter of the replies very systematically. He planned to read no more than ten a day, marking each bridal candidate on various different criteria, which he planned to tabulate on the foolscap paper that remained.

True to his intention, he used the edge of the clipboard to mark broad columns onto two sheets of foolscap, and having done that he clipped the sheets onto the board. He filled his blue fountain pen with ink and keeping it on his bedside table he proceeded to sharpen a thick red pencil. He wasn't quite sure exactly how he was going to proceed, but he was confident that the actual method of selection and rejection would reveal itself to him as he went through the replies. He fetched himself a glass of water and kept it to one side before he opened the first envelope. A photograph fell out as he unfolded the letter, and as he bent to pick it up he shuddered involuntarily. He felt sorry for this girl whose uncomely face stared back at him rather sullenly from the ground near his feet, for who would marry her?

Soon the pity that he felt for the first girl seemed to extend to several more, for every letter that he opened revealed a face that he was unable to look at except briefly. It wasn't that they were all ugly or repulsive, it was their resigned expressions, a certain dullness in their eyes and in some cases an air of disinterest that was apparent from their demeanour that he found unsuitable. The idea of marriage seemed to have saddened them, and not one so far had succeeded in enthusing Balu, who instead began to feel despair come over him again. He realised dejectedly that he had forgotten about his plans to tabulate each prospective bride and her family's salient points, and having rushed through over three or four dozen letters instead of the mere ten he had planned, prising out the photographs and rejecting each one of them in a matter of seconds on the basis of their looks alone, he felt he had betrayed his own principles. His mind full of remorse, he continued to go through the letters, slower this time but only in the tearing open of the letters, still drawn immediately to looking at the photographs first. He made an effort to examine at least the photos in greater detail, glancing briefly through the letter that accompanied each.

Quite a few of the sad, empty faces that he came across were more widow-applicants, their families all drawn to him in vain hope. That their hope was in vain caused him no guilt, for he was not to blame if people read more into his words than what was meant. Soon he realised that the pile of opened letters that he had cast aside had grown larger, while the space on the bedside table that he had cleared for the short-listed candidates remained empty. He felt compelled to fill that space with at least one reply, and since the photograph in his hand at that moment was the least offensive, he pushed it back into the thick manila envelope it had arrived in and placed it on the bedside table, aligning it precisely with the bevelled edge. There it remained short-listed and alone until a dozen letters later he came across another plain face that aroused no emotion in him. As soon as he had added this second photo and its accompanying letter to the short-list, Balu felt a good deal better, almost convincing himself that he was indeed making some inroads into the search for a bride. By the time he was ready to tackle the last bundle, he had four applications put aside and his spirits were much lifted. When his mother called out to him to come for his evening meal he walked into the kitchen with seven letters in his hand.

'Are they from good families?'

Balu picked at the embossed design on the yellowing plastic tablecloth that covered the small aluminium dining table and thought about the blank sheets of foolscap paper still attached to the clipboard. He felt a slight exasperation with his mother. He watched as she strained the cooked rice, saving the milky looking water to use later on to starch Balu's shirts. In terms of an opinion she had never given much to any of the major decisions he had made in his adult life, and if he stretched his memory as far back as he could remember, he could confidently say the same for his early years as well. For the first time in his life Balu wished his mother had contributed more than just her prayers; maybe then she wouldn't have found it so easy to be as detached as she now was.

While going through the last bundle of replies, the enormity of the task that he had undertaken started sinking in and he was overcome with uncharacteristic nervousness. The probability of getting it completely wrong, of choosing the wrong woman to marry was very high. To get it right was going to need a miracle and powers of divination, for it was obvious that crucial details about the girl and her family were quite likely to become apparent only after he had actually married her.

Balu's mother heaped the steaming rice on to his plate and waited for him to make a shallow well in the mound before she ladled some fish curry into it.

'You didn't answer me. Are they from good families?'

'It is difficult to say, Amma. I suppose the next step will be to make enquiries.' She had been like this ever since he could remember. A slight expression of interest on her part would then be followed by a predictable withdrawal into her solitary world of endless incantations and rhythmic pleas. For years he had thrived in the freedom that came with his mother's preoccupation with prayer, but for the very first time he felt he could do with a bit of guidance.

He ate, listening in silence as she outlined the rigorous schedule of special penances that she was going to start on the following Friday for the speedy resolution of matrimonial matters for him. It was only as he was finishing the meal that it occurred to him that his mother was offering him something far more valuable than practical help. She was offering him the possibility of a miracle,

45

heavenly intervention itself. He washed his hands at the tap outside the kitchen door, rubbing the sliver of hard soap vigorously between his palms to get it to lather. The smaller the cake of soap got, the more hard and shrivelled it became from sitting on the concrete windowsill in the harsh, unrelenting heat of the shadeless courtyard at the back of the house. He wiped his hands on the thin fraying towel that hung from a nail above the tap and then went back into the kitchen where his mother was peeling fruit for him.

He ate the oranges greedily, several segments at a time, his mind racing with the possibilities that had just struck him. Maybe his mother's devotion would pay off; maybe she would be able to intercede, ask for divine favours on his behalf. His final hesitation before he reached for his wallet was instinctive. He had always steered clear of his mother's obsession, not wanting to get caught up in the time-consuming rituals, not willing to give up the self-governing status that had been thrust upon him and which he now treasured dearly.

His mother expressed no surprise when he handed her the five-*rupee* note but tucked it into the folds of her sari at her waist. She told him she would divide some of the money between three of her favourite gods, draping

46

each of them in new sets of silk cloth and buying them the flowers that they were partial to. The remainder would go towards the making of clarified butter, which she would use to fuel the little terracotta lamps that she would light as a combined offering for the rest of the deities.

★ ★ ★

By the end of that week Balu had gone through the seven letters in great detail, and having rejected one on the basis that the prospective bride suffered from epilepsy, he wrote back to the six remaining families requesting a meeting. With each reply he enclosed a copy of his bio-data, the very same one that he had used when applying for his job as an apprentice accountant, though he had enhanced it considerably, putting in current details, outlining his bright prospects and the fact that he was going to sit the Banking Services exam. To each reply he also attached a copy of a glowing character reference from Mr Nath, one that vouched for Balu's claims of clean living. Mr Nath had been generous in his praise for Balu and had signed the letter with the proud flourish of a man whose wife had just presented him with a son and heir.

Four of the respondents were quick to come back, letting him know in a triumphant tone that he had been too late, the matters for the girls in question were already 'settled'. The fifth reply followed the next day, the father of the girl explaining that even before Balu's letter had arrived, they had been inundated with replies from interested grooms and thankfully he had managed to negotiate an excellent alliance for his daughter. However, he was writing to tell Balu of his younger daughter who was her sister's equal in all respects. If Balu would consider the matter (the photo was enclosed) and if he liked the alternative offering, a double wedding would be possible. The father declared he would be doubly blessed, the weddings would be auspicious occasions twice over and for a father of limited means with another two girls to settle, it would be a two-fold saving.

The idea that he was being palmed off with a substitute irritated Balu no end and his despair at having been beaten to the post by other grooms whose families were obviously old hands at this game, made him wonder if he should consider approaching his uncles for help after all. He toyed with the idea for a day or two, even thinking tentatively of independently approaching the broker on North

Temple Street. There were also the dozens of initial replies that he had rejected, which lay in a plastic bag under his bed. Balu was loath to go through them again, looking for a bride amongst letters and photos that he had thought not good enough in the first place. One morning towards the end of the week, he admitted to his mother that things had not worked out. She carried on with the task in hand, wiping clean the drips on the outside of his two-tiered stainless steel tiffin carrier that she had just filled with his lunch and placing it in the plastic macrameé bag along with a bottle of boiled and cooled water. She handed it to Balu.

'One family has yet to reply. Wait.'

To Balu, his mother's words sounded prophetic and when, on returning home from work that evening, he saw the neatly addressed envelope on the Formica table in the hall, he knew instinctively that this reply would not contain excuses, rejections or alternatives. He washed his face and hands and heated up the coffee that his mother had made and left for him before she had headed off for the temple. He did not open the envelope but instead searched for the initial correspondence with that family in the pile of six that he had banded together and placed under lock and key, in the large teak cupboard that dominated his room.

Shaking the contents of the envelope out, he picked up the photograph as it landed on the table and looked closely at the almost expressionless face, happy that it did not even this second time round, provoke any negative reaction in him. Her name, which he had not paid attention to earlier, appealed to him. It had a nice traditional ring to it. Janaki. He repeated the name several times as he read the reasons why her father thought she would be just right for him. She had failed her Intermediate exams and her family had managed to persuade her to discontinue her History BA degree in favour of marriage. The letter informed him that despite her academic mediocrity, Janaki excelled in every domestic matter, and being an obedient and loving daughter was a blessing to her father and mother. She was not being allowed to waste time at home but had been bought a sewing machine and was being taught tailoring by a tutor who came to the house. Balu read on, soaking in all the details that he had skipped the first time, when all that he had gone by was his initial and instant reaction to her photograph.

When he finally opened the newly arrived letter and realised that Janaki's father had requested a meeting and had kindly given him the choice of three auspicious dates on which Balu and the elders in his family could come to see the girl, his confidence was restored. Though he would never have admitted it, the reason for his despondency in the past few weeks stemmed from the humiliation that came from having had such a poor quality of response to such a well thought out and carefully worded advertisement. But it was a private humiliation and therefore easier to deal with. Very shortly, in a matter of days, he was able to totally put out of his mind the fact that, despite all the outstanding qualities that he was sure he had to offer as a prospective groom, this was the only reply out of over a hundred that had actually managed to move forward to this stage.

In the days before the visit to Janaki's house, Balu was overwhelmed with a feeling of well-being. He got great satisfaction in conducting an enquiry to ascertain that the girl's father and uncles did indeed hold the permanent and pensionable clerical positions in the Electricity Board that they claimed they did. He wished that Mr Nath hadn't gone off to Mysore to bring his wife back from her three-month-long confinement at her parents'. If Mr Nath had been in Madras, Balu would have requested him to make the enquiries on his behalf.

Matrimonial-related queries from total strangers were commonplace. An investigation could be helped along or hindered by eager busybodies willing to provide information or disinformation. The latter often happened when there was a degree of vested interest, and a blind eye was often turned for it was universally believed, and certainly hoped, that everything — be it a small foible or a major vice — would somehow correct itself after the marriage had taken place. Such was the belief in the benefits provided by the state of wedlock. Regardless of which side had initiated it, if details had been gleaned from friends of colleagues, acquaintances of relatives and former neighbours, that fact always found its way back to the family being investigated. The knowledge that even Balu's boss himself was taking a personal interest in checking out the bonafides of the bride and her kin would have eventually filtered down to Janaki's family, and it would certainly have created a favourable impression on them.

Balu spent a lot of his time at work thinking about the institution of marriage. It was a respectable position to have — to be responsible for someone, to take charge of their well-being, in effect to take over the reins of their guardianship. At work he found it was very easy to spot the married men. They shared a peculiar camaraderie that was enviable when, for instance, they seemed to so knowledgeably discuss life insurance policies that would mature, as planned, at precise moments in their lives. Yet the same camaraderie was pitiable when they some-times got together only to complain about the nuisance factor of irresponsible brothers-in-law or the vagaries of their pregnant wives. Their tribulations seemed to give them an air of maturity and, irritatingly, that slight edge over Balu. He had often heard them issue jocular warnings in the direction of about-to-be married colleagues, warnings which Balu had lately begun to resent for it seemed to him a perverse way of preparing someone for entry into their fraternity. They seemed to have a moral superiority that Balu in his bachelorhood could never hope to totally match. Still, it was easy to see that there were several who were unhappy, either through their own making or from having married difficult and demanding women. Failure was a sobering reality and even though he had never taken the matter lightly, he realised that the effort he would have to put in to be a good husband and have a successful marriage would be unrelenting. Having no doubts about his own ability to cope, he knew that much would depend on his future wife.

Balu's immediate concern however was the selection procedure itself. From his experience of the first part of the process, he knew that there was not much use in setting anything but the broadest of criteria. The suitability of Janaki would make itself apparent in a way that could not be fully foretold or measured by any definite yardstick. But what he wanted to be able to do was to find this out, to make that final judgement without the input of anyone else clouding his decision. Of course, Balu knew that this would be impossible, for he was going to be accompanied by several others. The inspection party would have to include his mother, his two uncles and their wives.

His younger uncle had in fact only the previous evening told Balu that Balu's two little nieces, would also be tagging along. The uncles and their wives had decided that the two girls, given their precocious natures, would ease the initial awkwardness that invariably arose when the groom's side arrived for the very first time in the prospective bride's house to see her and her family.

'Listen, Balu, you may not think it is the time and place for children to be brought along, but why do you think we had to suffer taking you with us when we went to look at brides? Whenever there was a lull in the conversation you provided the way out, you became the something everyone looked at, and whatever you were doing at that point in time gave us an issue to resume the conversation with. In my case you proved more than useful.'

Balu's younger uncle paused, puckered his lips and then leaning out over the front gates, let out an explosive stream of red-betel leaf juice, which landed as he had expertly intended on the road, in a stagnant pool of week-old rainwater. The two men watched a swarm of mosquitoes rise from the murk, startled by the velocity of the expectoration.

'You vomited into your father's lap and then all over the new *jamakalum* which had been spread on the floor in our honour. In the commotion that followed, I was able to have a good uninterrupted view of the girl, you know — your aunt. In a few days you'll want that fleeting moment of privacy for yourself. No one was watching me as I watched her, for five or six minutes at least.'

Balu had over the years heard many versions of the events of that day, but his uncle's confession about his opportunistic voyeurism startled Balu. He wondered what criteria his uncles had used to make their final choice and he was about to broach the topic when, preceded by a rasping clearance of the throat, the betel juice flew in an arc through the air again.

Balu's uncle didn't look up as he closed the gate behind him. 'Now you make sure you know where their house is. We must arrive within the auspicious time period that they have indicated.'

Balu had decided the occasion was important enough to engage a private taxi and he had already booked one a few days earlier. He spent the next day at work thinking about his uncle's parting remark. Would the taxi driver be able to locate the girl's house in the maze of small streets and alleys that was the traditional old quarter of town? There were two days to go and Balu made enquiries at work. The consensus revealed that it was an easy enough street to find if you knew where you were going. On his way home from work that evening, Balu impulsively headed towards Mylapore, cycling through the traffic lights instead of turning left at the Alwarpet Junction, his normal route home.

The roads narrowed and grew progressively congested as he made his way towards what he knew was the general direction of the address. As advised by the despatch clerk at work, he stopped at the A1 Juice Stall at the corner of Lingam Street and the Bus Depot, and asked for directions. He listened impatiently as the question of the shortest and easiest route was debated amongst the customers and the stall owner, and finally took up the offer of a departing patron, who suggested that Balu follow him for a distance up to the police station, after which the address he was looking for would be very nearly in sight. It was easy enough keeping up with his newfound guide, for even though the man was on a scooter, the press of people who had been jostled off the pavement and on to the road by vendors, and the volume of vehicles of every kind, noisily contending for space on the cramped road, meant that for most of the way Balu was actually able to cycle alongside the scooter and even engage the man in snatched bits of light conversation about the forthcoming Corporation elections.

When they did part ways at the police station, Balu was relieved to find out from a passer-by that the street he was looking for was, as promised, just around the corner.

It was a quieter residential area and cycling slowly, checking the numbers on the gate-posts, Balu became aware of a quickening of his heartbeat and a definite dryness in his mouth. As he rode past a nondescript bungalow with freshly painted green shutters on the windows, he realised that he had found the house. Balu continued to the end of the street where he turned around to head back home. He could feel his temples begin to throb and he found himself slowing down as he approached the house once again. He had an uncontrollable urge to go into the house, see the girl and straight away make up his own mind without being influenced by his family, and that meant immediately, without any further delay. He stopped at the gate and hesitated for only a moment before lifting the latch and then nudging the gate open with his cycle. He walked to the front door fully aware that what he was doing was completely inappropriate and against the grain of the centuries-old customs and traditions that he himself had subscribed to by using the matrimonial columns in the first place.

As he rang the bell, licking his lips and getting ready to say something, he knew not what, to whoever opened the door, he realised that he had made a mess of things. Yet, he stood rooted to the single concrete step at the foot of the front door, his curiosity now uncontainable and all reason put aside to satiate this immediate need. He knew that, even putting it mildly, his behaviour would be construed as very peculiar, and to have arrived unaccompanied by elders and on the wrong day and at what was almost definitely an inauspicious time, would guarantee rejection by the girl's side.

Just then, Balu heard someone lean over and call down from the terrace above the single-storey house. As he walked around to the side of the house he saw the girl in the photograph, Janaki, come down the steep out-door staircase. Her hair was damp and she had tied the ends in a loose-balled knot. Her sari was brightly coloured, but her face was plain and her look uncomplicated. It was relief that he felt uppermost as he immediately acknow-ledged her suitability. He was not sure why but he knew that he had found what he was looking for. It was just as he had thought it would be, a self-evident understanding.

'Appa has gone to the temple with Amma. What is it that you want?'

'Tell your father that I was making sure where the house was.' He turned around, grateful that the elders were not at home, and walked back to where he had left the cycle leaning on the gatepost. As he pedalled away, Balu conceded that other people's pious efforts — his mother's prayers and now Janaki's parents' visit to the temple — were paying dividends for him. He took it as an omen and never looked back.

3

Janaki was slightly out of breath when she looked up at the three faces. Her son and husband were hiding their mild exasperation behind patient smiles. Her daughter-in-law, Viji, whose face Janaki could see in the rearview mirror, was tucking loose strands of her short hair behind her ears with one hand; the other hand was on the gear stick, ready to get the car moving as soon as everyone was belted up.

'Your mother was never good with gadgets. Just pull the buckle, pull it hard across this way, Janu, and I will click it in for you.'

'Not too hard, Amma, or it will jam. The strap is meant to lock if it is wrenched or jerked, the way it would if we had an accident.'

'Don't say that at the start of our journey. Why invite trouble?'

'I'm not inviting anything, Amma, just telling you how it works. Pull it slowly across your chest — no, no keep your hand underneath it and now pull it across your shoulders and Appa will click it in.'

Janaki held her breath again; it was an

involuntary reflex that her body subjected her to when she was under scrutiny and concentrating. Balu had very purposefully unbuckled himself and shifting around in the back seat of his son's car, he was nearly facing Janaki as he took charge of the seatbelt with an impatient sigh, clicking it in successfully and then sitting back in his place and strapping himself in again with no difficulty at all.

Trouble with the seatbelt had dogged her since the start of their holiday, beginning with the journey back to her son's house from Heathrow. Even after a dozen times in the car since then, she had been unable to get the hang of it and her protest that there must be something wrong with the belt on her side was left unconsidered and unacknowledged. Even on the most scenic of drives that they had done over the weekend, Janaki had not been able to ignore the discomfort caused by both the restrictions the belt placed on her and an acute awareness of the chafing of the thick nylon strap against her neck.

As they headed off on this three-hour journey into London, Janaki was glad that for the next sixteen days at least she did not have to put up with diagonal seatbelts, and when she had discovered this fact on the previous night, her delight had been greeted with sighs all around. Yesterday, Balu had insisted on being packed and ready before Viji and Ram returned from work and they had spent the afternoon sorting out the clothes that they wanted to take on their coach tour of Europe. After dinner the four of them had sat down to watch the information video that Ram had ordered from the tour company.

'I wonder who picks the names for these tours?' Viji was reading off the cover of the video. ' "The information in this video applies to all tours except Alpine Splendours, Playgrounds of Europe and Italian Escapade".'

Janaki looked at her daughter-in-law, unsure whether she was appreciative of the names or just mocking them. Balu had been delighted when, months before they had travelled, Ram had written to them in India with details about the tour that he had booked for them, adding that it was called European Kaleidoscope. Balu had taken an instant fancy for the name, making sure that anyone who knew about their upcoming holiday also knew the exact name of the tour.

'Ours is the Kaleidoscope,' said Balu, who had settled into one of the fireside chairs and was looking at his son. 'I wish you and Viji were coming too.'

'Appa, neither Viji nor I have enough leave, remember? Anyway, if we did, we would have done it differently. Driven you and Amma around England and Scotland perhaps, or even across to Ireland. We'll do that the next time you both come.'

They were fifteen minutes into watching the video, being shown the comfortable interior of a typical coach, when Janaki spotted the detail about the seatbelts. Ram had rewound the video to the clip showing the adjustable seating, the vents for air-conditioning and the lap belts. Balu hadn't been impressed with this interruption of the video on Janaki's behalf. He was eager to hear the rest of what were labelled as 'typical questions' being asked by a mock passenger and the assuaging replies being given by a cheerful, enthusiastic tour guide in a smart suit in the Allsights Tours' company colours. Janaki had wondered then if Balu was a bit nervous about the journey. It was difficult to say, for though he had, in the last few days coming up to the start of their coach tour, displayed short bouts of impatience with her, he had also insisted, on three separate occasions, on sitting her down at the dining table and showing her, on the map that had come as part of the tour pack, what he thought would be their most likely route from London to Amsterdam. Her eyes had strayed across the map, taking in instead the vastness of the continent that they were going to traverse in sixteen days, and Balu had to call her attention to what he was saying.

'If you don't know where we are going you will not enjoy the holiday, Janu. All the rest of the passengers will have a good idea of the route and we should show them that we are no less.'

'It is so difficult to understand the English of these foreigners. What conversation can one have with them anyway?'

'We must make an effort to mix, leave our opinions about these Westerners behind. See this information pack? It says that most people take back more than just memories but also new friendships. We must give a good impression of us Indians, make international friends, invite them to India, show them our hospitality.'

Janaki sensed the underlying anxiety in his broad sweeping statement of intent and though she would have liked to say something to him, she knew he hated it when she spotted his nervousness. 'I don't want you to worry about what I am worrying about!' was his standard admonishment and over the years she had learnt to couch her words, sometimes placating him by expressing her own anxieties in the matter. She knew he felt immediately duty bound to ease her worries and often, in doing that he would have shed his own doubts and mastered the situation for himself.

Now, as they were being driven from Norwich to London to be dropped off at the hotel from which their tour was to start the next day, Janaki found herself wishing for the peace and familiarity of her son's house. She would have been quite happy to spend the rest of the holiday in Norwich. Each morning, after Ram and Viji had left for work, she found the silence of their empty house therapeutic. She had for the last week pottered about the house, touching and marvelling at appliances and gadgets that made housekeeping such a novelty compared to Madras. This coach holiday suddenly felt like too much of an effort. She closed her eyes and tried to picture in her mind's eye the little temple across the street from their house in Madras. She had just begun to pray for a safe journey to London and back for Ram and Viji, when Balu nudged her. When she opened her eyes, he directed her attention to what looked like acres of red that now and then swayed slightly in the breeze.

'Poppies. They grow wild,' Ram explained, yawning as he spoke. She felt sorry for her son. He worked very long hours and Janaki was glad that Viji was driving. She worked too, but wasn't that out of choice?

'Why don't you sleep, son? If you didn't have to wear these seatbelts you could have slept comfortably at the back with your feet up and your head in my lap.' Janaki was offended by the burst of collective laughter in the car. 'You are laughing, but didn't you insist on doing exactly that even as recently as the year before you got married? Every trip that we made out of Madras you slept on my lap. Ask your father.'

'That was India, Amma. Anything goes.'

Balu intervened. 'Yes, but it was both of you. You and your mother were great for sleeping in the car. Do you know, Viji, when Ram was ten years old and we had just got our first car, I drove the entire eighteen-hour journey from Madras to Kodai all by myself. And that was the story for all the journeys we ever made by car. I did all the driving while my good wife slept. When Ram did learn to drive he had left Madras to study in Delhi. He doesn't really know, does he, Janu, how lucky he is that his wife is such a capable driver?'

'You could have taught Amma to drive, you know.'

'She never wanted to.' Balu was looking at Janaki for confirmation.

'It was quite rare for women to drive in

those days. It attracted a lot of attention — the wrong kind. Anyway, where would I have driven to? Everybody I knew lived on the same street as us and they still do. Except for the Bhaskarans. They moved three years ago to live with their son in America. I miss her. We always made our Diwali sweets together. Do you remember her, Ram?'

'America! I wonder how they are coping?'

'She was a troublemaker, Janaki, even you would admit that. She was fit for America all right, with all her talk about that women's lib business. None of the ideas were her own, mind you. She just read a lot and thought that these newfangled ideas could just be transferred willy-nilly to women in India.'

'Oh, come on, Appa!'

'It is true, Ram. Your mother has held the most important position in our house. She didn't need some modern theories to tell her that her husband's and children's welfare depended on her. Indian women are the backbone of our society — and why? Because they know the role they have to play.'

'Do you agree, Amma?'

'Leave me out of this. They always do this to me, Viji. Father and son argue and then drag me in.' Janaki looked at her daughter-in-law's reflection in the rearview mirror. Viji was smiling back at her.

Since the start of their holiday, Janaki had often wondered what her son's wife really thought about them. She was a quiet girl, convent-educated and well brought up. Ram had met her while studying in Delhi and had announced his intention to marry her shortly afterwards. Balu had been taken aback but had eventually given his blessings. As for Janaki, Ram had assumed from the start that his mother would not stand in the way of her son's happiness and he was right. It was Viji's academic achievements that had impressed Balu the most. She had completed her post-doctoral degree in Mathematics and was now teaching degree students at Norwich University and he was proud of this fact.

Janaki and Balu had found it difficult to deal with Viji's parents, Balu in particular. Viji's parents were typical South Indian Delhi-ites. They suffered from that peculiar social affliction that comes from having a claim on both South Indian intelligence and North Indian sophistication. They belonged to a set that was a breed apart, a group with a superiority complex that could cleverly be exercised over both their native South and their adoptive North. They intimidated Balu with their quiet, stylish house and clothes, and Janaki was grateful that when Viji's father retired a year ago, the couple had decided to remain in Delhi, which had after all been their home for over thirty years.

Janaki looked out of the window as they sped by the flat fields of Norfolk. Even though Ram had been married for four years, the role of mother-in-law did not come easily to her. As a married couple Ram and Viji had never lived in India, let alone in Madras. Both of them returned after their wedding to academic posts they held in Singapore, and now in the UK. This was the first time Janaki and Balu had ever stayed with their son, and far from feeling proprietorial about her son's house as most mothers were supposed to do, Janaki felt more like a visitor. Balu was in fact far more at ease than she was, and Janaki put it down to the fact that men were not naturally wedded to their own homes like women were, and were therefore unable to experience the emotions that came with staying in another woman's house. She closed her eyes and tried once again to pray.

When Balu's loud snoring, which seemed to echo and re-echo in the small confines of the car, woke her, Janaki realised that she had somewhere along the way fallen asleep herself. Ram had nodded off as well and Viji was listening to the radio as she drove.

'We are just getting into London, Amma.' Viji lowered the volume on the radio as she spoke. 'The traffic will slow us down quite a bit now. Do you want a sandwich? Or a drink? Ram has packed a few things into that plastic box — why don't you have a look?'

'Will you have something? You must be tired with all the driving.'

'Ram is going to do the driving on the return journey after we drop you. I'll eat and nap on the way back.'

Janaki watched her daughter-in-law skilfully manoeuvre her way through traffic that got increasingly heavy as they drew closer to Central London. Ram was duly woken up when Viji decided she needed a navigator to read the *A to Z* and direct her to the Thistle City Hotel. They woke Balu only on arrival at the hotel, and when Ram and Viji had left after a brief leave-taking in the hotel lobby, Balu and Janaki went upstairs to their fourth-floor room. With the room door shut, Balu turned on her unexpectedly, annoyed that nobody had seen fit to wake him as they drove into London.

'Ram said to leave you to rest as we were going to do the tour of London later this evening anyway.'

'Ram said! You should have known. Who drove in London? Did Ram take over?'

'Ram was going to drive on the return. Viji drove all the way here.'

'I admire that girl. It is an achievement, you know, to be able to drive in a metro city like London. It really is true, what they say about Delhi girls — they are smart.'

'She was given an opportunity to learn and she took it. That is what was smart,' said Janaki.

Janaki had taken the pins out of her bun and her thinning hair rolled out, unravelling itself slowly. She undid her sari and left it on the upholstered chair. Quickly loosening the strings of her petticoat she proceeded to retie it, but this time for comfort. Then shaking out the towel that she had fetched earlier form the bathroom she lay on the bed, arranging the towel to modestly cover her chest and stomach. She had a headache that she knew she could shake off if she could just close her eyes for half an hour, but looking at the tray with tea and coffee-making facilities, it struck her that Balu would come out of the bathroom in a minute, having had a quick wash, and would want a cup of tea. She got up reluctantly and with the towel still draped across her chest and shoulders she walked barefoot up to the bathroom, loving the novel sensation of the soft thick pile against her toes, and asked him what he wanted to drink.

'We'll take a walk around the area,' he replied, his answer muffled as he wiped his face and neck dry. 'We can come back and have tea. Why have you taken off your sari?'

Janaki put her fingers to her forehead and Balu sighed. 'If you had asked me I would have told you that some fresh air would do you good. Take two tablets and we'll go. How often do we get a chance to see London? I'll fetch the tablets for you while you get ready.'

Janaki began draping her sari on again, tightening the strings of the petticoat firmly before she started tucking in the yards of silk. 'I wanted to lie down for a while, for half an hour.'

'How could I go without you? I want to be able to tell everyone I saw London in the company of my wife. Do you know, Janu, how envious they all are? My son fully settled, my promotion to Branch Manager and now us having this holiday? Did I tell you that the company's half-yearly newsletter is going to carry a small item about us? We must remember to take a nice photograph to give to them for publication. I was thinking that one with Ram and Viji would be good. Let people know that we have done well for ourselves.'

'They will cast eyes on us. You yourself say they are envious.'

'I know, and this is what I cannot understand. To be envious of someone who has worked hard, planned his life and achieved the things that he set out to in a systematic way — people should learn from example rather than be envious.'

Janaki pinned her hair back into a bun and took the tablets that Balu had managed to locate in his leather pouch. He patted her on her back as they waited for the lift to take them down to the lobby. 'Don't speak till you feel better. It won't be long before you do.'

The lobby was busy, and faced with the prospect of actually leaving the security of the hotel and heading out on their own into London, Balu hesitated in front of a row of racks with brochures and leaflets detailing every sort of tourist attraction. Janaki headed for the nearest sofa and waited there, her head now throbbing. She watched Balu as he picked up and put back several brochures, looking around intermittently as if he was browsing in a shop and expected any minute to be served. As she continued to gaze around the lobby she spotted a desk being set up with the Allsights Tours logo prominently displayed. Balu had as well, for when she turned to him he was striding purposefully towards the desk. But so were nearly all the other people sitting in the lobby. They smiled at each other sheepishly, nodding and shaking hands as they formed an orderly queue in front of the desk, not wanting to jostle ahead but not wanting to be too nice about it either. They looked at each other slyly as they waited to register, aware that first impressions mattered, taking stock of the oddballs they would definitely want to avoid and making note of the couples that seemed like-minded, even if that judgement had been gained by the most superficial of methods.

Janaki tried to avoid Balu's eye, knowing that he would be impatient for her to stand alongside him in the queue, but she relented when she found that the effort of doing so was just making her headache worse. He introduced her to the couples ahead of and behind them in the queue. Janaki strained to understand the unfamiliar accents and tried her best to make herself understood as they asked her to repeat her name slowly. Impatient with her, Balu finally decided to spell it out.

The Australian couple in front of them repeated her name again and again, waiting for her to say that they had got it right. Not getting any affirmation, they introduced themselves as Don and Pat. The couple behind them seemed more reticent. They said they were teachers and nothing more.

'In India we worship our teachers.' Balu looked at the Australians who were laughing in response to what he had just said. 'No, it is not a joke, they are held in veneration. My son and daughter-in-law are both teachers. At university level, of course.'

The Australians irritated Janaki. She ignored them and turned to the teaching couple instead. 'Teachers empower us with knowledge and we are taught to give them the highest respect in return, on the same level as our parents. It is the way things should be.'

'We are science teachers — from South Africa. William is my name and this is my sister Karen.'

There was a round of quiet handshakes by which time they found that the queue had moved on. The Australians began to rummage in their stylish leather backpacks for their papers and Balu turned to Janaki and asked her how her headache was. Janaki rubbed her temples slowly and then pressed her fingertips against the top of her cheekbones. Balu turned away, unhappy with her reply. Janaki was well used to being subject to the subtle pressure that he put on her to recover quickly from any ailment, but she was annoyed that he would show his displeasure so obviously. After all, she was the one who had agreed to forgo a short rest, which she knew would have helped her headache.

It was an aspect of Balu that she had never been able to comprehend. Janaki appreciated his brisk concern for her when she was unwell, but she could never understand his need to hurry the process of recovery along as fast as he could. She had once, a couple of years ago, asked him if he perhaps felt she pretended to stay sick longer than she really was. It was after a four-day bout of gastroenteritis that had left her weak and irritable. He had come back from work earlier than usual because Janaki was unwell, and yet he had been bothered by the fact that she had not been able to give the servant girl any instructions regarding the house. Her question offended him deeply and he had chastised her for thinking that he did not trust her. It was all a matter of making a concerted effort to get better, to return to normality, he had tried to explain. But she was in defiant mood; her body exhausted and caution thrown to the wind, she turned around in the bed where she lay, her back to him, her tearfulness apparent in the slight heaving of her shoulders. Yet it was Balu who somehow managed to remain the one slighted, and Janaki eventually felt compelled to sit up in bed and call out to Muthu who had, true to form, given herself a complete break from work while her mistress was ill.

Ram, home on a week's leave from his job in Singapore, had come as close as one could in explaining his father's behaviour.

'He bullies you, Amma. Bullies you into getting better.'

'You young people always see things differently.'

'There you go again — you provide the support, the props for his behaviour. Can't you see, Amma? He loses control of you when you are sick. He needs you to get better quickly so that he can go back to being the husband instead of the helpless bystander.'

Janaki had been taken aback by her son's assessment of his father's motives. Father and son were close and Balu had always encouraged debate between them, telling Janaki it was part of the making of a man, to question. She wondered what Balu would think of his son's opinion. Ram seemed to have almost read her mind. He took the watering can that she had in her hand and directed the sprinkler over her beloved roses. 'I've told Appa that many times. He of course insists his only concern is that you get better. Quickly.' Ram had laughed, repeating the word 'quickly'.

Janaki had laughed too. 'We are what we are and at the end of the day we are happy.'

Standing in the hotel lobby now, Janaki

remembered saying that. She reached out to tug Balu's sleeve. He looked back at her over his shoulder without turning around.

'I will be okay once we have had a cup of tea after this. After we finish with the queue.'

Balu swung around and nudged her in the direction of the sofas. 'Go and sit down till then, Janu.'

Janaki sat down and tried to close her eyes but she was too shy to do so, convinced that if she did, the entire queue would have an opportunity to look at her unhindered. So she sat sleepy but wide awake, facing the queue and watching Balu go through the booking confirmation forms, reading each one in great detail. He then opened their passports, examining them one by one, page by page. When she looked at the others in the queue, nearly everyone seemed to be doing exactly the same thing, looking up now and then to have a good, brief stare, soaking in as much visual detail as they could about the people who were going to be their travelling companions for the next sixteen days.

Janaki saw the Indian couple before they saw her. They had emerged from the area around the lift and had headed for the queue straight away. Once they got into line, they had what looked like a short, sharp argument, with both of them glancing at their watches several times. They didn't speak to each other for quite a while but when Balu left the line, having finished the registration, carrying on each shoulder a sling bag with the Allsights logo emblazoned across it and in his hands bits of paper stickers and badges, the lady poked her husband with her elbow. Together they followed Balu with their eyes and when he reached Janaki they realised that she had been watching them. There was much nodding and smiling and even a short wave of a hand on Janaki's part. Balu could hardly contain his excitement and even folded his hands together in a formal *namaste*. The lady returned the *namaste* after a short hesitation and this made Balu call out to them.

'We'll wait here for you. Till you have finished. They are giving out these bags, free.' He held one up and winked. 'Make sure you get one each.'

Balu turned to Janaki and sat down next to her. He unzipped the bags and examined the compartments. 'We'll carry one between us. Pack away the other one. You'll get your tea, don't worry. We'll have it with them, Janu.' He looked up towards the couple and rubbed his hands together in pleasure. 'Sheer luck, you know this is. To have one of our own kind on this tour will make us feel a little bit at home.'

'They look North Indian. Delhi-types.' Janaki was looking at the manner in which the woman had draped her sari. South Indian women wore their sari more modestly, there was no doubt about that.

'Outside India we are all Indians.'

Balu made himself as comfortable on the sofa as he could and waited. Janaki closed her eyes, safe in the knowledge that with her husband awake and alert beside her no one could look at her too intently. She knew that Balu would not approve of the woman when he finally met her. He never cared for women with pointy heels on their shoes: it made them look like a certain type, he said. When they were first married she had found it amusing that he had expressed many of his likes and dislikes using cinematic examples. She hadn't realised that men could also be mesmerised by celluloid images, though she understood very quickly that Balu did not seek escapism in the cinema. Instead he seemed to look for inspiration, using selected aspects of particular movies almost as a guide on how to live a virtuous life. Over the years, he had became very picky about the movies he chose for them to see, preferring the genre that sanctified the simple routes to achieving the high ideals of duty, fidelity, honour and sacrifice. He was a willing recipient of cinematic messages, telling Janaki firmly that it was good to have an ideal to emulate.

Balu shook her awake just as she was dozing off to sleep, drifting into memories of their early years together when she was more than happy to conform to the image of the kind of wife he wanted her to be. It wasn't very different from what she had been brought up to believe, and it wasn't very difficult either, for Balu showed his pleasure at her acquiescence with praise that was public. Her capabilities were a reflection on him and he wasn't ever reticent in letting all and sundry know of how well he had chosen.

When Janaki opened her eyes she found Balu standing up and introducing himself. Inder and Romi Singh followed suit with their names, but seemed unsure what reciprocative gesture they needed to make to a couple who had waited for them so patiently.

Balu beamed at them. 'Singh? Our daughter-in-law is from Delhi. Perhaps you know her father? He is in the Finance Ministry.'

'Actually, we are from London.'

'Ah! I thought your accent was slightly foreign. Born here, is it?'

'No, we came here in the late sixties. Seems

like we have been here all our lives, isn't it, Romi?'

Romi gave her husband a look before she turned to Janaki. 'Too long. I have been doing the dishes for too long. I dream of servants and now I have become a servant.'

Balu drew Janaki closer to him. 'We were going to have some tea.'

'I need a drink. The hotel has a bar somewhere — let me find out. Okay, Romi love?' Inder Singh headed off in the direction of the reception desks.

Janaki looked at Balu who was smiling weakly at Romi. Janaki knew he was looking for something to say. Then something struck him and he seemed to struggle with it, shifting his weight from one foot to the other and then looking at Inder's returning figure he finally leant closer to Romi and nearly whispered, 'Is your husband a shaven Sikh?'

Romi nodded mutely as her husband joined them. Inder's spirits seemed lifted and he announced with satisfaction that the bar was in the basement.

'*Chalo ji*, let us start the tour.' He slapped Balu on the back. 'A few drops of the holy water, eh?'

Janaki took a while getting used to the gloom of the windowless bar. No sooner had they sat down on the uncomfortably low stools than she found herself alone at the table. Romi had headed off in the direction of the toilets and Inder in the direction of the bar. Balu had followed right behind him, having gone through the motions of asking Janaki what she wanted to drink. She sensed he was buying time, not wanting to arrive at the bar at the same time as Inder Singh, only to place an order for two teas.

It was a momentous occasion for Janaki. She had never been inside a public bar before. She looked around shyly, wanting to take in all the sights and sounds of the place. The smell was not totally unfamiliar. She took in deep breaths again and again to confirm the memory of clothes tainted with the smell of smoke. Balu wasn't what anyone would call a drinker. 'Other people's brand is what I drink,' he would say, proud of his moderation. There was never drink kept in the house until a few years ago, when Ram brought him a bottle of Johnnie Walker Black Label from the duty-free in Singapore. Father and son had shared a drink from that first bottle in the house and since then Balu would occasionally pour himself a small shot, keeping the bottles that Ram always replenished under lock and key. Balu was aware of the danger of the servant girl Muthu supplying a drop or two to the neighbour's servant, a rogue if there ever was one.

Occasionally Balu would have to go to a bar. Even Janaki knew that it was not out of choice. Sometimes he would know in advance, sometimes he would ring her from the office and tell her he was going to be home late. If there was a Branch Managers' conference or if the Deputy General Manager was visiting from Head Office, the circular bar at the Southern Palace Hotel was the place where the business would be shifted to after office hours. Janaki knew it was circular because you could see it from miles away, a huge, slowly revolving disc that sat on top of the nine-storey hotel, one of the tallest buildings in Madras. It had darkened windows that had, from the day it was opened, unfortunately lent it a degree of uncalled-for notoriety.

Whenever Balu returned from the Sky Bar, he would leave all his clothes in the bucket in the bathroom rather than in the laundry bag that hung behind the bathroom door. 'That smell is contagious,' he would tell her every time. 'Make sure Muthu washes them separately.' Janaki would listen to him later as he described how, in the smoke-filled atmosphere, he had impressed the other managers to a point of jealousy and the Deputy General Manager to a point where

84

Balu was poured an additional drink on the company account. She had met the Deputy General Manager only once at the company's silver jubilee celebrations. He was a lecherous man and she had been taken aback by the way he had leered at her. Balu had been upset, upset enough never to discuss it, though Janaki knew that he blamed himself for having left her in the man's company.

She shuddered slightly at the unpleasant memory and sniffed her sari discreetly, wondering if it had already been tainted by that familiar smell. Would Balu insist on washing their clothes? She had planned on wearing this sari for two days at least. Romi returned and sat down, fussing over her recently applied lipstick. Janaki looked on, fascinated with the way she moved her lips, pressing them with tissue and then looking at them in a tiny lip-sized mirror that for some reason she held concealed in the palm of her hand. A couple of times she ran her tongue over her lips leaving them glossy for a few seconds before she decided that they needed to be dabbed with tissue again and coated with lipstick one last time.

Satisfied finally, Romi turned and offered the mirror to Janaki. 'Want to touch up?'

Janaki put her fingers to her lips. The coat of Vaseline she had applied had nearly dried up and she self-consciously licked her lips. 'It is okay. I don't use lipstick. My husband Balu, he doesn't care for it.'

'But you have other make-up on. On your eyes. You have powder on your face.'

Janaki laughed at the other woman's outburst. 'You know how men can be. He won't let me leave the house without a careful application of kohl on my eyes. To be unadorned he says is to be unkempt. But lipstick — he thinks it is unnatural. After all these years I myself can't imagine using it.'

The women were interrupted by the arrival of a young waitress. 'Tea and a Baileys, yes?'

'Well, that's just the way they wanted it, isn't it? The two of us here and them next to the bar.' Romi was trying to look over the young girl as she lowered her tray, to where Balu and Inder were standing. The two men had turned away from the counter and were looking at their wives benignly.

'What can a man want to discuss with a stranger that he will not want to discuss with his wife? No offence meant though, Janaki. It is Janaki, isn't it?'

As she poured out the tea, Janaki wondered about it herself. There were certain things that Balu would not discuss with her. She knew that some men would come home and talk to their wives about their work and the politics that they claimed to despise and yet so obviously thrived on. Balu on the other hand totally left work behind at the office, but the would instead entertain her with domestic details about those who worked with him and under him.

'It is far more interesting for you, Janu,' he would say.

From the peon in his office to his Assistant Manager, Balu was able to tell Janaki of their misfortunes and sickness, of the birth of sons and grandsons, of the marriages of sisters and daughters and of the building of houses, of the selling of family homes, of the buying of jewellery and of the pawning of the same, of the pilgrimages made and the vows taken — all that, but nothing more. Nothing about the drive for new customers, the new rules for fixed deposits, the raid by the Income Tax Department or the work to rule by the Clerical Union. All of that she gathered in her own time from newspapers and issues of the company newsletter. She didn't do anything with the information but it still gave her pleasure to know a little of what it was that her husband did at the offices of the Golden Life Chit Fund.

Romi was looking at the men again, her drink in her hand. Janaki was curious about the Baileys. It looked like milky coffee but smelt like alcohol. It seemed a good way to strike up a conversation.

'If you don't mind me asking, what is your drink?'

'Mine? This? Baileys. Here, taste it. It is made with cream and whiskey. My daughter introduced me to it.'

'I don't drink.'

'Oh, I was like that too. Very traditional and Indian. Then he brought me here halfway across the world. Now I am neither here nor there. Everything with us is half and half — we are bastardised English and bastardised Indians. I wear my *salwar kameez* with trainers and I wear a *bindi* when I am in trousers. I am happy sometimes but most of the time homesick. To tell you the truth, this holiday is a present from our children — our two daughters. The elder one is an Immigration Officer and the younger one is a pharmacist. This European tour was a joint anniversary gift from the two of them. Last Saturday we were thirty years married.' She paused before adding, 'That is why my Inder is sitting with your husband!'

Both the women laughed. Janaki warmed to this woman who was able to speak her mind with such apparent ease. She put her cup of tea down.

'I think women are the ones who open up

to other women, even strangers,' she said. 'I remember the time I was returning to my father's house for my confinement. He had retired and left Madras for the hometown in Kodai. By the time the train got to Kodai Road Station, I knew the life history of the three other women in the ladies' sleeper compartment and they knew all about mine. Even my sisters, to this day do not know the things I told those women. Of course, I knew I would never see any of them again.'

'That sort of thing happens in India. Not here. Not on journeys, anyway. But I have my friends, many of us in the same boat like I was telling you, neither here nor there. It is better with friends: some things you can't discuss with your sisters. I find that with younger sisters you don't want to sow ideas in their heads and I'll tell you, in my experience older sisters can be so judgemental — you know, criticising you and your husband and your children too, sometimes. No, friends are best — no criticism, lots of advice. A good friend and a kettle is all a woman needs. And the men, they are best left by the bar. I'm telling you.'

Janaki looked towards Balu. Even from this distance she could tell just from his shoulders that he had begun to relax. He had taken his jacket off and it hung from the back of the barstool. She thought of all the women over the last thirty-three years of her married life that she had met on trains and bus journeys. She could not remember a single face and yet some of them had been entrusted with her most personal thoughts and worries. It wasn't that Balu was not a good listener. There was nothing he liked better than to come home from work and listen to her talk about the day's goings-on. If she didn't tell him, he would ask her, demand that she come and sit down and fill him in on the details of her day while he drank his coffee and read the evening papers.

She would tell him practically everything and she knew that behind that paper he was listening carefully, for he would often lower it, swiftly if he was angry and slowly if he was surprised. If it was something funny, he would fold the paper away temporarily and laugh. While Ram was growing up and still at home in Madras, he would join in the sessions as well, staying away only if he knew that he was going to be the complaint of the day. Janaki was aware that Balu was unusual, for most of the women in her circle grumbled that their husbands didn't want to know anything about the domestic routine of the house.

When Balu and Janaki eventually left the

bar half an hour later, it was in a flurry of quick goodbyes and promises to see each other the next morning. The Singhs naturally were not going to do the London optional and they remained in the bar in each other's company, fortified with fresh drinks in their hand.

Janaki half expected to see them in the lobby when they came back to the hotel but it was late and the lobby was deserted except for those returning from the London tour. Balu had been mesmerised by London, almost overcome with emotion at seeing long-familiar landmarks up close in stone and mortar. But he had not been impressed with the Tower of London. He was incensed at what he called a blatant display of stolen goods.

'These Crown Jewels should be returned to where they belong, Janu. Most of them to us in India,' he muttered darkly and spent the rest of their brief time in the Tower pointing out to her various treasures large and small that he confidently declared were rightfully India's.

Janaki was struck by the orderliness of the crowds and the queues, the abundance of the flowers in window boxes, in hanging baskets, in elaborate colour coordinated flowerbeds at roundabouts and traffic islands. Flowers that seemed sacred almost, for they remained untouched, protected by some amazing sort of unwritten civic code.

Once in the room, Janaki washed and changed and lifted the heavy quilted bedcover back. Underneath were more neat layers of blankets and flannel sheets, clinically folded and precisely tucked. She lay back and looked at their bags, all packed and ready for the next day's six a.m. departure, while the clothes they were going to wear for the long journey to Amsterdam hung neatly on the two chairs. She wasn't surprised when Balu's feet reached out to hers almost as soon as he had switched off the bedside lights and got under the sheets. She stretched her fingers as far down towards her knees as she could and pulled up her thick cotton nightdress. He turned heavily in the bed, nearly losing his balance in this deep mattress into which elbows and knees seemed to sink so easily. She opened herself to him as she always did, only just as he lifted himself over her. He was mindful of any discomfort that he might cause her, not by the look on her face nor by what she said for she always remained silent, never having known what to say; but by the way she shifted her body under him, easing her hip or turning her shoulder. Sometimes he would fondle her breasts, but not tonight.

It had been two weeks since they had left Madras and since he had turned to her, in this his customary fashion, at night. He was sated within minutes and she drew her legs back together as he rolled off her, panting softly.

Janaki drew her nightclothes down, repeatedly smoothing imaginary creases across her stomach. Balu had dozed off, lying on his side, his hand on her shoulder. When she closed her eyes she knew that sleep would be a while in coming, thwarted by the nagging, achy restlessness in her feet and ankles. She turned and twisted her ankles clockwise and anti-clockwise, the clicking of her joints giving her a satisfaction that was inexplicable. Her eyes flew open when she realised that she had not thought of Ram since having left the hotel bar late that afternoon. He had promised to call to say he and Viji had reached home safely. Janaki was sure he had left a message at the reception desk and a small cry of regret left her lips. She consoled herself; after all, the message would still be there, to be picked up before they left for Amsterdam tomorrow morning. Still, she thought, as she pulled the sheets up closer to her chin and then turned to do the same for Balu, it would have been nicer to know that they had driven home without any incident.

Balu normally got irritated with her for what he called her needless worrying, but all these years of his mocking admonishment could not stop what came to her naturally. So she had learnt to worry silently, trusting in her frequent but brief entreaties to the powerful resident deity in her local temple.

They must have reached home safely, she said to herself again. It was Balu who had taught Ram to drive, so Janaki was surprised that she actually felt safer when Viji was behind the wheel. Her daughter-in-law didn't seem to take as many risks as her son. On the last journey the four of them had done together, a day trip to Cambridge, she found herself jamming on imaginary brakes as Ram drove in what seemed to be a needless hurry. If I had learnt how to, I am sure I would drive like Viji, she thought. She knew that driving a car was not something that she had needed to know like cooking or sewing or praying. If it were, her father would have ensured that her mother had organised to have Janaki duly instructed, well before they had felt she was ready to get married.

Balu had felt no differently from her father. He had laughed heartily when the subject of her learning to drive had come up. Janaki had never dwelt on that incident, but now twenty years later she felt a degree of irritation with herself. Perhaps if she hadn't so readily joined him in his laughter he might have actually considered it. But his reaction, all those years ago, to her casual question had been so spontaneous that she had believed without question his inference that she was incapable of learning something so complex.

But one only had to see the speed and skill with which she used the hand-operated sewing machine — why, even today the same friends who would laugh when she said she preferred her beloved old Singer to the newfangled foot pedal ones, would shake their heads in admiration when they saw the dexterity with which she used it. The brass fittings on the machine had been polished to a shiny smoothness with years of usage and sometimes, as she held the wooden handle of the wheel steady for a second before she set it spinning, she could almost feel her fingers fit into their own impression. Three decades of usage embedded lightly onto the wood. Even before she was married she was able to have the machine going for far longer than any of her sisters, guiding the fabric with one hand, able to follow the contours of the tailor's chalk without having to slow down, even if the fabric was silky and slippery. The tailoring master that her father had employed for Janaki and her sisters had declared her to be an exceptional pupil, though Janaki found out only years later that he had in fact not headed for the Middle East in search of a job, as she had been told, but had stopped coming to the house to teach them because he had been dismissed by her mother for the excessive attention that she thought he had begun to pay Janaki.

Janaki turned in the bed and lay on her side with her back to Balu. There was no point in thinking about it now, and what use would the ability to drive have been to her anyway? But she was still not happy, having realised for the first time the true extent to which she had colluded in putting herself down. Her frustration had made her hot and she pushed the sheets off her chest and pulled up her feet till she was able to pop them out of the cocoon of the tightly tucked linen. It was a very long while before she slept, Balu's stentorian snoring pre-empting any chances of her being able to sort out her troubled thoughts before morning.

4

When Balu stepped into the Allsights coach for the first time he was thoroughly impressed. By the time they were all boarded and on the way to Dover he was familiar with every gadget, button, vent and concealed pocket that surrounded his seat. This was definitely the king of coaches, unlike any other he had ever seen. It was a hundred times better than the Super-Luxury Deluxe A/C coach on which he normally booked a seat for Janaki all those years running when she used to go back for her annual stay with her parents in Kodai. Even though she would never have insisted on it, he considered it his duty to send her back in comfort, a reassurance for her parents that all was well with their daughter. But that was years ago and since then Janaki's father had died and her mother had, as was proper, gone to live with her son in Jamshedpur where he worked as a chemical engineer at the Tata Steelworks.

Soon after her father's death, Janaki had broached the subject of her mother coming to live with them for a while and Balu had tried to explain his decision as firmly as he could.

But she had been unwilling to see reason and had retreated into one headache after another until her brother's letter arrived. The brother questioned Janaki's good sense, stating that their mother was now his responsibility, and sending her to Balu and Janaki in Madras so soon after she was widowed and that too for a prolonged stay, would leave him open to criticism of having shirked his duty. Moreover, his own wife's reputation as a responsible daughter-in-law would be compromised and if their mother were unhappy in Jamshedpur, as Janaki felt, she would soon get over it.

Balu had read the letter and asked her if she would now at least concede that he, Balu, had been right about the way her brother would feel.

'Which is more important — my mother's happiness or my brother's sense of duty?' she had answered quietly and finally on the subject.

Balu had let the matter rest but it remained an unsatisfactory episode in their lives, for he had found it unreasonable that she would blame him for predicting her brother's reaction so accurately. He had tried since then to have as little to do with Janaki's brother as possible, resenting him for the unsettling effect he had on her. To add to

Balu's annoyance, the man had the temerity in the following years to try and exercise control over Janaki as if trying to replace the father that she had lost. In spite of all that, Janaki had, even this morning as they were settling into the coach, reminded Balu that her brother had asked her to buy him a cuckoo clock from Switzerland. She had seemed oddly defiant, mentioning the cuckoo clock almost to annoy him on purpose.

The sun hadn't as yet risen, and as they sped down the dual carriageway, London's sprawling suburbs fell behind to be replaced by smaller towns and villages all shrouded in the dark. He had caught a glimpse of Inder and Romi when they had boarded the bus but the tour guide, a tall burly man with a head of tight curls and khaki chinos with sharp creases, who had a grand designation as 'Tour Director', had insisted on everyone's attention as he went through a lengthy explanation about seat rotation, the currency packs that he had on sale, the safety procedure and the day's travel ahead.

Balu reached out to adjust the spotlight above his head and to test the fresh-air vents. Janaki had her eyes closed and he nudged her elbow to ask if she wanted to have her seat angle changed or footrest lowered, for he had figured out how to do those two tasks. But she was actually asleep so he left her as she was and settled down to read the itinerary and map, readjusting the spotlight so that it fell precisely on the London to Dover section that he was looking at.

Though the map stayed balanced on his lap Balu, along with other passengers, was soon listening to the individual conversations that the Tour Director was having with people, as he worked his way from the front seats towards the back.

'I'm your TD. Call me Thierry.' This was followed by handshakes and as Thierry got closer, having gained far more information from each of the passengers than he wanted, Balu shook Janaki on the shoulder. He shook her more urgently when she did not respond straight away. Balu watched her as she woke with a start and then within seconds, recovering her composure, she began to neaten her hair, loosening a couple of pins in her bun and pushing them back in what always seemed to him to be random fashion. She then aligned her index finger with her nose in order to ensure, with her fingertip, that her stick-on bindi hadn't shifted and was dead centre to her forehead. Finally, she made as many minor adjustments to her sari as she could given the constraints of doing so in a sitting position.

Balu was familiar with this rapid sequence of actions that Janaki always followed when she felt that she was going to be under scrutiny. The TD was listening to the group of four women in the two sets of seats ahead of them. Despite Thierry's impatience, which was obvious to everyone else watching, the women, who were clearly members of some yet unknown club for they all wore identical, indecipherable lapel pins, began to enthusiastically regurgitate the details of their long and tedious journey from Chicago to London. Soon they forgot about Thierry and proceeded to dispute each other's versions and opinions about the service on board the long-haul flight. But no sooner did he make a move towards Balu and Janaki than they grabbed him quite literally by his wrists, reminding him that they had yet to buy the currency packs from him.

As the money changed hands, they bombarded Thierry with questions about the manner in which he would ensure that the seat rotation would be fair, the best way to use the tiny on-board toilet while the coach was on the move, how much shopping time they would have in Paris. When he had answered all those questions as clearly and as fast as he could, they asked him why, when his French parents migrated to New Zealand soon after they married, had he, Thierry, come back to Europe. Was he searching for his roots? However, they paid scant attention to his pointedly brief reply, for the shrillest of them suddenly remembered her son-in-law's yet unsuccessful quest for his Irish ancestry. She began to relate that saga, starting with the initial enquiry at the New York City Public Records Office.

Balu shook his head in disapproval. He could see the profile of one of the women through the slim gap between the backs of the two seats. But looks would not have mattered anyway, for he had taken an instant dislike to these loud women who seemed to have no hesitation in being so opinionated.

'No wonder Mrs Bhaskaran is so happy in America. Her kind of women come from there.'

'Mrs Bhaskaran on our street? Our Mrs Bhaskaran?'

'Don't these four remind you of her, Janu?'

'She was a well-meaning person.'

'Huh! She with her BA degree in Social Work. Just because she had that, she thought it gave her a licence to become well-meaning. Her husband never forgot to remind me, and the rest of the world, that he had married an educated woman. What did she achieve anyway? Seeding so many desperate women in the slums with notions of escaping their fate, when they never had a chance given the men they married. Always trying to cure the symptoms. Always short-term solutions.'

'But it was a good cause. She helped so many.'

'The trouble is, Janu, none of these do-gooders have any vision. 'Go to the root of the problem' is what I told her once, the time she came to my office looking for donations from the Chit Fund. 'Take the same slum, give the men some hope, a future to look forward to and the life of the women will change.' I told her that. Gave her my solution, told it to her face without any hesitation. But do you know what she said? She lectured me with some long theory about breaking the dependency culture. Tried to impress me with big words. Anyway, why are we discussing her?'

Getting no reply he turned to look at Janaki and saw her going through the motions of busying herself by pulling out a hairpin or two from her bun and pushing them in again. It irritated him no end when she did this. Balu always felt, in fact he knew for certain, that she did this on purpose. She had an infuriating habit of indicating her disagreement with silence instead of just saying what he knew she wanted to say. This attitude of hers gave him no avenue for a satisfying conclusion. The mention of Mrs Bhaskaran, and to a certain extent the old odd-job man Patta, often had this effect on conversations that he had with Janaki. Balu knew he had to tolerate Patta, for the odd-job man was admittedly useful in many ways. Not only did he do the queuing and the waiting outside the milk booth early every morning and the ration shop once a month, he was somehow able to give Janaki advance information about impending shortages of any domestic necessity, of electricity failures, of telephone lines being repaired and of water mains being turned off. Patta knew when the Corporation's anti-malarial fumigation squad were going to be around and he was almost always able to give Janaki half an hour's notice if the temple elephant was doing the round of the local streets.

It would give Janaki sufficient time to arrange an offering of fruits on a platter and, in the early years when Ram was still a child, to have him waiting impatiently at the gate with a coin in the palm of his little hand. The elephant's set routine of sniffing up the coin and blessing the donor's head with the warm, wet and inquisitive tip of its trunk would leave Ram squealing with nervous excitement and Balu, on his return home from work, would be spared no detail of the pachyderm's fund-raising visit.

Patta seemed to be able to gather all this vital information by just sitting at the street corner for long periods of time, squatting on his haunches in the meagre shade of the milk booth. He washed Balu's car early every morning and raked the dusty garden of fallen leaves twice a day. He ran numerous small errands for Janaki and was a useful source of sundry information about all the neighbours in the street. Yet, Balu disliked him. It had nothing to do with the fact that he seemed to do very little most of the day, or that he was constantly cajoling Janaki for Balu's old clothes, or that he always managed to wheedle a week or two's salary in advance. No, what thoroughly irritated Balu was the fact that right from the very start, when he had first come looking for a job, whenever Patta spoke to them it was always Janaki whom he addressed. If Janaki was not available he would wait on the verandah or come back later to divulge his information straight to her or to take his instructions directly from her. This subtle exclusion incensed Balu, and his annoyance was compounded by the fact that Patta's jobs were so menial that they came firmly under Janaki's domestic realm and to take offence openly would have been below Balu's dignity.

Mrs Bhaskaran touched a different nerve, far more raw. She lived diagonally opposite Balu and Janaki's house in a brand new bungalow, which she and her husband had built on a quarter of an acre plot that had lain empty for years. When she used to come around occasionally it was Janaki's behaviour that caused Balu most concern. He would find it very difficult to catch his wife's eye, for Janaki seemed to be mesmerised by her neighbour's talk, which was almost always about the plight of the women who attended the Slum Welfare Centre of which Mrs Bhaskaran was the Secretary. She told stories of desperation and misery in which the men drank away their meagre earnings and then battered their wives, always quoting names, dates and figures to authenticate her 'case studies' as she liked to call them. Janaki was constantly awestruck by her good works and grand plans, never taking her eyes off the portly woman. The only time she would look at Balu, if he happened to be present, was when Mrs Bhaskaran would urge Janaki to contribute her time towards one of the many causes that needed the input of 'committed' women.

This was invariably the point where Balu would assert himself, standing up and pushing his chair back, running his fingers over his neatly combed hair.

'Charity begins at home, Mrs Bhaskaran. My wife is already a very committed lady. It is plain for anyone to see that she is devoted to her family and we are grateful to her for it.' He almost never stayed around to hear her reply and, if Mr Bhaskaran was also present, Balu would make it a point to smile genially as he spoke, for he did not want the man to think that he was casting aspersions on Mrs Bhaskaran's devotion to her family.

These confrontations with their neighbour would always result in recriminating silence on Janaki's part, and now on the coach, it maddened Balu to think that a harmless comment on the woman, who had after all exited their lives when she had migrated a few years ago to America with her husband, would make Janaki slip back into using an old ploy — and that, now, while they were just starting out on the tour, even before they had got to Dover! The Tour Director, Thierry, was nearly done with the women in front and was about to move on to Balu and Janaki, but Balu was determined that he would not let Janaki have the mute last word on the subject.

He spoke with one eye on Thierry's progress towards them. 'What is the use of Mrs Bhaskaran having stirred things up for those wretched women anyway? After all that incitement she went off to America and left them to their own devices. Left them to flounder with half-baked ideas of independence. I am telling you there was never any hope for them because there was never any hope for their husbands.'

Janaki was looking at her feet. 'I could have learnt to drive as well as Mrs Bhaskaran.'

'Let me guess. You are both from Pakistan?' Thierry was upon them at last, with one hand outstretched towards Janaki.

Balu looked at his wife and then at Thierry in confusion. They were shaking hands oblivious to his reaction. Had he heard Janaki right? What was she talking about? Driving like Mrs Bhaskaran? And why was this Tour Director fellow calling them names? He found himself floundering, unsure of how to break into their conversation. Thierry was pointing to Janaki's *bindi*, nearly touching her forehead as he did so.

'I was told that this spot that you are wearing covers a woman's third eye. Apparently, without its protection anyone could look into the woman's soul.'

Janaki looked hesitant and Balu recovered his composure. 'It is a symbol of marriage actually, a Hindu symbol. My wife and myself, we are from India.'

'Ah ha! Very clever, so only the husband can have a look into the woman's soul. But tell me, what about your wife? Does she have a window into your soul?'

'We have no secrets.' Balu was serious.

Thierry winked at Janaki. 'That's what we all like to think.'

Balu forgave him for being so forward, making a mental note to tell Janaki that she should also do the same; after all, the Tour Director was crucial to the enjoyment of their trip and it was a known fact that these foreigners were sometimes insensitive to the cultural traditions of others.

★   ★   ★

When they got to Dover, there was a great flurry of excitement with bags, cameras and coats being pulled from the overhead racks with unnecessary haste, only to end up being organised and reorganised several times over on people's laps, while the Allsights coach inched its way behind at least a dozen others in the agonisingly slow queue for passport control.

When Balu got off the coach he could hear Janaki, who was right behind him, cracking her knuckles in nervousness. She was convinced she was going to be seasick and he knew from past experience that there was not much he could do to help her. Janaki was biddable, but the one thing he had not been able to do, despite their years of marriage, was exercise any control over her fears. Balu found it difficult to totally ignore it as well, for Janaki's coping mechanisms, the wringing of her hands, the brief closing of her eyes, her under the breath prayerful mutterings — all drove him to distraction and finally to rebuke which he knew, even as he said it, was completely in vain.

Inder and Romi Singh had got off the coach as well and were waiting by the footbridge that led directly onto the ferry. They waved to Balu and Janaki to catch their attention.

'We were planning to go on to the upper decks and take in the view. We could go to the restaurant together afterwards.'

Balu was pleased that the Singhs had waited and as they led the way on board, he pointed out the fact to Janaki.

'Typical Indian courtesy. In spite of living in the West they haven't lost it at all. It is in our blood I tell you, in our blood.'

The route to the upper decks was confusing and crowded with sluggish streams of people passing each other down the narrow corridors and stairs. Everyone stopped to read each sign and every deck-plan, and yet it was clear from people's dithering manner that most were slow to get their bearings. The upper deck, when they reached it, was very exposed, cold and wind-swept, and the air had that familiar smell of salt, diesel and fish that ports all over the world share. They stood next to each other in silence, leaning against the rails watching the cars, coaches and articulated lorries disappear into the bowels of the ferry. Janaki's sari had caught the wind and it ballooned around her like an upside down tulip exposing her slim ankles and threatening with every gust to rise even further. She pulled the three-quarter length woollen coat that Viji had lent her closer around herself and shivered.

Romi stepped back from the rail and stuffed her hands into the pockets of her jacket. 'This is complete madness. It was your idea, Inder. If I stay out here any longer I am going to get chilled to the bone. Shall we go below, Janaki?'

Realising that Janaki was looking almost grateful for the suggestion, Romi turned on her husband again. 'We are going to get warmed up. A shot of brandy in our coffees — okay, Janaki? Come on.'

Balu was a little taken aback at the speed with which Janaki scurried behind Romi

Singh as she headed for the stairs. 'My wife doesn't drink,' he shouted out as the women turned the corner. Inder was blowing his nose, trumpeting into a paper napkin that Balu recognised as being from the London hotel. Inder shook his head as he folded the paper over a couple of times, getting it ready for another blow.

'My wife Romi, she never used to drink either. But my daughters, when they left home, became independent and totally, you know — English. They introduced her to it. 'Let her have a life, Dad,' is what I was told. So she drinks occasionally. Still, she sticks to the ladies' tipples.'

Balu looked at him sympathetically. 'It has medicinal qualities, brandy.'

The two men stood side by side, not saying much, trying to shake off the embarrassment that both felt for having had that unexpectedly personal exchange by occasionally pointing out the obvious to each other as they watched their cross-Channel ferry slowly pull away from the docks.

The top-heavy, many-tiered vessel headed purposefully for the opening in the harbour walls. The imposing and thick grey-green ramparts were under constant and spectacular assault from gallons of spray, whipped up by the wind, and the heave and fall of the swell revealed steps, at regular intervals along the wall, leading down to the sea. The water contained within the fortification was a muddy brown while the open sea ahead presented a dirty grey vista. As they drew further away, they watched with admiration as the petite DHB *Doughty* skilfully shepherded the enormous Sea France *Cézanne* into the berth that their own ferry had just vacated. Now, as they drew away, the true extent of the sprawl of the port became clear, nestled right underneath the famous cliffs.

'They are not as white as I remember,' said Balu, following Inder's cue but finding himself stuck. He was still fumbling with the zip to his camera case, while Inder was already clicking away in what seemed to be a sudden frenzy of picture-taking.

Inder lowered his camera. 'Oh? You have been here before?'

Balu shook his head. 'No, but I have a good memory. My wife says a photographic one. I remember seeing these cliffs on the *Pathé* newsreels. The beaches of Dunkirk. Retired RAF pilots looking up at the flypast in the sky. The famous Vera Lynn. So many anniversaries and commemorations I have seen on screen, but the images and footage rarely seemed to change. Don't you think the cliffs are actually more creamy than white? Of course I am talking about cinema in the black and white days. Nowadays everything is in colour, the *Pathé* newsreels have long gone and so has the national anthem. Do you remember those days? But then there was so much disrespect shown to the anthem that they had to stop playing it at the end of the show.'

Inder was nodding vigorously so Balu continued, appreciative of his assenting audience. 'It is a collective cancer we suffer from, this contempt for authority. Look at the British, see how they queue for everything. The only thing Indians will line up for is cinema tickets. But what's the use? They don't even make movies like they used to. The black and white days were the best. Those were movies that had some meaning: they gave you something to think about.'

'Romi is cinema crazy. Hindi movies have been her lifeline to India ever since we left. I have no time for all that running around the trees but she enjoys it.'

Balu slung his camera back on his shoulders. 'Yes, the new productions are like that. I myself rarely go these days. Heroines with no substance and this new angry-man type of hero — a complete waste of time.'

'But you surely can't blame the industry really. Tastes are changing. People don't want the Sati Savitri, goody-goody heroine any more. They want to see more, you know — more flesh, more fights.'

'What was wrong with that Sati Savitri type of a heroine as you put it, anyway? How can virtue go out of fashion?'

'I suppose the audience just got fed up with the same formula.'

Balu felt he didn't know Inder well enough to really pursue the argument. What was lacking in the formula heroine? Which man in his right mind would spurn an obedient daughter, a faithful wife and a selfless mother? Balu stared at the dull grey horizon ahead. For a brief moment he thought again about that first time he had seen Janaki. He had long ago admitted to himself that there had been a cinematic quality about the way she had descended the steps, so conventional and decorous, and that probably was what had given him that immediate sense of assurance that he had made the right choice.

At the outset, in the early years of their marriage itself, he had appreciated her guilelessness and her impressionable nature, traits that contributed to her very agreeable personality. She was hardworking, had a propensity to please, and once she had overcome her initial nervousness around him, he found that she was an amenable wife, non-confrontational and happy with her lot. He was proud of the fact that he had in return spared no effort to be good to her, making allowances for her very occasional lapses into silence. Balu ensured that Janaki could hold her head up high in front of her sisters and their families at festival times by buying her a reasonable number of new clothes for the occasion, and after Ram's birth even a modest set of jewellery now and then. He sent her to her father's house for a holiday every year and pleasantly surprised his in-laws by continuing this practice even after Ram was born. He never withheld his permission for her to make short, unscheduled visits home for weddings and funerals as long as the relative involved was close kin. By doing his duty Balu knew he had gained Janaki's complete loyalty. Why change things when they were so right?

Balu was aware of Inder standing beside him, looking out to sea, blowing into his cupped palms and then patting his warmed fingers against his cheeks. Though he did not want to argue, Balu felt compelled to say something in support of the traditional model of womanhood, the Sati Savitri image that Inder had dismissed so perfunctorily.

'Why look for another formula when this one works?'

'Cinema audiences are notoriously fickle. Romi's brother had a film producer friend. He told me that once. Today's hero is tomorrow's zero.'

'See? This is the reason why the moral climate is deteriorating. When tradition is cast aside, the natural equilibrium of things gets upset. I am a firm believer in that.'

Inder did not reply and Balu wondered if his theorising had hit a touchy spot, given that Inder's daughters were obviously beyond his control and had even succeeded in influencing their mother, Romi. Balu felt bad, for the last thing he wanted to do was to have caused this man any distress. He thought hard for something palliative to say but Inder pre-empted him quite cheerfully.

'Too cold up here. Let's join the women in the bar, shall we?'

Balu quickened his steps. He had assumed the two women would be in a restaurant, and as he and Inder wandered around looking for their wives in the numerous bars that seemed to dot every deck on the Sea France *Renoir*, he wished Janaki had not gone off. If only she had just put up with the cold and stayed a little bit longer, she wouldn't have found herself in a bar of all places! So he was rather relieved when the ladies were eventually located in the main self-service restaurant, the very grandly named International Food Court, at a table with a few others from the Allsights group. The six Malaysian women, who had been sitting a couple of rows behind Balu and Janaki on the coach, were passing around photographs of their children and one or two of them were suddenly overcome with emotion and pressed the corners of their eyes with the back of their hands and sniffed, twisting their noses from one side to the other as they did so.

Inder took it upon himself to cheer them up. 'What about photos of the husbands? Save some tears for them.'

At this there were smiles all around and more photographs were produced. The group of close friends, all paediatric nurses from Kuala Lumpur, soon headed off for the shops on board. The ship was beginning to roll and toss slightly, and Balu turned to ask Janaki if she felt okay and then changed his mind at the very last moment, reasoning that if he brought it to her notice, there was a greater likelihood of her feeling seasick. Moreover, his attention had suddenly been caught by the Australian couple Don and Pat who were in a passionate clinch even as they queued to pay for their meal, but it was the manner in which they were gripping each other's buttocks that made Balu avert his eyes. Inder had followed Balu's gaze and he snorted quietly. Balu wished he hadn't, for it had unnecessarily drawn Janaki's eye to the uninhibited display. She looked away immediately as Balu knew she would and Inder laughed at her reaction.

'I keep telling Romi that if we can't beat them we should join them. After all, we came from the land of the *Kamasutra*: we could teach these *angrezi* fellows a thing or two.'

'*Chee*, Inder!'

Inder leant back in his seat, drumming the table with his fingers, licking his lips and grinning at his wife's discomfort. Balu was unsure about the sincerity of the embarrassment, for even as she had expressed her feelings so explosively, a small smile played at the corners of Romi's mouth. Next to her, Janaki was looking down vacantly at the palms of her hands. Balu's mind raced in various directions for he felt it was his turn to say something, to add a jestful aside, and he felt a small twinge of irritation with his wife. Could she not at least make a little bit of a pretence at not being shocked? A small laugh, a sage nod, something that would give the Singhs the impression of being at least a little bit worldly? He felt compelled to look towards the cash till where the Australians had progressed to in the queue. They now

119

each had a hand stuck into the other's back pocket and were nuzzling each other's necks in turn.

'This is nothing. Wait till we get to Amsterdam. They are world leaders in the art of public displays.' Inder winked at Balu and then leant towards him in a conspiratorial way. 'Pure non-vegetarian stuff, as we say in India.'

Balu smiled at Inder, all the while thinking about Perumal, his old friend going back all the way to their apprentice accountancy days. Far from being at a loss for words, Perumal would have been in his element had he witnessed the Australians' behaviour and would have been able to match Inder's confident ribaldry with something equally crude. As for Perumal's wife, she would be tittering in a corner, the act of covering her mouth with her hand a sham, a mere symbolic gesture of demureness. Thank God Janaki wasn't like that. When Balu thought about the kind of woman she could have turned out to be if she had married someone else, he felt sorry for his earlier brief irritation with her.

Balu had remained friends with Perumal, who had for some inexplicable reason taken on the task of helping him with the arrangements for his marriage to Janaki. Balu had been mollified, flattered by Perumal's efforts and had quickly forgotten the offensive references he had made at the very start of the matrimonial process. That was, until the day, nearly a year after Balu's wedding, when Perumal returned from two weeks leave of absence, having gone with his parents back to their hometown to get married to a girl of their choice. He had been unhappy the day before he left, nervous and unsure of what to expect. After all, unlike Balu, he hadn't even seen the girl he was going to marry, just her photograph. But fifteen days later, it was a different man who returned.

'I am very happy,' he confessed to Balu at lunchtime. He had persuaded Balu to abandon the tiffin that Janaki had packed for him and insisted on buying him a mutton *biryani* at the newly opened Military Lunch Home, striding straight into the gloomy air-conditioned section and brushing aside Balu's protests at the expense he was going to.

'I am very happy,' he repeated, lowering his voice despite the fact they were the only two people in the bitterly cold room. 'She has watermelons, that's what she has. Not mangoes. And she wasn't afraid at all — you know what I mean.' He looked satisfied as he pushed his empty plate away and lit a cigarette, blowing huge puffs in the direction of the No Smoking sign.

Balu had kept his head down, pretending to shake out the rice clinging to the large chunks of mutton by tapping the bony pieces on the plate and suddenly realising that the reason why the grains of rice were dyed a patriotic saffron, green and white was because Independence Day celebrations were only three days away. The awkwardness that he felt at being privy to Perumal's personal life was acute, more so because he knew exactly what Perumal meant. Why, he could remember his own terror at finding his bride of half a day, Janaki, lying rigid in their bed, fully clothed and trembling like a leaf. Not knowing how to deal with her he had stayed on his side of the bed avoiding even any accidental contact with her and, listening to her shallow breathing, he had eventually fallen asleep. The situation remained unchanged for weeks, and soon Balu began taking a constitutional twenty-minute walk at night, returning to his bed well after Janaki was asleep. In his mind, Balu would always acknowledge Mr Nath as being instrumental in ensuring the consummation of his marriage.

Mr Nath had seemed completely nonplussed when Balu had approached him with his problem, Balu's inability to come to the point in itself a clear indication to Mr Nath that the matter was of a highly delicate nature. Mr Nath had in fact surprised Balu with his astute and clever reading of the situation, advising Balu even before the problem had been fully divulged.

'Just close your eyes and do it, or your good wife will wonder what is the problem. Okay, you say today she is afraid, but tomorrow she will think that you feel there is something wrong with her. The real problem is that, the day after tomorrow, she will begin to think there is something wrong with *you*.'

Balu was still thinking about Perumal and Mr Nath when Inder and Romi got up, saying they were heading for the hot food counter. Janaki looked up and watched them walk away.

'Let us eat as well, Janu. We will reach the French port before we know it.'

But Janaki was feeling slightly queasy and refused to take any chances, urging Balu to join the queue with the Singhs on his own. Three hours later, having driven past the Fields of Flanders in the distance, they sped down an extremely dull motorway through Belgium and into Holland. Balu regretted that he had not forced Janaki to have something, even a glass of milk or some fruit. Now she was feeling terribly nauseous, more

123

than she did on the ferry, and Balu had no doubts that the cause was just plain hunger. Annoyed with his own poor judgement over the matter, he took it out on Janaki, urging her in angry whispers to at least try to sleep, and then got more infuriated at what seemed to be a dogged determination on her part to make things difficult for him.

Janaki held one hand over her mouth continually in a sort of dreadful anticipation, only ever moving it to replace it with the other, all the while straining to look at the sights which were anyway still few and far between, the banks of trees, dense shrubs and earth on either side of the motorway providing a sound barrier for the communities who lived along it, but completely masking the view for eager tourists on coaches such as theirs. Now and then, she made small gurgling sounds which alarmed Balu and embarrassed him greatly, for the ladies from Chicago had twice peered through the gap between the seats in front, the second time asking if she wanted a mint to suck on. Janaki had compounded his annoyance by refusing the mint with nothing but a shake of her head and before Balu had a chance to thank them, they had shrugged and turned away.

The pre-dawn start from London, the

never ending drive from Calais to Amsterdam and the fact that Thierry was constantly filling them in with details about distant spires, barely discernible castellations and shedding light on the finer historical points of famous towns and fascinating cities that they seemed to always be on the edge of but never actually in, proved to be too much for Balu and he fell asleep just as they finally left the monotony of the motorway and actually headed into a city.

When Janaki nudged him awake, their coach was crawling slowly through Amsterdam's evening rush-hour traffic. It seemed to be a great opportunity to use cameras that had been primed for so long, poised on laps ever since they boarded the coach at Calais, but the stopping and starting of the coach as it lurched through gaps in the Dutch log jam, frustrated all but the most eager of photographers. Their coach was headed for a pre-arranged rendezvous with a canal cruiser, which was to be the highlight of their first day on the tour. Thierry kept up a non-stop commentary on everything they passed, making occasional asides in French to the Belgian driver who smirked but didn't say too much in return.

Janaki had begun the rearranging of the hairpins in her bun and the tidying up of her sari. She had been so difficult earlier that Balu, when he woke, was surprised to find her smiling at him, a couple of hairpins clenched in the corner of her mouth. Her very obvious change of mood made him curious. When she turned to talk to the elderly lady sitting on the other side of the aisle, he immediately began to fret. Right through their married life, Janaki's tendency to befriend the elderly had caused him a considerable amount of nuisance.

After Balu's mother had died following a mercifully short illness, Balu found that he did not miss her presence as much as the people coming to condole him had assured him he would. What he found instead was that he was nervous about not having a back-up plan any more. While his mother was alive, there was a quiet confidence that he had got used to. If all else failed, he could at least rely on his mother's prayers to see him through whatever obstacle or crisis he had to overcome. His attitude towards his mother's piety had undergone a sea change after the arrangements of his match to Janaki had been finalised, and he had gone from tolerance to healthy respect for her fervour. Yet, when Janaki had arrived as a new bride he had discouraged her from doing what would have been considered very natural, in fact very nearly a duty for a daughter-in-law.

'Leave the praying to Amma.' He made it very plain to Janaki that there were more pressing things to be done on an everyday basis and that he considered his mother's efforts adequate. When his mother died, the taking over of the religious duties should have been seamless, for Balu would not have raised any objections to Janaki providing the buttress that he now acknowledged his mother had done all these years.

Janaki's compliance with this new require-ment of her had not been as straightforward as he wanted. Having been initially deterred by Balu from getting involved in lengthy daily rituals, she had taken to expressing her religious convictions in action and deed instead and finding great satisfaction in her method. Convinced that she had slowly but steadily built up a cache of favours with the gods that she could call upon if needed, she was unwilling to turn to the more passive methods of supplication that her mother-in-law had followed.

Balu was convinced that it was this attitude that had given her a reputation for being a soft touch, one whose simple-minded com-passion could be counted on to get a week's wage in advance or a loan of Ram's old cycle, or to be wheedled successfully out of old clothes. It was this misguided sort of charity that had often landed Balu with the payment of a variety of bills for people who were not his responsibility. From the extraction of Patta's teeth to the school fees for Muthu's widowed sister's children, Balu had been cajoled and morally blackmailed into agreement. Elderly people were Janaki's particular weakness, and she had a habit of preceding representations on their behalf with references to their agedness as if that in it self was reason enough to grant them whatever it was they were looking for.

'It is not a matter of money, Janu,' he would try to explain, hiding his sheer exasperation and annoyance behind an outwardly calm manner. 'These people take you for a big ride and then do they show any gratefulness at all? It is your attitude that makes their own kith and kin so irresponsible. They take us for fools and that is what I have against them.'

Looking at the way Janaki was leaning over the aisle now to talk to the older woman, Balu could see trouble looming. Ten minutes later on the canal cruiser he had the opportunity to ask her about her conversation with the woman and her even more elderly companion.

'Imagine, they gave me a homoeopathic remedy for my motion sickness! I thought it was only Indians who believed in it. I told them how homoeopathy cured Mrs Bhaskaran's piles and they told me that the Queen's son uses it too. I have taken the name down. Ram will buy it for us.'

'If you had had something to eat as I had told you, you wouldn't have had to take anything from those old ladies.'

'They are sisters. One is a retired nun.'

'Huh! Where is her veil? Why is she in trousers?'

'I didn't ask all that.'

'You are too simple — you believe anything. Next they will be asking you for some donation or the other. Did you tell them Viji was convent educated?'

Janaki had turned her face away, pretending, he was sure, that she was very interested in the canal boat that was being pointed out to them. It was a famous canal boat, the cruiser guide explained, beloved of the people of Amsterdam, and it housed at any one time over a hundred rescued cats. It was a feline sanctuary, started by a Dutch woman who adored the creatures.

A home for homeless cats, thought Balu, shaking his head. These people in the West had no idea, did they? Balu's irritation with Janaki returned. He thought about her nausea again. If she had listened to him she would not have had to rely on the charity of these so-called nuns. He turned around, as casually as he could, to look at them where they were sitting side by side, gawking at the cat boat. A large silver cross hung from the neck of one of the women, the older of the two. She must be the nun, thought Balu, and he was about to look away when she caught his eye and smiled, and then putting her hands together and bowing her head slightly, greeted him with a small *namaste*. Balu was taken aback, his return *namaste* to her a result purely of reflex.

The boat was glass-covered and Balu longed for some fresh air and an opportunity to stretch his legs. They had been shepherded straight from the coach into the canal cruiser and he was fed up of sitting. It seemed to be all they had done since leaving London, sitting on a coach and then on a ship, back onto a coach and now on a boat. Janaki handed him the complimentary drink that was being passed around and she smiled tentatively. He decided to be patient with his wife and was soon providing her with his own interpretation of what the rather hippie-looking guide was saying.

Balu was thoroughly impressed as he listened to the account of how the Dutch people had, over the centuries, tamed the power of the sea with their complex system of canals, dykes and levies, successfully draining and putting to good use vast tracts of their country that lay well below sea level.

'There was a time when we were good at this sort of thing as well you know, Janu,' he said shaking his head sadly and knowledgably. 'How technically advanced we were in ancient India! The provision of running water, ingenious sewage systems and the damming of rivers — it was a recognised science and considered a civic necessity. That fellow Marco Polo was all praise for us then but what would he think of us now? From floods to drought — if we aren't drowning we are dying.'

He turned to Janaki and satisfied that he had her attention, he carried on with his commentary. When they disembarked an hour later it was nearly dusk and Balu was disappointed to find that they had to get back into the bus again.

But this time it was a short trip to Dam Square where they huddled around Thierry in half circles, everyone looking towards the coach doors accusingly to see who would be the last off. It was Inder and Romi and they hurried around to where Balu and Janaki were standing.

'Some action at last,' Inder whispered,

zipping up his jacket, patting his pockets and finally, rubbing his hands together. Romi dug him in the ribs with her elbow and rolled her eyes.

Thierry was giving them cautionary instructions about pickpockets and impatient cyclists, and when he turned around and used his very large umbrella to point out the church across the square from which they would be starting their walking tour of the Sailors Quarter, there was much tittering. Thierry set off at a brisk pace, his unopened umbrella held high, a rallying marker for the sixty strong group who, for the first few minutes at least, marched behind him purposefully. Balu had steered Janaki clear of the nun and her sister, not willing to be slowed down by them, and instead he sternly urged Janaki to keep up with him so that they could be within hearing and querying distance of Thierry, for Balu had decided, in London itself, to ask plenty of probing questions, to have his curiosity about the history and culture of all the countries they were visiting to be fully satisfied.

Janaki was out of breath within minutes. 'What are we going to see at this rate?'

'Make an effort, or we will never find out. It is difficult enough to understand that man Thierry at close quarters.'

As Dam Square disappeared around a corner behind them, the streets began to narrow and, in the deepening dusk, the water reflected the lights from the windows of the gabled houses that lined the canal sides so snug and tightly. Trees overhung the water at many places and the small bridges, some of which had illuminations outlining their arches and their parapets, gave the canals an atmosphere that was nearly attractive, had it not been for a certain seediness that cloaked the streets that ran alongside the canal banks, and the pimpish-looking characters who stood languidly around, leaving no doubts in anyone's mind about the real unsavoury nature of the place they had come to sightsee.

Inder fell into step beside Balu. 'We are too early for business,' he commented. 'They must all be recovering from last night. Either that or they know that we are with our wives.' He looked over his shoulder. 'What do you say, Romi love?'

His wife pretended to ignore him, waving him on with a flick of her wrist, but she couldn't help adding with a small laugh, 'All talk.'

'Plenty of action too, love.'

Behind him Romi laughed out aloud and then murmured something to Janaki. Balu was shocked to hear his wife laugh along.

But before he could look around to gauge the true expression on her face, he saw a very large sign across the canal flicker a couple of times and then come on. It was unmissable and Balu was taken aback at the blatant graphics of it. When Thierry had briefed them in the coach, the idea that a red-light district could actually be toured was in itself so bizarre that Balu had hardly known what to expect. But when he realised from the banter on the canal cruiser that even the nun and her sister were not planning to opt out and that the teachers from South Africa were looking forward to it, he had been lulled into a false sense of security.

Now, try as he might he was unable to peel his eyes off the shapely neon lady, lurid and smiling, with pulsating red pinwheels for nipples and blue eyes that rolled heavenwards every few seconds, who sat straddling a giant yellow banana that rocked suggestively. Minutes after she had been switched on, more neon appeared around her but this time in the form of text, detailing, for those whose imaginations wouldn't stretch that far, the quirky extras that were part of the live show on the premises.

To Balu's consternation, Thierry led them across the bridge directly past the establishment, though he did not have much to say in terms of commentary, except to re-issue his warning about not taking photographs. Crossing the bridge seemed to have brought them into the very heart of the district, for business appeared livelier and brisker, speciality bars and clubs advertising permutations and combinations to satisfy every sort of appetite, shops selling erotica and pornography vying with other establishments providing many varieties and variations of the real thing.

Thierry's group derived a smug legitimacy from the fact that theirs was a collective gawking, and despite grave individual reservations about ogling too obviously, as a group they window-shopped in as matter-of-fact a manner as they could, letting their guard down however whenever confronted with a truly outrageous accessory or deviation. When this happened there was either an averting of eyes or muffled giggles, but more often than not, disbelieving shakes of the head.

Balu found the visual titillation very difficult to cope with. He was shocked and mesmerised and, more worryingly for him, slightly aroused. Thierry had led them on to a small side street, waiting at the corner to make sure that the stragglers in the group had caught up. The hypnotising effects of the past twenty minutes or so became apparent to Balu when he realised that he had unwittingly let Janaki slip behind. She had somehow ended up walking with the nun, Sister Bernadette, and her sister Breda, on either side of her, the nun holding on to Janaki for support, the threesome making up the very tail end of the group. Balu was remorseful and thankful all at once, ashamed that he had in the heat of the moment forgotten his wife and grateful to the two elderly women for providing Janaki with something to do, rather than have to suffer the indignity of looking around. He tried in vain to catch her eye but having caught up with the rest, Janaki and the elderly women began to take stock of the spot that Thierry had them waiting at. Inder and Romi had paired off together again and as they walked ahead on Thierry's signal, Balu was torn between waiting for Janaki and her companions or setting off in the relative privacy that came from being partnerless in the group.

As he debated the issue in his head he began to walk slowly, letting others in the group overtake him if they wanted, assuring himself that if he did so, Janaki would anyway not be too far behind. Soon he was practically dragging his feet, moving along only because he felt that decency demanded that he not come to a full stop in front of one of the tiny, garishly lit rooms with huge windows that overlooked the street. Nothing could have prepared him for the sight of naked women wearing only minuscule pieces of lingerie, some of it mere string, ensconced as objects in what could only be described as three-dimensional living pictures, with other items — a bed bathed in bluish-red light, a selection of condoms, paper towels and creams — all arranged beside the female centre-piece, like a still-life montage.

Balu had never seen such nakedness, so much bare flesh being flaunted so wantonly. It was a sleazy spectacle, but he couldn't help marvelling at the milky-white skins of the European girls and the gleaming ebony of the black women. He was shocked at the presence of Asian women, who stared back him defiantly, almost as if they could sense his disapproval. He was confident they were from other parts of the subcontinent, not India. He felt under assault from his mixed feelings, immediate ones that made him mentally recoil with aversion, and as he went past window after erotic window, inexplicable voyeuristic ones that bordered on desire. When he realised that he had slowed down so much that Janaki was right behind him, he turned around deliberately and, forcing a considerate smile onto his lips, made way for the three women, letting them go past.

'I'll walk behind you all,' he said, his lips dry and his eyes a little bleary.

He kept close behind them, but was able to stare unhindered at every window, licking his lips every now and then. One oriental-looking woman posing right up against her window, took this as a sign of indecision and pushing aside the tiny triangles of gold sequins that covered her ample, round breasts, she thrust them out at him, teasing her nipples with one hand and pushing the other into the only slightly larger triangle that covered her shaved pubis.

Balu staggered on; his only thought at that moment was of Perumal's wife. So this was what watermelons looked like. Seconds later he was thoroughly ashamed of himself, and not fully able to understand his behaviour and his unacceptable train of thoughts, he did the first penitent thing that came into his head.

'Janaki, Janu — I will walk with Sister Bernadette.'

Minutes later, Balu found himself paying morbid attention to the three or four thick hairs growing out of a large mole on Sister Bernadette's chin. She clung to his forearm, which he had obligingly offered, not hesitating to put her full weight on it as she walked. Soon Balu's shoulder began to ache and he wondered how long he would be able to hold out, wishing he had taken on the nun's much fitter, younger sister instead, for Janaki and Breda had quickened their pace and had caught up with the Malaysian nurses. At any other time, Balu would have found Sister Bernadette's nonstop reminiscing about her life as a young nun in India interesting, but the nun was completely unaware of the turmoil in her companion's mind. Balu felt sure that if he kept his eyes on her face, he would be able to get past this part of the tour without any more deviant thoughts. But the memory of those watermelon breasts filled his mind's eye and when, a quarter of an hour later, they boarded their coach that was waiting for them opposite the Royal Palace, Balu was in a sweat.

'Hot stuff, wasn't it?' Inder shuffled past, heading for his seat.

Balu nodded without looking up. Janaki waited till Inder and Romi had gone past and then murmured, 'It was shameful.'

Balu was glad to hear his wife's sensible and honest assessment, her tone calm and her demeanour unruffled. It soothed him, made him realise that what had happened to him was just a temporary insanity, a perfect example he thought, of what can happen to even the most upstanding man when unsuspectingly exposed to vice.

He patted her hand gently. 'Yes, those women have no shame.'

'No, it is the men who are shameless, the men who run those places and the men who frequent them. Sister Bernadette was telling me about it.'

Balu was stung by Janaki's retort which, though not directed at him, seemed to point a finger at the guilt of which he had only a few seconds back absolved himself.

'What will she know? Nuns! They hate men. That's why they become nuns.'

'No, she had dreamt of the Virgin.'

'Of being one?'

Janaki cracked her knuckles. 'How can you be so disrespectful? She is old and she is a nun.'

Balu put his hands to his ears. 'None of this would have happened if you had stayed by my side.'

'What is it that has happened?'

Balu snorted and kept quiet. He was aware that Janaki was fidgeting in her seat; she did that when she was aggrieved. Burdened with his guilt, Balu sulked, unwilling to make it easy for her when things were so difficult for him.

The dinner at the hotel was a boisterous affair, with constant references to the group's evening walk through the red-light area. The staid and sterile surroundings of their city centre hotel provided the perfect backdrop to the recounting of their tales of shock and embarrassment. Righteousness was expressed but it was accompanied by that all-important final shrug, that rider to all the theorems that examined deviancy, that grudgingly tolerant clause that admitted that it took all sorts to make the world.

Towards the end of the meal, word went around that if there was enough interest, a group might stroll back to the red-light district again just for a lark. It was reputed to really come alive later on in the night. There was much hesitation and posturing at this suggestion, and few takers were forthcoming immediately.

When Romi and Janaki headed for the dessert counter, Inder turned to Balu.

'What do you say? Shall we join them?'

'I have no interest. It is difficult when you are diabetic.'

Inder took a while replying; when he did, he was laughing. 'I meant after dinner. You know — along with the others.'

Balu was taken aback, for the thought had not even crossed his mind. Janaki had tried,

141

several times before they had come down for the meal, to find out what was bothering him but he had brushed aside her roundabout probing, for he could hardly tell her the truth and he was in no mood to think of a plausible explanation for his outburst. When they came down for dinner he noticed to his satisfaction that she studiously avoided Sister Bernadette and Breda as he had insisted she do. Balu spotted Inder and Romi already seated at a table with the Malaysian contingent, and had promptly headed in their direction. No, he had not given the idea of going back to the red-light district any thought at all.

Inder brought his napkin up to his face and spoke as he dabbed at his lips, stopping now and then to examine the resulting stains on the white cloth. 'To tell you the truth, I want to buy something for Romi. A surprise — you know, something romantic like.'

Balu felt uncomfortable and at a loss for words. He had seen the sort of things that were on sale as they had walked through the first time. What would a man like Inder be able to get for his wife there of all places?

'Look, our friends here — the nurses — are planning to head for the karaoke in the bar. Romi and Janaki can join them. Does your wife sing? Romi has a great voice.'

Half an hour later, Balu walked alongside

Inder, aware that he had put up very little resistance to the other man's suggestion. If Janaki had been taken aback she did not show it, while Romi's reaction of fake outrage had overshadowed her expressionless response.

There were more than a dozen or so of them who had opted for the impromptu excursion and they walked in a huddle, not sure exactly what they were going to do and no one really keen to be the leader. A live show was suggested and someone remembered seeing signs for an act with pythons. There was a collective explosion of disbelief, followed by much speculation about the cost of the tickets to such a show, the legalities of bestiality and the cruel possibility that the creatures would be drugged. It turned out that none had the stomach for it and, with the relief that followed that discovery, much of the bravado and backslapping returned and they progressed into the red-light district, now definitely looking for a live show to see, but one that was more mainstream, one that would suit the sensibilities of the three women in the group.

'Nothing too weird,' said somebody and they all agreed.

Balu wished the women hadn't tagged along and he said so to Inder.

Inder shrugged. 'Things are different on

this side of the world. Why, did you want to see the pythons?'

Balu shook his head violently. 'No, no. I meant none of this is for ladies really, is it?'

Inder sniggered. 'This is an equal opportunities tour.'

Balu wished then that he had never come, that he had stayed back, had had a cup of tea in the room, which Janaki would have made for him with a little extra milk, knowing that he was tired.

When Inder stepped into a large shop saying, 'Just a minute,' Balu followed, mopping his forehead with a handkerchief as he walked in. While Inder wandered around the lingerie section with a serious look on his face, Balu waited near the till, trying to figure out the most graceful way of saying that he wanted to go back to the hotel. Looking down into the display cabinet that he was leaning against, he jumped back with a start. Fully erect penises of every size and ethnic colour lay in neat rows, each with a descriptive label indicating race, size and battery requirements.

'All hand-finished — very realistic, you'll agree. Have to keep them locked. Shoplifting is a major problem around here. Just point to the one you want to have a look at.'

Balu looked up at the woman behind the

counter and shook his head.

'Okay, we have a good selection of vaginas too. Soft latex with internal suction, none of that rough and rubbery Made in Taiwan stuff. Just step this side.'

Balu looked towards Inder at the other end of the shop.

'Oh, he's doing the choosing, is he? It is nice to be surprised, isn't it? Where are you from?'

'India.'

'Have you seen our fridge magnets? The twelve positions of the *Kamasutra*? They are right behind you on the racks there. It is a boxed set.' The woman continued in her friendly monologue until Inder arrived at the till.

'Hmm. Chinese love balls, medium-sized. Let me check the price. Have you seen the deluxe version? They come in a velvet bag.'

Inder looked embarrassed and when the woman walked away he waved in the direction of the lingerie. 'She'd never wear that stuff. Too raunchy.'

Balu nodded, accepting the explanation but wanting to get away from the till and the upcoming transaction, for the shopkeeper had come back with two velvet bags which she was turning around this way and that, examining them for a price sticker. As he moved away and wandered around the shop he fell into a hypnotic daze, his senses confounded and stimulated all at once. These were props from the world that Perumal dreamt about living in, things he had spoken about in innuendo, the erotica that he had slyly implied he knew all about. He had always been coy about where he gleaned his information from, revealing only, in what was probably an attempt to coax Balu, that for those who had an inclination and an interest in such adult matters, the sources were many and forthcoming. All these years, Balu had never doubted that it was Perumal and not he himself who was the odd one.

Balu considered himself normal and his own sexual needs standard. They were regular and his wife satisfied them whenever he wanted. He had never looked upon sex as a recreational activity, but had accepted it as a natural desire that had to be fulfilled. Janaki was quiet and chaste in this regard and Balu's own sexual sobriety had ensured that she had remained that way. She was happy to be left alone, never once, in all the years of their marriage, having initiated anything herself and yet she was dutiful and, until a few years ago, uncomplaining even if he woke her in the early hours of the morning.

As they stepped out of the shop Inder

hesitated. 'Do you mind, I think I'll head back. Romi will be waiting.'

Balu couldn't look him in the eye, but nodded as he looked across the street to the Banana Club where the rest of the group had headed. 'I'll come with you.'

★   ★   ★

Looking back on the events that followed his return to the hotel that night, Balu was sincere in his inability to apportion blame for his behaviour fully on himself. He reasoned that if Janaki had not, during the course of the evening at the karaoke bar, allowed herself to be persuaded by the others to have an Irish coffee, she would not have gone on to foolishly agreeing to have a second glass. He was sure that if she hadn't been under the influence of the alcohol content in those two glasses of coffee, she would not have recklessly joined the others when they had ordered pegs of brandy to finish off the evening. Janaki had only herself to blame for the fact that Romi had to help her upstairs to the room and then wait for Balu to return to give him the key.

He hadn't known what to expect when he opened the door, for in the hotel lobby Romi had ominously insisted that, despite what it looked like, Janaki would sleep it off and be fine in the morning. She lay across the bed, her head on one outstretched arm, her sari in a loose pile on the floor. The strings of her petticoat and the buttons on her blouse had been loosened and she was uncharacteristically exposed, with her legs skewed apart and her breasts pushing out of her bra. She looked wayward, like a villain's moll in an old black and white movie. This was not his wife Janaki, this woman who was sprawled there unashamed and uninhibited. Balu turned on the bedside lamps and stared at her for a while. It was a novelty, being able to see her in such a revealing position in full light; the anonymity that the cover of darkness usually provided her with during his lovemaking had never given him any visual gratification. Balu reached across the bed to pull down her petticoat which had bunched up around her waist, but he stopped short, touching the inside of her thighs instead, running his fingers up and down her legs.

This was not the Janaki he knew; her painful modesty and his encouragement of it had meant he had never seen all of her naked at one time. When they were first married, it had its own appeal: her reticence unless she had the reassurance of the dark aroused him, but it wasn't long before it had become just another pattern of their everyday lives. Now, as she moved in her sleep, flinging an arm to one side, Balu stayed where he was, his hand still between her legs as he slipped into a new world, a man surrendering, slowly sucked into unfamiliar but pleasurable fantasies that flitted through his mind and electrified his body. Balu touched her underwear, rolling it down resolutely. She shifted again, sighing deeply, her body so pliable in her alcoholic stupor. This is okay, he told himself as he lowered his face between her legs, not sure of what to expect, but just following his instinct of the moment. This is not Janaki. This is not my wife.

5

Janaki had not enjoyed the visit to the diamond factory at all. The whine of the diamond polishing wheels and the bright fluorescent lighting added to the desperate throbbing in her head, and her fingers had not left the sides of her temples since the time she had woken that morning. In the showrooms she quickly found a seat and stayed there watching the others scan every tray of jewellery for something affordable. The Malaysian women were wild with excitement, each waiting impatiently to try on rings and earrings that someone else was contemplating buying.

Balu was looking at the dress watches when she saw the ladies from Chicago crowd around him, successfully muscling him away from the counter. He moved away to the mineral-water dispenser in the corner of the large room, examining the strange conical paper cups that were provided in a holder alongside. He had been very attentive to her since the morning, not hurrying her at any juncture, digging out tablets for her from the leather pouch and producing them at the breakfast table, seeking her opinion on Romi's singing voice and asking if she had enjoyed the company the previous evening. He made no reference to her intoxication, nor to the fact that she had been helped to her room and put to bed by Romi. Normally she would have dreaded this tactical game of magnanimous benevolence that he loved to play. He was very good at making her feel every bit of her guilt, when he thought she had overstepped her mark, by being overly forgiving. He would resort to this device mainly when they were in company, when any overt displeasure on his part would only reflect on his own capabilities as a husband.

However this time she was slightly defiant, bolstered by her conviction that she was not entirely responsible for what had happened to her. After all, Balu had dumped her in the company of the other women when he had known she was very tired and wanted just to go to bed, and then he had gone off to that infamous area that was of such ill-repute that people came from all over the world to see it. Why, even Sister Bernadette had looked at her pityingly this morning, and Janaki was sure that the nun would no longer be approving of Balu, as she had been the previous day when she had had the use of his arm.

151

No, this time wasn't like any of the occasions before when she would have been ready to put up with his double-edged good-humour because she knew his annoyance was justified. This was more like the time when Mrs Bhaskaran had called unexpectedly at the door, her arrival coinciding with Viji's parents' first visit to Balu and Janaki's house. The arrival of Ram's in-laws-to-be had been an occasion fraught with anxiety for Janaki, for neither Ram nor Viji had been able to get away from Delhi to join them in Madras, and she had been left to cope with her own worries about the occasion as well as with Balu's insecurities. He had not wanted her to overdo the preparations, unhappy as it was that she had cajoled him into having the house whitewashed and the grilles on the windows painted. A week before the impending visit, he had discovered on his arrival home that she had got Patta to paint the gates and the garage door as well. Janaki had reasoned her way out of that excess by saying that Patta had been idle, doing nothing, and that she had merely got him to make use of the leftover paint.

'Like a lot of things I feel strongly about, Janu, it is not a question of money. After all, we are the boy's side. Why are we bending backwards in this fashion?'

Janaki had tried her best to calm him down. 'It is a matter of Ram's pride.'

'Ram has impressed their daughter. That is enough.'

His irritation with the painting of the gate had spurred him on to keep a close check on her, making sure that everything else she did was in total moderation.

'Not too much show now, Janu. There is no need for all that Delhi-type of vulgarity.'

He insisted that there should be no more than two sweets and two savouries offered to the visitors when they came, and that it would be adequate for both the savouries to share the same chutney, which it would be easy to do if she used the leaf-shaped, divided wooden platter he had brought back from Calcutta, when he had gone there some years ago on a Regional Managers' conference. He debated with her about whether the items for the tea should be homemade or shop bought. Neither alternative was to his satisfaction; the former would be an indication of the trouble that Janaki had gone to and the latter would signify that considerable money had been spent on them, both of which would give Viji's parents the feeling that the boy's side was out to impress.

To make a good impression was the duty of the girl's side, and Balu was loath to admit

153

that they had succeeded in being so impressive, they were actually intimidating. He was jumpy and on the defensive when the couple arrived and Janaki, having gauged his mood, knew she had her work cut out. Mrs Bhaskaran's unexpected arrival eased the strain before it became apparent and Janaki began to relax, confident that her neighbour's bearing and amiability would help the evening along. But Janaki hadn't catered for Mrs Bhaskaran's reaction to Viji's father.

Mrs Bhaskaran had never before had the ear of a senior civil servant in the Finance Ministry in Delhi and she immediately launched into a complex and thorny exchange with Viji's father, debating and arguing the Central Government's attitudes towards women's causes, charitable bodies and NGOs, occasionally addressing issues to the mother too. Janaki sensed Balu's agitation immediately and refused to catch his eye, knowing that what he was going to ask her — what would in effect be the eviction of Mrs Bhaskaran — was going to be impossible to achieve gracefully.

For not having made that vital eye-contact with him and for having therefore contributed to the prolonging of Mrs Bhaskaran's stay, Balu had used the same tactic he was using on her now in Amsterdam. Although she had been resentful then, this time she was far more indignant and found to her personal satisfaction that she did not feel as cowed. Balu was heading back in her direction with a conical cup of water, which he held out to her, coaxing her with an encouraging nod to take it.

Janaki took small sips, and thought of all the things she wanted to say to him. 'Why don't you say what you want?' she blurted out finally.

He seemed startled at her outburst and then pointed to the dazzlingly lit sales counters. 'Do you want to buy something for yourself?'

Janaki was taken aback. Balu had clearly allocated the funds that they had available for their holiday under various headings, and the purchase of jewellery was definitely not one of them. He was eagerly looking forward to buying a few useful gadgets — 'quality stuff' was how he referred to them, preferably Japanese designed and German made. He had set aside a sizeable portion of their money for the purchase of the obligatory and token gifts that they would owe to people on their return to Madras. Balu had made a list of potential recipients while on their long flight from Madras to London and the list grew alarmingly long, with no possibility of anyone being dropped for fear of the long-term offence such an exclusion would surely cause. With every name that he put down in his little diary especially purchased for the trip, filing them under the various headings — 'token', 'souvenir', 'bottle', and 'substantial', Balu cursed them, the named friends and relations who had in the past, on their visits abroad, brought Balu and Janaki a small present, perpetuating a social ritual that now necessitated expensive reciprocation on his part.

Balu had grumbled terribly and Janaki had shared his sentiments until the moment when he had suggested that she buy the cuckoo clock that her brother had asked for in Madras itself, in the smuggler's market, the famous Burma Bazaar.

'Sitting in Jamshedpur, what will your brother know? Whether it is bought in Switzerland or in a Customs seized-goods shop in Madras, a cuckoo clock is still a cuckoo clock. Think of the space we will save and the chances of breakage.'

Janaki would have none of that and she countered the suggestion with one of her own. 'We could buy Mr Nath's crystal vase from there too.'

Balu had given her a black look. He had never forgotten Mr Nath, his supervisor 'and mentor' as he always liked to add grandly, and the purchase of a crystal vase for him had been at the top of Balu's list, in a category of its own under the heading 'Mr Nath'. Janaki was glad that the lights in the aircraft had been dimmed just then and Balu had been distracted, temporarily lost in admiration for the technology that enabled a large cinema screen to appear out of practically nowhere in the bulkhead above them.

Now, remembering all that painstaking budgeting and the continuous grumbling that had gone on with it, Janaki wondered why Balu had offered to buy her something at this diamond factory. She looked at Inder and Romi, who were at one of the counters surrounded by a selection of trays. Was Balu just going through the motions, not wanting to be the odd couple out, thinking she would say no? Balu seemed to have read her thoughts, for he put his hand out to her elbow.

'Let us have a look. There must be something, something small.'

Janaki got up warily. He had never before carried this game of amplified forgiveness, this charade of putting her in her place, this far. Romi had tried on diamond rings, two on nearly every finger, the miniscule tags with the weights of the diamonds printed on them fluttering as she held up her fingers to Janaki as she approached the counter.

'So difficult to choose for my daughters.'

Inder smiled through teeth that he gritted dramatically. 'So difficult to pay for my daughters.'

'He always complains. I don't know what he would do if we lived in India.'

'Balu wants me to buy something. I thought I would pick up a ring for my daughter-in-law.' Janaki glanced sideways to check Balu's reaction. He seemed delighted and Janaki knew she had done the right thing. Romi had inspired a flash of genius, and Janaki was sure that in making that clever choice, she had called Balu's bluff and mollified him at the same time. They chose the ring together with little fuss; their limited budget denied them any difficult options. Janaki had cheered up a great deal by the time Thierry had managed to gather them all up and march them out of the factory, down a couple of quiet side streets and around a corner, to where the coach was parked.

The Allsights group headed for the Bloemenmarkt, the famous floating flower market on the Singel. I will never forget this sight as long as I live, thought Janaki with a big sigh. She envied the flower sellers their jobs. How pleasant it must be to be surrounded by such incredible beauty all day, so many delicate colours and bold hues, such amazing flowers! She wished she could buy a couple of bunches, just bending down and choosing whatever she wanted, like she had seen Viji do so casually in Norwich. If Balu given her the go-ahead, Janaki would have picked a bunch of the double coloured tulips, the bright yellow ones their frilly-edged petals tipped with a shocking pink. Perhaps she would have also asked for half a dozen of the nearly black roses, each bloom so velvety and so perfectly formed that they in fact looked artificial. For a while she was lost in the imaginary dilemma of having to make such a choice, succumbing hopelessly to almost every bunch of flowers that she set her eyes on, coming back to reality only when Balu called out to her to pose for a photograph.

Their optional half-day trip to Volendam and Marken, which followed the visit to the Bloemenmarkt, was ruined by the incessant rain. Much of the excursion to the two seaside villages was spent dashing between the awnings of one souvenir shop to the shelter of the next. The locals, who were famous for going about their daily business in colourful traditional Dutch attire, were hardly to be seen and the motionless windmills that dotted the landscape near Volendam looked ghostly in the damp haze that surrounded them. In the one brief break in the rain, Balu, with his camera at the ready, made Janaki slip her feet into the giant pair of wooden clogs that had been strategically placed outside the clog-makers' workshop in Marken where they had spent a fascinating quarter of an hour. Inder was watching.

'Join your wife and let me take the photograph instead,' he offered. 'You don't want people to say she wears the shoes in your house.'

'It's trousers, Inder,' said Romi, laughing. 'He always gets these English expressions mixed up.'

Inder was squinting behind the camera. 'Trousers, panties — what's the difference?'

'*Chee* Inder!'

So Balu stood behind Janaki, holding on to her shoulders to steady himself as he stepped into the giant shoes.

'Get closer! Come on, pretend it is your second honeymoon!'

Janaki blushed and Balu came closer, his breath hot on her neck and his grip on her waist firmer than necessary. She wondered then if he was okay, for he had definitely not been himself from the time he woke, and ever since they left the diamond factory, he had oscillated between being morose, staring wordlessly out of the window, shifting in his seat constantly and then snapping out of that mood whenever he became aware of her. She had never known him to be in such a strange frame of mind and she began to worry a little. Was he unwell?

She remembered Mrs Bhaskaran detailing the events leading up to Mr Bhaskaran's first heart attack. He had not discussed the symptoms with his wife — the tiredness and indigestion, the unease, the feeling of foreboding, the pain in his jaw. If he had, Mrs Bhaskaran, who had a St John's Ambulance Society's first aid diploma, would have spotted the signs straight away. Was Balu feeling uneasy? She decided to watch him closely. It was all she could do anyway, for any questioning on those lines would only annoy him.

★ ★ ★

Back in their hotel room that evening, Balu drank a cup of tea and watched his wife as she combed out her hair. Janaki was watching him too. He seemed to be slow even in taking his cup to his lips, and she was quite sure that when she saw him look at the bed, he had shuddered slightly.

'Do you want to lie down for a while?'

Janaki tried to sound as casual as possible.

He stood up quickly and ignoring her question, walked to the opened suitcases. 'I'll sort out these bags and you get ready quickly.'

Janaki had no option but to carry on putting up her hair. Thierry had warned them about their seven a.m. start for Cologne the next day, and the last meal in Amsterdam for the Allsights group was going to be an early affair. Balu had been very determined to sit with the Singhs at dinner, telling Janaki that they were excellent company, and to Janaki's surprise he had eagerly agreed to meet them in the bar half an hour before dinner was to be served.

When Janaki opted for an orange juice, there were smiles all around. Inder patted her hand comfortingly and Romi gave her a thumbs up. Janaki felt a little embarrassed with the attention and she fiddled with her sari, keeping her eyes down, ostensibly on the pleats.

Balu looked at her with an eyebrow slightly raised. 'What about a small brandy, Janu? To keep Romi company?'

Janaki felt a rush of blood to her face. Why would Balu want to bring up the subject of the brandy? She did not think after his fairly amiable behaviour all day long, he would taunt her publicly about the previous night.

He even looked like he was actually waiting for a reply. Janaki looked at Inder and Romi and smiled. What a shock he would get if she said yes! But he would deserve it, for mocking her like this in front of them all. She thought of the difficulty she would have sleeping tonight if she was going to be upset, as she knew she already was. She reached for her bun and felt for a pin, running her finger over its smooth surface, and as she pushed it in further she nodded in Balu's direction.

'Okay, I'll have one. To keep Romi company.' She felt wretched and regretted her words immediately.

'You don't have to, you know. My wife will drink anyway.' Inder looked worried.

'I'm not that bad, what are you making me out to be?'

'Romi love, what I meant was — oh, what's the use?' Inder flung his hands up in the air and grinned at Balu. 'You get this round and I'll get the next.'

Half an hour later, just before they went into the large function room for the buffet dinner, which Thierry had promised them would have some excellent Indonesian fare, Inder headed off to the bar.

'Don't wait for me, just reserve a table and get into the queue.'

The three of them knew exactly what he

was talking about. When the coach pulled up for a break it was crucial that they decided, as they were descending the steps, the direction in which they were going to head. One could rush for the toilets first and take intense pleasure in the sheer relief that came with having an empty bladder. If they chose this option, there was the inevitability of being stuck in a long queue of indecisive people using sign language or very loud English or sometimes even both, in trying to fathom what lay encased inside various breaded and fried objects that were being tossed out of the deep fat fryers or what the black bits in the sandwich filling were, before moving on to the cash till where the struggle continued with unfamiliar currency.

The alternative was to head for the food queue, making use of the initial patience exercised by the serving assistants, to choose something adventurous and know what it was that was being eaten. Of course, this meant that an entire meal would be eaten in discomfort, with discreet squirming and then a final urgent desperation to shove everything down and head for the toilets, where things were pretty grim, having had a coach full of people pass through them.

It was a tough choice but not one that had to be made tonight. Tonight there would be a single-minded rush for the food en masse, and it was important that they position themselves to be able to make a dignified dash. Under Balu's supervision they accomplished this with ease and when Inder arrived they were all seated, with Romi having served him too. The Malaysians had once again joined them at the table, large smiles on their faces, ready to discuss the day's purchases, forming what Thierry had begun in jest to call 'the Asian axis'. When Inder arrived with the drinks, Janaki was taken aback. He had brought her another brandy. She was still lingering over the first one, which she was drinking with very little enthusiasm.

'Well, I wasn't too sure,' he said in explanation. 'It is a small one anyway, a *chhota peg*,' he added, looking at Balu. Janaki let it remain where he put it down, unsure of what to say, not wanting to sound churlish and yet having no intention of drinking any more. Sitting right next to her, Balu had not commented at all, concentrating pointedly on the food heaped on his plate, a sign Janaki interpreted as one of disapproval. His behaviour was so bewildering — she had not wanted to drink at all in the first place, and wouldn't have been in this situation with half a drink in one hand and another waiting on the table beside her plate if it had not been for him — and now, bafflingly, he was being censorious.

She wished she were back home in Madras, in familiar surroundings where the pattern of her daily life remained peaceful, unchanged and predictable, where she knew exactly what was expected of her and where the fulfilling of those expectations caused no disruption to her life. Her sisters had always envied her for precisely that. Ever since she had got married, she knew that she was the one the others had envied. They had told her that once, as they had all sat together on the verandah of her father's house in Kodai, enjoying a prolonged post-mortem of the family wedding they had all come to attend. Their respective children had all been put to bed, their husbands asleep, probably, on various buses and trains, making the return journey to their own homes alone, a day or two before their wives were to follow.

The sisters sat on the parapet of the low concrete walls, massaging each other's hair with sesame oil and swatting mosquitoes with rolled-up newspapers. The next day, they would wash their hair out with *shikakai* powder that their mother would have had her servant maids prepare in advance of their arrival. But that cloudless night was reserved for sisterly gossip; the ritual rubbing in of the warm oil into their scalps relaxed them, for they had had a couple of tense days, each one of them trying to make life in their cramped parental home easy for their husbands and children.

They caught up on news about each other's lives, and there was an outpouring of sympathy and advice for each other. One sister was besieged with problems since her husband had joined the Rotary Club. Now he wanted her to dress like the wives of the other Rotarian men, to be stylish, wear sleeveless sari blouses and to shave her underarm hair. There was stunned silence when she had told them this, and it was only when she began to sniff, that they did what she expected of them and commiserated with her. The youngest sister revealed that her husband was after her to get a job so that he could afford to buy a scooter. She felt he was trying to insinuate that he should have got one as part of her dowry. They debated that for a while, making soothing clucking sounds and shaking their heads. None of them said anything to their eldest sister. Her husband had, long ago, been accidentally discovered wearing her bra and petticoat, and ever since then, the eldest sister tended to keep quiet on such occasions, happy just to massage her sisters' hair and to thank God that she was not the only one with problems.

Janaki rarely had anything extraordinary to say, her news so mundane that her sisters tended to hurry her along, eager to get to more problematic and fraught stories where even if help couldn't be proffered, at least judgements could be passed. There was a highly therapeutic satisfaction to be gained in the whole process of listening, placating and exonerating. They chided each other for minor self-confessed vices and failings, and then as the night progressed, they were lulled by the emotional succour provided by their apparent sisterliness, into revelations that grew bolder and more explicit. Sitting in the shadow of the tiled roof, they nudged each other knowingly as they spoke about the goings-on in their marital beds, but not venturing beyond innuendo to articulate their husbands' sexual preferences.

Janaki remained quiet and tight-lipped as she listened to coy accounts of how her sisters coped with the demands that were made on them, and when they goaded her collectively, accusing her of listening intently but disclosing nothing, all she would say was, 'Balu, he is not like that.' This admission, more than any of the others, seemed to dampen their spirits completely and was almost always the cue for them to tell her, like they had many times before, that they wished they had a husband like hers. The men they had married were not like him. Balu was unwavering in his control, consistent in his beliefs, sober and virtuous in his tastes and, very importantly, he knew what a wife needed in order to hold her head up high in front of her family and he provided Janaki with those accoutrements. They laughed at her attempts to play down her luck; after all, they reminded her sarcastically, her problems arose mainly from the misbehaviour of her maid Muthu and the occasional power-cut or water shortage.

Janaki wished she were with her sisters right now — now that she had at last something to tell them — and Balu's behaviour would certainly give them something to mull over. Immersed in her thoughts about Madras, she didn't even realise that she had slowly sipped away the remaining brandy in her glass until Inder called for all at the table to raise a toast to the next day's journey. She looked around to see what the others were going to do, wondering if anyone would notice if she lifted an empty glass.

'Use the other glass, the full one,' Balu muttered urgently to her. 'These things have to be done properly.'

Janaki did as she was told and self-consciously raised her glass along with the rest, clinking it with Balu's and Romi's, quickly copying the actions of those around her. Everyone returned to eating and Janaki toyed with her food, unable to eat and feeling slightly light-headed. Balu smiled at her now and then, but he seemed to be more interested in listening to Inder who was looking very seriously at each of the Malaysian women in turn and telling them what their facial features said about them. His interpretations evoked much nodding of heads, hands flying to cover open mouths and embarrassed laughter.

'This face-reading business is his party piece,' Romi confided. 'Our daughters have stopped bringing their boyfriends home because of him. Just look at him, he won't stop now. He always starts with the women first. Tell me Balu, do you think we women are just more gullible, or do we like to find out things about ourselves, or to have others affirm what we know already?'

Balu was about to answer when Inder turned to him from across the table. 'In your case your forehead says it all. You are a self-made man, Balu, and strong-willed. Let me see now, show us your profile please. Maybe I should discuss this with your wife.

Heh, heh, does he like to get his own way, Janaki?'

Janaki looked around the table at the faces smiling at her. Was she expected to reply? It was not an answer she needed to think about. The few times she had dwelt on it in the past, she had felt helpless at her inability to effectively counter his opinions and do things the way she wanted. She was aware of his one weakness — an uncharacteristic nervous respect for the family deities — but he was fully aware of it too and was thus able to very quickly nip in the bud most attempts she made to use the religious route in order to circumvent his resolve on any given matter.

It was only after Balu's mother died that Janaki really understood how much Balu depended psychologically on his mother's powers of prayer, though his own communing with the gods remained, as always, by proxy. It was as if he considered it a woman's job to plead on behalf of the family. So, he looked on from afar and, to most who knew him, it appeared to be a look of unconcern, nearly disdain. He had ensured that Janaki continued where his mother left off, keeping the gods on the right side with consistent, simple placation and minimum offence. She was sometimes able to make use of this need for divine goodwill and thereby do things the way she wanted, couching her plans as good deeds, presenting other ideas of hers in the guise of sacred acts that would invite heavenly blessings.

Balu was not a person Janaki had found easy to question. How could she? He held his beliefs with such conviction that it was difficult to see how he could be wrong. But it was some of those very beliefs that had impressed her father enough to make him give her away in marriage to him with such little hesitation. A man who made no demands on the bride's side was a godsend for a father of four daughters and a son. Janaki's dowry had been diverted to furthering her brother's education and Balu was elevated to the position of demi-god in her parental home.

'She's not going to tell us. I knew it. You can see it clearly in her. Yes, I can see it clearly — loyalty is her middle name. See the way the eyes are set? That's how you can spot it.'

Janaki couldn't help smiling and when she did, Inder turned to Balu.

'I can also tell from looking at your wife that you are a lucky man.'

Balu seemed momentarily lost for words and then glancing at Janaki, he very dramatically raised his glass. 'To my wife. To all wives.' There was a round of applause from the Malaysians. Romi slapped her napkin down and joined them. Once again Janaki watched the others raise their glasses and she followed suit. The brandy no longer burnt her throat as it slid down. She tried hard to remember where she had seen Balu behave like this before. She was sure she had seen him, or was it someone else, acting so dashing and confident, raising his drink and saying 'Cheers!' She remembered the frenzied music, the women dancing around Balu and then the doors bursting open and gunfire, noise and arrests.

Janaki shook her head and tried to think straight. No, come to think of it, that wasn't Balu at all: it was someone else. It was the hero in a movie, the hero who had set it all up. The dancers were his friends and the drinking was merely a clever plot to fool everyone, to lull them into lowering their guard. Heroes always did that sort of thing, she thought, smiling at Balu. He seemed pleased and raised his glass to her again.

6

Looking up at the twin spires of Cologne Cathedral, Balu felt dizzy. Viewed at such close quarters, against the backdrop of a blue sky with a few puffy clouds scuttling swiftly by, the magnificent 515-foot high spires seemed to sway alarmingly. He put out his hand to Janaki to steady himself but she had moved away and instead he staggered into a large group of Japanese tourists, who scattered in terror. Balu apologised as he regained his balance but they had quickly moved on, like felled and resurrected skittles, reassembling quickly in an orderly fashion in front of their guide.

Janaki hadn't gone far, barely a couple of yards away but she had her back to him, totally unaware of what had happened. He knew she was scanning the huge raised plaza, the Domvorplatz, which surrounded the Cathedral, checking all the seats and some of the low walls for somewhere to sit and eat their lunch. Balu pointed out a place that had just been vacated and strode towards it. He waited impatiently while Janaki dusted the stone seat with a paper napkin that she

174

produced from her handbag, and then carefully examined the area she had cleaned before sitting down with a loud sigh. She handed him one of the huge filled rolls they had bought from a busy bakery across the road and then lifted a coffee cup out of its disposable tray and placed it next to Balu. He grunted an acknowledgement, his mouth full and his eyes back on the spires again. As Janaki fussed over her own lunch, pushing back into her roll the cheese, tomatoes and lettuce that were spilling out, Balu wished she would pay some attention to the Cathedral instead.

It was an awesome sight — enough, he thought, to fill anyone of any faith with reverence, though the conducted tour they had been given had made him question his own Hindu religion. He had explained his feelings to Janaki as they waited to be served in the bakery after the tour.

'Just look at these fellows, Janu, these Christians: they allow anyone into their churches with no fuss, all the way inside with no restrictions. What have we to fear in India? Why do we have 'Hindus Only' outside every sanctum sanctorum in every temple?'

'Because the others, the non-Hindus, they eat beef.'

Balu was surprised by the swiftness and the

assuredness of her reply but he wasn't going to let his point of principle get brushed aside with such a simple explanation. He pointed to the array of sliced meats, cheese and prepared salads in the deli counter that they were queuing alongside.

'That is beef there, the pinkish-brown slices. Are you going to eat the chicken that is next to it?'

Janaki began to crack her knuckles. 'Ever since we left London you have been acting strangely. If there is something I have done, why don't you come out and say it? I wish I had stayed back with Ram instead. Am I to blame if non-Hindus aren't allowed into temples? How can I eat now?'

Balu looked at his wife with a degree of irritation. She always denied him intelligent debate by getting emotional about the smallest of matters in question. He took in a deep breath and did what was his duty. He pacified her because he knew it was important that she ate before they got onto the coach again. It was only now, as she placed the coffee next to him, that he felt a twinge of guilt, realising that she was fiddling with her lunch, still hesitating because of what he had said earlier.

'It is not unlike Tirupathi back home, is it, Janu? Gods always live in high places, don't they?' He realised from her look that she was suspicious of his efforts to get a conversation going, but he persisted. 'What do you think?'

'About what?'

'That gods like to live in high places.'

'They deserve to.'

'Yes, yes.' Balu looked at her as she took a bite of her roll, deflated that she had managed once again to stall his efforts at having a normal chat. She looked tired, eating in a listless fashion, chewing her food on one side of her mouth only. He looked away, in the direction of the stone paving of the plaza a few yards ahead, where the efforts of the chalk artists had managed to attract a crowd of admiring onlookers. Balu had seen the art works earlier, before they had begun the tour of the Cathedral; they were faithful renderings of famous paintings, painstakingly drawn and coloured in, but he was unable to shake off his initial opinion of the artists. Which shortsighted person would waste their talent drawing on a canvas as impermanent as the Domvorplatz? Why not draw on something sellable? But right now, that was not really the question that troubled him.

Instead, Janaki's weariness had once again forced out to the present time the memory of his behaviour of the previous night. It was a disturbing recollection, for as much as it debased him in his own eyes it was also one that stirred him. Janaki's inebriation had been total and undramatic; she had just nodded off to sleep at the dinner table itself and later, when he had managed to get her to their room, she had nearly passed out as they entered, just making it to the bed where she allowed Balu to divest her of her sari. He pulled out the pins in her bun and watched her hair loosen and unravel as she finally collapsed onto her pillow.

For a while he just looked at her; the need he had felt all these years, the need that he satisfied when he turned automatically to his wife, was nothing like the new lust he felt for this woman. But what he remembered most from last night was her faint but definite response to his touch as his fingers and lips explored her body, and her almost inaudible sighs that aroused him further, leaving him with no control over himself.

Sitting next to Janaki in the bright daylight that bathed the Domvorplatz he tried to find a reason for his temporary insanity, for he had no doubt that that was all it was. Maybe, thought Balu, this was a passing madness like the one that had hit Mr Nath a few months before his retirement. Balu had at first been angry and dismissive of the rumours of the aging Mr Nath's office fling. When Balu had initially heard the gossip, it had seemed totally incongruous, laughable even, that Mr Nath, a grandfather by then, would be obsessed with Joyce Johnson.

Joyce had risen out of the secretarial pool where she was notorious for being the only one who wore bright lipstick — purchased in London, she claimed proudly, by her brothers who were in the Merchant Navy. She wore trouser suits with shiny buckles and large silver hoop earrings and pointy-heeled shoes. She had been engaged twice, once to a German with long hair and bloodshot eyes, who had lived off her in comfort before leaving her suddenly to join a commune that practised free love. She had pursued him in the company of the tabloid evening papers and, following that unsuccessful but public attempt to retrieve her fiancé, she had been tearful in the office for nearly a whole week before she had found solace in Mr Nath.

Perumal had been the source of all this information, though Balu had noted that his colleague's unhealthy interest in the titillating goings-on in the commune was far greater than the attention he had paid to the scandal in the office.

'Three or four men and women, at it together they say. Can you picture it? Real blue stuff. Nirvana, they call it. Why do you

179

think they don't admit Indians?'

When it was all over between Mr Nath and Joyce, and when Joyce had been transferred out of the section, Mr Nath had been very matter-of-fact about it.

'All this is very natural, to be expected. Remember Balu, when you get to a certain age, danger sometimes presents itself as an opportunity.'

Balu had not known why Mr Nath had wanted to explain himself, particularly when no one in the office really blamed him for what had happened. Balu could now see the precise wisdom of those words yet, analysing the situation as he sat in the Domvorplatz, he was not ready to accept that he was playing with fire. It was Joyce Johnson who had seduced Mr Nath by leaning over his desk and offering to light his cigarette with the fancy foreign lighter that her German lover had left behind. That was Joyce. This was Janaki, his wife, so where was the shame in it? In fact, in his eyes it wasn't even really his Janaki — and anyway, hadn't he done the right thing? Hadn't he spared her any ignominy by not expecting her to participate? Balu glanced side ways at his wife. Was she really as oblivious to what had happened as he hoped? He would have to be extra careful, he thought, just till this madness passed. It was temporary and he knew it.

Janaki had put her coffee down to wave to Sister Bernadette, who had at long last come out of the Cathedral along with her sister. They had queued up to see the relics of the three Holy Magi that were housed in a jewel-encrusted shrine behind the altar, and as a consequence had forgone their chance to have a decent lunch.

'They don't really know what it is like to wait to see a god. They should come to India. Remember, Janu, how we queued for six hours at Thirumala for the *darshan?* And that too after having climbed three thousand feet to get there?'

Janaki became animated immediately. It was merely a chance remark, a stroke of luck that had made Balu speak his mind out aloud and he was glad that he did, for he knew straight away that he had cheered her up. The memory of that pilgrimage had remained vivid in both their minds and for the same reason: it had been a happy time for each of them. Janaki had luxuriated in a well-deserved sense of achievement, for having persuaded Balu to do the pilgrimage with her had been no mean feat. She had worn down his resistance to such a blatantly religious act slowly but steadily, having started with feeble attempts immediately after their marriage.

Balu had dismissed these as wishful fancies on her part and he had been content to pay his obeisance quietly in the privacy of his home, but Ram's birth had sowed the seed of acquiescence. Balu began to feel that perhaps he needed to make a public gesture of his gratefulness for the gift of such a happy and healthy child given the very difficult pregnancy that Janaki had had and the emergency Caesarean that had been required to save the baby's life. Janaki had sadly ended up having a hysterectomy, but Balu didn't spend too much time mulling over the fact they would not have any more children. He knew that, considering how easily things could have gone completely wrong, he was lucky he had both his son and wife alive. He couldn't help however, allowing himself to go through the motions of being cajoled till the very end to do the pilgrimage, declaring to Janaki's father that he did not really believe in what he considered was a drum-beating style of religion. Once again, he was fêted by his in-laws for both his unwavering moral stance and his obvious consideration for their daughter in having agreed to accompany her on the arduous walk up the famed Seven Hills despite his misgivings. Balu would never know that his attitude had actually made them very nervous, for who would dare go to see the Lord reluctantly?

In the end, to the satisfaction of all concerned, Ram had been left in the safe custody and loving care of his maternal grandparents while Balu and Janaki left Madras on an overnight train to Tirupathi. Once there, Balu accompanied Janaki as she visited the temples that were scattered around the foothill town, taking each god or goddess the offering that they preferred — fruit, flowers, cooked food, small silk pieces, thick cord necklaces smeared with turmeric — all of which were conveniently on sale outside each shrine. Janaki, along with thousands of others, prayed for specific favours from each of the deities, most of whom had special powers that covered a particular aspect of life: health, wealth, marriage, fertility, longevity and knowledge were just the principle few.

At many of the temples Balu remained a bystander, hanging around in the inner courtyards of the sanctums while Janaki performed the required rituals. He watched as people lost their inhibitions when face to face with their god, beseeching or thanking loudly and with great feeling. He very quickly found there were other men like him, who hadn't the driven fervour of their women — the wives, mothers, grandmothers and sisters they were chaperoning. These were

183

men who hadn't been able to carry through their enthusiasm beyond the first few temples but who, in the main, waited patiently and listened companionably to each others' stories, though Balu was reluctant to be as forthcoming as some of them were with regard to the reason for their pilgrimages.

From these conversations Balu also gathered information about the difficult climb that lay ahead of them. There was excited talk of rogue monkeys who had become too lazy to forage in the forests, of clever pickpockets who had no compunction about going about their business even in these holiest of hills, and of jewellery snatchers who could cut a woman's skin to shreds when the gold chains they grabbed refused to break easily. In all cases, the consensus was that resistance was futile and dangerous, though if alerted immediately, fellow pilgrims had sometimes been known to catch fleeing pickpockets. However, everyone agreed that such heroes were a dwindling breed and that most people wanted no trouble, for the constant struggle with the steep and never-ending steps was enough of a challenge in itself.

It was nearing dusk when they arrived at the final temple that Janaki wanted to visit. While she was inside, queuing to have her offering placed at the feet of the goddess,

Balu learnt, from a small crowd that had gathered around two of the local constabulary, that a panther had been sighted in the forest, very close to the path that the pilgrims were meant to stick to. The matter was being given the most urgent consideration, for the men who had spotted it had insisted that the animal was injured, that it limped horribly. Such was the seriousness of the incident that the District Collector had abandoned a scheduled inspection of the Vasectomy Clinic to visit the area of the sighting himself, in the company of armed Forest Officers. The crowd listened with rapt attention and even Balu was so carried away with the thrill of danger that he, like the rest, was not able to spot the fact that the two Constables embellished the story with every telling.

At last, Balu saw some sense of real purpose in his journey. He was determined to protect his wife from all the wide variety of menaces, human and animal, that he had heard of in the course of the day. He decided not to worry Janaki by telling her about the various perils that lay ahead, except to warn her that they had to have a very early night so that they could seek safety in numbers and start their climb along with the main body of pilgrims. Those in the know tended to start the ascent as early as four in the morning, both to avoid the intense post-dawn heat as well as to beat the queues at the main temple on the sacred summit at the township of Thirumala.

The climb had begun with very little ceremony, and soon after the first hill that was renowned for its steepness, Balu found that far from having to protect his wife from the troops of audacious white-faced langur monkeys that they encountered on the way, or from the legendary thieves that roamed the footpaths, he had to put all his energy into encouraging her to take that next excruciating step for, despite her fervent desire to complete the pilgrimage, Janaki had not catered for the extreme physical difficulty that it would present. Almost immediately after they had climbed the first hill and were faced with the second, she was tearful and afraid, for it was inauspicious to say the very least, to abandon the ascent. Such an action would have been soul-destroying for someone who was as god-fearing as Janaki, for to her it signified one thing only — an awful pre-destiny, a divine wish from the Lord that he did not want to see her.

Janaki had hung on to Balu's arm, also hanging on his every word of encouragement, resting when he told her to do so and resuming the climb when he thought she was ready for another short go at it. At one point when she was overcome with exhaustion, he took it upon himself to vow to her that she would finish the walk as long as he was there beside her. Having made that dramatic statement, he was determined that neither his wife nor the Seven Hills would get the better of him and they made their way to the summit at a painfully slow pace, arriving at Thirumala seven hours later, having taken twice as long as the average person would have done.

Janaki was ecstatic at the summit, and as they walked in the direction of the main temple complex, she told Balu time and again how she would never have managed without him, reminding him, repeating in detail what she had said to him a few hours ago in her despair and what his encouraging reply had been. She relived her agony, continually acknowledging his role, going back in her mind's eye to the exact spots where she had stopped and where people had looked at her in pity and at him in admiration. Her successful pilgrimage to Tirupathi had been a commendable feat, a physical victory over the odds, but for Balu it was a triumph of a different kind, for not only had he done the climb, he had, to all intents and purposes, carried her up too: it was a moral victory that put him on a wonderful high ground that she, with all her piety, could not reach.

Janaki was shaking her head at the memory of it all. 'Seven hours of such difficult climbing, followed by six hours of patient queuing. If it hadn't been for Lord Venkateshwara waiting in his divine abode at the summit I would never have been able to do it. God is truly great.'

Balu was taken aback but he hesitated. He knew it wouldn't be right to end up vying with Lord Venkateshwara for the glory of having helped his wife overcome the climb, but he did remember whose name Janaki had called out as she had struggled up the steps.

'I don't remember you calling out to Venkateshwara that day.'

'I didn't need to. He knew my difficulty.'

Balu absorbed this interpretation of the events of that day, nearly three decades ago. To argue about it, to debate the matter even in his head, to insist that *he* should have been the one she should have gratefully remembered, would pit him against the gods and that surely was a dangerous thing for any man to do. Balu nodded his head in a frenzied manner and tried to shake off such heretical thoughts. He scanned the plaza to see if there was anybody or anything that would divert his attention.

'I want to buy a folding mini-penknife,' he declared finally. In the shop that overlooked the plaza, he was like a child, and when they walked out with the tiny pocketknife with four gadgets that slotted into the knife handle, Balu was all smiles, having almost forgotten the matter with the gods.

Hours later, on the Rhine cruise, he was able to pull out his knife and extract the tiny screwdriver from it and hand it to Inder very casually.

'Try this on Romi's glasses.'

The repair was successful and the penknife, with its handy little screwdriver firmly back in place, was passed around carefully and admired.

'Romi can't do without her dark glasses,' Inder said, and slapped Balu on the back. 'I tell you one thing, Balu, in her eyes you are a hero.'

★ ★ ★

They had boarded the large Rhine cruiser, the Lorelei Line's *Pegasus*, at the village of Boppard, a couple of hours after having left the Domvorplatz. Heading out of Cologne, the road had hugged the banks of the Rhine for a good distance and Balu had looked out of his window, totally mesmerised by the absolute mightiness of the river. It was swift flowing, with massive swirling eddies, and the size of the heavily laden cargo ships that plied it in both directions were an indicator of the river's great importance as a waterway.

Old war movie scenes flashed through Balu's mind as they drove past expansive bridges beneath which navigational buoys bobbed, looking ominously like landmines. If he closed his eyes, he could very nearly hear the rumble of the German tanks as they rolled menacingly over the bridges, led by a pair of outriders on motorcycles with sidecars from each of which screaming soldiers would hurtle through the air when the British officers, hidden in the wooded hillside opposite the bridge, pressed the plunger down on the explosives cleverly packed around the foundations well below water level.

Balu instinctively scanned the steep slopes on the other side of the river, looking for the likely spots where the men who had been parachuted down would have hidden, using the cover of darkness to don their frog suits and shake hands with each other poignantly before wading into the mine-infested waters to undertake the most difficult part of their dangerous mission. After the final moments of destruction had faded from the screen, the elegant Morse code operator, with the plucked eyebrows and dark lipstick of the period, seated at the intelligence headquarters in London, would turn to the anxiously waiting white coats and political leaders holding smouldering cigars, with a symbolic smile of relief, one set of finger-tips still pressed against the headphones that she still wore.

It was at this point, towards the end of the movie, that Balu would usually stand up reverentially, almost at attention, to read the invariable epilogue that would follow, rolling upwards on the screen, sometimes to triumphant crescendos, sometimes to dramatic silence. Most of the cinemagoers would have started shuffling out but Balu loved this bit, and he felt cheated if he was not able to learn what finally happened to the heroes. It fascinated him that so many of them would go back to their mundane lives after such a traumatic war. He would try to explain to Janaki his admiration for the dam-buster who resumed growing prize roses after the war, or the veteran RAF pilot and the tunnel-digging prisoner of war who returned to England to drive a bus and run a fishing tackle shop respectively. How could these men suddenly stop being heroes?

Janaki could never understand his largely

rhetorical questions. In fact, she had often irritated him by reminding him in a consolatory fashion, when they were on their way home from the cinema, and when he was right in the midst of just such a philosophical quandary, that the war movies he so loved were merely that — movies. At first, in the early days of their marriage, he used to pity her for not being able to grasp the collective importance of all the various acts — big and small — of heroism to the final outcome of the war or, in fact, the historical importance of the wars themselves. Later, when she grew bolder and began to make complaining remarks about the absence of heroines or any entertaining song and dance sequences in most of these movies, he resigned himself to the fact that his wife's view of worldly affairs was, and would probably remain, very narrow.

Balu knew that Janaki considered it a lucky bonus to have married a man who, apart from having all the virtues of a good husband, was also fond of the cinema. It had pleased him greatly to have once observed her lap up the envy of her sisters when she had told them that Balu had insisted on seeing *Mother India* thrice, when it had been re-released for matinée shows. On that occasion, much to their surprise, he had butted into their sisterly conversation.

'It is a story from which we can all learn something, particularly women. There is a moral in it for every mother, daughter and sister.'

Balu had been a cinemagoer for a long while. Ever since he had begun to earn a stipend in his first job as an apprentice he had indulged in an occasional movie, often going with Perumal, but it was only after he got married that he began to go regularly. Initially, it had been a way of getting Janaki out of the house and away from his mother's obsession, for he was afraid that his wife would quickly get sucked into that time-consuming world of rituals and rites.

Every Saturday, his mother would devote the first half of the day to cleaning out her cupboard full of deities, dusting them with soft cloth squares that she kept exclusively for that purpose, checking for spots of lamp oil and then changing, if required, the brown paper sheets with which she so neatly lined the shelves. After that first step, she would move on to washing all the brass lamps, fishing out the old blackened cotton wicks before decanting the oil from each lamp carefully. This would be followed by the gathering up of the various small brass dishes and plates that held the daily offerings of flowers and fruits. She would scrub all the brass vigorously with fibrous tamarind pulp carefully saved from the week's cooking for this express purpose.

Lining up the brass in neat rows to drip dry on the iron mesh that covered the well in the rear courtyard, Balu's mother would head in briskly to start the rearrangement of all the statues big and small, pictures and framed calendar prints, putting them back in precise positions that were determined by the importance of each deity and sometimes the inter-relationship between the gods. Married gods like Lord Venkateshwara and his Consort, the Goddess Laxshmi, would be placed next to each other. Lesser deities or saints, who were themselves known for their devotion to one of the major gods, were placed at the feet of each of their respective revered ones. Thus a kneeling papier-mâché Hanuman with his mace slung across his shoulders was placed at Lord Rama's terracotta feet, while a tiny, roughly hewn stone rendition of the sacred bull Nandi sat beside a brass Lord Shiva.

It was a difficult task making sure that all the gods got their due respect and that the protocols were maintained at all times. This half-day ritual was only the start, for Balu's mother would then proceed to have her ceremonial bath, after which she would begin her very long special Saturday prayers, addressing each of her deities individually. The whole evening would similarly be fully occupied, with visits to the four local temples, where she would first jostle with the crowds to pray to the resident gods, after which she would sit in the temple courtyards, often reading aloud the reams of devotional inscriptions carved into the stone walls.

Though it was easy enough for Balu himself to completely stay out of it all, he was aware that, given her upbringing and being the daughter-in-law, Janaki could very easily get drawn into the routine rituals too. Balu was content to have one woman praying for him, and at that time in his life, his mother sufficed. In order that his bride would not feel morally obliged to take part in the entire goings-on of that day, he quickly arranged a routine of his own for her. He began, every Saturday, to take Janaki to see a matinee, following which he took her by auto-rickshaw to Marina Beach.

He himself would book the cinema tickets on the previous Friday and if he had liked the theme or the songs in any movie, it was natural that they would see it again. Very soon he began to feel that the movies, with their glorification of good and the upholding of the traditional virtues of obedience, sacrifice and honour, were like a training session for both himself and his bride. He was sincere in his conviction that they had so much to learn from the storylines, and he always came away with a strengthened resolve to be a tolerant and providing husband to what he hoped would be a patient and obedient wife.

Janaki loved their Saturday outings from the very start, and though she would make a show of him in front of her mother-in-law, expressing surprise that they were going to go for yet another cinema show and that too, yet again on a Saturday, she would wake early in order to complete all her household duties well in advance. This meant cooking all the meals for the day and then giving her mother-in-law as much of a hand with her laborious Saturday rituals as was possible, right until it was time to leave.

Soon, Balu began to place great emphasis on their trips to the beach that followed each movie. There, having looked carefully for a clean and uncrowded spot, they would sit cross-legged on the sand that was still hot despite it being near dusk and Balu would start analysing the story to his satisfaction, pointing out the parables about love, friendship and family ties. He particularly loved to examine the subplots, identifying the lesser virtues that these stories exemplified. Janaki wasn't always attentive to his fervent monologues, particularly if the movie had dance scenes or dream sequences filmed in foreign locations. The lush green Alpine slopes, the flower-filled gardens, the fountains that danced to music and playful snowball fights of the courting hero and heroine on top of jagged mountain peaks that were reached by spectacular cable-car rides — all caught her imagination and she would talk of little else as they sat at the humid and litter-strewn beach.

He tried to be patient with Janaki when she rushed headlong into discussing the songs and the dances, humming the tunes even as he spoke to her. He would let her prattle on until his patience wore out and then he would try to steer the conversation back to the moral points he was trying to bring to her attention. It was an impatience similar to the one that he felt when, as they sped onwards from Cologne, he realised that Janaki had once again promptly nodded off to sleep. Snoring gently with her lips parted slightly, she lay back with her head and neck twisted to one side, in a position that would no doubt make her wince in pain when she did get up.

Of all the people, he thought as he tried to control his temper, Janaki was the one who should have been awake and looking appreciatively at the magnificent scenery that had for so many years enchanted her on celluloid. What was the point, he muttered to himself, shaking his head in disapproval, of sleeping through this picture-postcard countryside when she had spent years longing to see just such scenery, yearning to take in the sights with her very own eyes?

Even now, as they sat on the Rhine cruiser, Balu was sure that behind the dark lenses of her sunglasses, her eyes were shut. He shot quick glances at her every few minutes, looking for any telltale signs that would confirm his suspicion — a gradual and barely discernible loosening of her tight grip on her handbag, a certain slackness in her jaw and the slow relaxing and parting of her knees which, if she were awake, would normally be held demurely together despite the fact that her legs were at all times out of sight anyway, wrapped in a petticoat and then swathed over modestly in five metres of sari fabric.

When he saw her actually nod off, he looked away rather guiltily, holding his breath for a long minute, admitting to himself once again, as he had done when they were in Cologne earlier on in the day, that his real problem was that he knew why she was so tired. It was the drink that he had so deviously encouraged her to imbibe, the brandy that she had sipped so defiantly the previous night — not much by the standards of most regular drinkers, but the three *pegs* had been potent enough to have left her with a hangover and, he hoped, no memory of what had transpired last night. As Balu distractedly went through the motions, along with the others sitting on the deck of the *Pegasus*, of marvelling at the ingenious harvesting techniques in the vineyards that had been planted on the acutely steep and, in some places, sheer slopes on either side of the Rhine, he had to admit that it wasn't just Janaki who had lost control of herself. At least she could blame the drink, but who could he blame? What could he use as an excuse for his own behaviour?

He did not know why, contrary to all good sense, he had goaded her into having a drink last night. At least I did not pre-plan it, he told himself, and yet it was small consolation, for he knew that he had not hesitated at all, even for a moment, to seize the opportunity to make sure his wife got intoxicated for another evening in a row. Just thinking about what had followed, his tentative explorations into a hitherto unknown sexual world, which had grown bolder still on the second night, reminded him of the new pleasures he had experienced. He shuddered slightly in excitement. How much more pleasurable it would be for him if Janaki would be a participant.

For one wild moment he thought about telling her, asking her to join him in his titillating new discoveries, but his return to reality was quick. To do that to his own wife, to expect her to perform even the simplest kind of oral act, the sort that he had seen advertised so explicitly in Amsterdam, she who was so chaste and modest — why it was unthinkable! Anyway, he was not the kind of man who would expect his wife to actually indulge in that sort of licentious behaviour, even though he had been consumed with exactly that very fantasy, having seen it on a continuous video clip, a taster of the blue movies available for purchase, at the shop he had gone into with Inder.

As far as this, his own sudden deviancy in the past two days was concerned, well — at least he could say that the woman inebriated and so supine on his bed, whose body he had explored so intimately for the first time in their three decades of marriage, wasn't really Janaki. To reveal his behaviour of the past two nights to a sober Janaki was not an option. Why, he wouldn't even know how to articulate what he had done, to put into words the path his lips had followed, the tastes his tongue had discovered on parting her legs, to explain the sexual emotion of seeing her fully naked in plain light, her breasts so languorous, to describe the arousal that he had experienced when he had turned her over slowly onto her side, his hands cupping her buttocks firmly, wanting to squeeze them, drawing her legs up to her chest, arranging her so that he could see the cleft concealed in the wiry mass of her pubic hair.

He had been left speechless then as he had indulged all his senses, feasting his eyes on what he had only known fleetingly in all these years, tasting, touching and smelling her, listening out for her very small sighs, imagining they were signs of her subconscious pleasure and waiting as she shifted in her sleep before he started where he had left off. So how could he ever spell out to Janaki the things he had done in a way that she would comprehend, for it was unthinkable that she would have any knowledge or notion of such incredible sexual possibilities. Not only could he imagine her immediate disbelief, her silent mortification and horror, he could also picture the disgust she would feel for him.

How many times more did he need to have this novel, libidinous experience before he would be satisfied and allow the madness to pass? For he was sure that was what it was — he was caught in the grip of a temporary depravity that would shake off once he had had his fill. Balu found himself struggling with regrets about the past; he knew they were foolish, and yet he ran them through his mind, hoping perhaps to find in his tortured and illogical reminiscing a reason for his more recent behaviour.

He was sure things would have been different if he had demanded all of this and more when he had first married Janaki. She would have satisfied me then with anything I asked for, he thought, for she would have known no different. I wouldn't need to feel so guilty now, wouldn't have had to resort to getting her drunk. I would have enjoyed my conjugal rights in a manner of my own choosing, would have had every one of these fantasies that now have me in their grip come true. Each morning I would have gone to work like Perumal — all puffed up and crowing like a well-satisfied rooster, winking and boasting about my wife's willingness to please and in Perumal's shameless fashion never failing to make some sly innuendo about being the sole proprietor of her generous breasts.

He felt the blood rush to his head thinking

about Perumal's wife. All reason returned immediately and he knew that with all these thoughts of what might have been, he was merely deluding himself. The reality was that he had never ever wanted to have a wife like Perumal's, with her sly giggle and knowing look. He had instead, fashioned Janaki into the ideal wife, using as his model the famed Sati Savitris of the silver screen, the virtuous all-sacrificing heroines of the innumerable melodramatic and morality-packed movies that he and Janaki had seen together.

No Sati Savitri he had ever seen on screen had even a hint of wantonness about her, and sex was something that was barely hinted at, with coy shots of flowers nodding together in a gentle breeze signifying intention, and a bee alighting on a blushing rose being the traditional celluloid representation of the act itself. He had never any doubt in his mind, from the very start of their marriage, that Janaki would respect him for the high moral standards that he had set for her and for their relationship. He was sure that over the years, his sexual sobriety had contributed to and become part of those standards. As for himself, Balu had thrived on the respect and deference that his wife had continuously paid him, growing more paternalistic in his treatment of her with each passing year of their marriage.

He looked towards Janaki now, with all her pretence of being awake done with, her head slumped forwards, her chin nearly touching her chest, and he called out to her sharply in Tamil.

'Enough, enough Janu, wake up! There is so much to see on both sides of the river. You can sleep later. At this rate it will be a wasted trip, totally.'

She coughed apologetically as she woke with a start and immediately straightened herself, taking off her dark glasses and cleaning them with the corner of her sari.

'I'm okay now,' she replied in Tamil. 'Will I get you some tea?'

As she left, clutching the money he gave her and heading for the tiny restaurant below deck, he knew that what he had was too valuable, too good to sacrifice for the unhealthy carnal desires that had struck him like a bolt out of the blue. No, there was no question of revealing anything to Janaki. All he needed was a bit of resolve to overcome his current predicament.

A few minutes later when his attention, along with that of the others, was directed at the legendary Lorelei Rock, Balu almost felt he could empathise with its victims, understanding fully the sheer helplessness of the sailors who were seduced to their watery ends.

7

The Chicago ladies, who were in very high spirits after the evening's rousing and thigh-slapping entertainment by a traditional German folk group, had started the sing-song at their table after dinner and boisterous tunes were soon doing the rounds of the other tables in turns. Janaki wished desperately it would stop before it reached theirs. There was no backing out of this public display, for when the Malaysians had balked, the ensuing slow hand-clapping died only when they had hurriedly decided on a song that they all knew and had started singing.

'Romi will do the honours for us.' Inder was looking at his wife with a large grin on his face.

'Forget it. I mean it, Inder.'

'Okay. What about you, Janaki?'

'My wife hasn't the confidence.'

Inder turned to Balu with one eyebrow raised. 'But has she the voice?'

'Oh, she sings, but you know ordinary, mainly devotional songs.'

Romi knocked on the table with her fork. 'Shall we ask Janaki?'

They all turned to look at her. Janaki was adjusting her sari, neatening the folds across her shoulder.

Balu coughed apologetically. 'Perhaps some other time, not in this — you know — hotel setting.'

'I'll sing.' Janaki looked at the surprise on their faces. 'I have the perfect song for the occasion,' she added, half hoping that that would explain her unexpected willingness to perform.

Inder thumped the table and Romi clapped her hands. Janaki turned to look at Balu. He was toying with his glass and she knew that he was speechless and when, aware that the others were also watching him, he raised it to her she knew that, far from being the gesture everyone thought it was, it was probably the only automatic acknowledgement that had come to his mind given he had a glass in his hand at that moment.

As for herself, Janaki was not sure what had come over her. It wasn't just that she had found Balu's comments objectionable, his mention of her devotional singing had reminded her of a *bhajan*, an old favourite of her father's called 'Yatri'. A traveller's prayer song, it made entreaties for safe journeys and beautiful vistas, for welcoming shelters out of harm's way; it pleaded for bridges over treacherous seas, unwavering resolve and above all, the comfort of faithful companions. Janaki found herself standing up, compelled by what she thought was the appropriateness of the song, to explain the allegorical words to her audience who, when she finished, had all quietened down considerably and were suddenly nodding reflectively, as if she had spoken to each of them about the anxieties and the directions of their own lives. She was astonished by the round of applause that followed her short speech, even before she started the song.

Romi pushed a glass of water towards her and Janaki gratefully took a sip to calm her nerves, which were just beginning to catch up with her new-found bravery. The song was brief and though her voice had faltered once or twice, on the whole it had not been too bad a rendition. Halfway through the song, Inder began to keep time beating on the table with a fork and spoon. Glancing towards Balu as she sang the last stanza, Janaki realised he had his eyes closed, and was swaying imperceptibly as if he had been moved in a very devout way.

She doubted very much that it was a true reflection of what he really felt. He was probably afraid she would make a greater fool of herself than she already had done. As she sat down, accepting the applause and the good-natured hooting and whistles, her hands covering most of her face in a sudden rush of embarrassment, she wished Mrs Bhaskaran had been there to see and hear it. Or her father — yes, especially him.

If only her father could have seen her, standing up as she had explained the meaning of the *bhajan*, one of his favourite songs, to this group of total strangers — and that too in a foreign hotel, with only a few hesitations and an occasional mispronunciation — perhaps he would have thought twice about not allowing her to complete her university degree. Perhaps he would have begun to understand why she felt so inadequate and had such an inferiority complex, for she had no educational qualifications beyond the very basic ones that she had acquired at school and the little she had gained with a mere year in university.

How difficult it had been for her when she had failed her second year exams! The whole family had stood around and wrung their hands, as if she had, overnight, become a cumbersome liability. They had looked for every possible solution to this setback that would in some way or the other affect them all. Her failure was discussed with family, friends and well-wishers, and no one had spared her the indignity of knowing that she was the problem. Of course, the easiest way out would have been for her to repeat the year and pass the examination. But that would have thrown into complete disarray the order of marriages, with her younger sisters behind her having to wait longer than planned and more importantly, longer than was advisable. Then there was the question of her father's retirement.

Janaki's father had planned his entire career around the marriage of his four daughters and the education of his son. He aimed to find suitable matches for each of his daughters in their final degree year, each time starting the process in the month of January and hoping that a bridegroom would be found at the very latest by April. This would mean an alliance could be arranged for the marriage to very conveniently take place soon after the final examination in May. Things had worked according to plan for the eldest girl and Janaki's father was confident that he would be finished with his responsibility for his daughters, perhaps with even a year to spare to have his son properly settled with a wife, before retiring.

There were innumerable advantages in being in service while having matrimonial matters sorted for his daughters. Any manner of favour could be asked, for he was a serving clerical officer of over twenty years' standing in the Electricity Board. He was known to be an honourable man in these matters, keeping his side of the bargain and fast-tracking files, letters and petitions safely though the labyrinthine system in return.

There were other, additional benefits. The peons — office boys who worked in his section under him — could be called upon, in the hectic few days before the wedding and on the day of the wedding itself, to perform general duties, to ensure that all the arrangements worked smoothly. As had been proved at the eldest daughter's marriage, the peons had turned out to be nearly essential, for they could be assigned menial responsibilities. They could be directed to duties like keeping the beggars away from the gates and opening the doors of cars arriving with the groom's family — tasks that even the most helpful of relatives could not be asked to do. Being in service meant that the Electricity Board linesmen would ensure that there were no power cuts in the marriage hall during the crucial hours of the wedding, and they could be relied on to contact their counterparts in Metro Water to ensure that the water supply in the house was kept topped up, even at a time of severe shortages in the city.

Retirement would have brought to an abrupt close all such facilities, and it would have left Janaki's father to cope as an ordinary citizen. The helpless position that would leave him in could not be tolerated — it was unthinkable.

Janaki had been unable to put up any sort of spirited resistance. How could she, when her father and mother had been in such complete agreement about the difficulties that would follow if she were allowed to repeat the year in college? Nor was it possible, as she had tentatively suggested, that they could skip Janaki's place in the queue and make arrangements to marry the next sister in the following year. The social pitfalls of not following the right order for matrimony in terms of the ages of the sisters were many and insurmountable.

Families of prospective grooms would always be suspicious about the story behind the unwed sister. Girls' families were known to use the pursuit of education as a ruse to hide far more worrying predicaments than mere academic failure. Speculation would be rife even amongst friends of the family. Did the girl have a health problem that was being treated, and was it a gynaecological matter or some psychological difficulty? It wouldn't really have made a difference which one it was for, given that everyone was convinced about the hereditary nature of such medical conditions, once a suspicion had been raised, neither Janaki nor her younger sisters would be considered suitable brides.

Other questions and fears would also be raised. Was the girl modern and rebellious, or did she perhaps have a secret paramour for whom she was stubbornly holding out? If either of those turned out to be true, this would definitely be a family whose daughters had to be avoided because, despite the assurances of the parents that marriage would rectify all such faults, it was always too big a risk for the groom.

It was Janaki's brother's contribution to the subject that quickly sealed her fate.

'What if she fails her exams again?'

The following Sunday, Janaki's father pored over the matrimonial columns and set in motion the process that would ensure that his second daughter got married according to plan.

At that point in time, Janaki was not heartbroken not completely devastated; she felt her regrets only in later years. That Sunday, watching her father scouring the papers intently, using a bit of her blue tailor's chalk to circle advertisements that sounded promising, and listening to her mother instructing the maid to grind a variety of herbs and oils into pastes and emollients that she, Janaki, would have to start using for the beautification of her face, hair and skin, she was in fact relieved that she was now in the limelight for a different reason, not for having failed her examinations and upset her father's plans, but because she was the bride-to-be and as such would be given special treatment while she remained in her father's house.

When her match with Balu was finalised, Janaki was very nearly praised for not having passed her Intermediate exams, as the family now considered her academic failure to be one of the most fortunate twists of fate: if she had passed and gone on to complete her degree, they would never have landed Balu — a genuine, no-dowry son-in-law. A year later and he would have been someone else's.

Despite the way her father had made her cast aside her education in favour of marriage, she had never held it against him alone; in fact, the couple of times she had discussed it with Mrs Bhaskaran or even with Ram, Janaki had laid the blame entirely on the attitudes of that era. Mrs Bhaskaran, however, was never that charitable about Janaki's father's role in the whole affair.

'See your attitude, Janaki? So forgiving! That is why things remain unchanged. Excuse me for being frank, but how long can we keep blaming society?'

The first time Mrs Bhaskaran had pointed out that her father was far more to blame than Janaki would let herself admit, it made Janaki very uncomfortable. When the topic of her unfinished degree had come up with Mrs Bhaskaran, Janaki's father had been dead only a few years and she was very reluctant to speak ill of him. She had nodded in a noncommittal manner to everything her neighbour said, hoping that Balu would not arrive home early from work, for he would have been furious to hear Mrs Bhaskaran's assessment of a decision that he always maintained his father-in-law had taken in good faith.

Mrs Bhaskaran had not let the matter rest for too long. She turned up a few weeks later with her husband under the pretext of inviting Balu and Janaki to attend the opening ceremony of a Shelter for Battered Women for which she had helped to raise the funds.

'It is based on the American model for such institutions,' she had said as she reached for another biscuit to dip in her coffee.

Mr Bhaskaran had handed Balu the invitation. 'The Chief Minister is going to be there. As the chief guest, of course.'

Balu was always more tolerant when Mr Bhaskaran was around. He had told Janaki many times that he was like that only out of sympathy for the man who had to live with a woman like Mrs Bhaskaran.

'Yes, yes, congratulations are most certainly in order,' he said as he made a show of opening the invitation with the greatest of care.

Mrs Bhaskaran wanted to make sure that as many neighbours as possible were in the audience to see her presenting the huge bouquet of *rajahvarti*, that she had been personally responsible for ordering, to the Chief Minister as soon as he had been escorted to the dais. She had wanted to have the honour of doing both, ushering him to the dais *and* handing him the flowers, but had to settle for the bouquet alone when objections about unfair procedure began to circulate amongst the women in the Inauguration Committee.

'I will be presenting him with flowers as soon as he arrives on the podium. He has been very supportive of the project, has expressed a keen interest in the way we help these poor abused women.'

Balu had looked at the invitation intently. 'So who is he bringing with him? His wife or his mistress?'

There was silence for a while and Mr Bhaskaran coughed as he reached for the plate of biscuits.

Mrs Bhaskaran turned to Janaki. 'Oh, by the way, Janaki, I have made some enquiries on your behalf. You can complete your degree under the mature students' scheme if you so wish, but you will have to wait for eight months.' Mrs Bhaskaran was looking at Balu now. 'She will not be able to register till the next academic year.'

Janaki was convinced that Mrs Bhaskaran would not have mentioned the mature students' scheme if Balu had not incensed her with his remark about the Chief Minister's choice of companion. She remembered very well holding her breath and waiting for someone to say something. It was Mrs Bhaskaran who spoke, her voice emotionless.

'It will change the way you look at things, Janaki. It will be good for you.'

Balu had said nothing, simply continued to look down at the card that he held in his hand. When the visitors had left, he tore the invitation into many pieces and threw them carelessly onto the tray of used cups and saucers that Janaki was carrying out of the room to the kitchen. It was an unnecessary gesture on his part. Janaki already knew that because of Mrs Bhaskaran and Balu, she now stood no chance of getting her degree.

They had both tried to console her in their

own ways. Mrs Bhaskaran came around to the house the next day, while Balu was at work. When Janaki passed on the opportunity to accompany her neighbour to Pondy Bazaar to make the final selection of the bouquet for the chief guest, the older woman had looked at her with pity and sighed.

'Mr Bhaskaran, he is always saying I am hasty. Do you blame me?'

Janaki found herself making excuses for Balu but it wasn't long before Mrs Bhaskaran butted in.

'Of course, I know it wasn't *my* fault. You see, Janaki, sometimes well-educated women find their learning a handicap. It intimidates men and that is precisely the attitude that I want to change.'

By the time Mrs Bhaskaran had left, Janaki was filled with great trepidation, having quickly realised that once the Shelter had been inaugurated, she herself was going to be Mrs Bhaskaran's next project. The very thought of the unpleasantness that would ensue if it came to a battle of wills between Balu and Mrs Bhaskaran made Janaki nervous, and she wished then that she had never told her neighbour about the events that had taken place when she had failed her Intermediate exams all those years ago. She spent many anxious days trying to think up something to say to deter Mrs Bhaskaran, something that would put her off trying to get Janaki to enrol for the mature students' programme.

But knowing Mrs Bhaskaran's way of thinking, it wasn't easy to hit on an excuse that she would accept without putting up a concerted effort at thwarting it, and that was just what Janaki wanted to avoid. If she had tried to express a lack of interest in the matter, Mrs Bhaskaran would have considered it her duty to subject her to several persuasive lectures, and if Janaki had passed the blame onto Balu, God alone knew what terrible confrontation might have followed between the two of them!

Apart from worrying about how to fob off Mrs Bhaskaran, Janaki also spent several days waiting for Balu to say his piece, for she knew that it was yet to come, and in that anxious interim, she convinced herself that she had absolutely nothing to gain from any sort of attempt at formally completing her education, nothing other than trouble and humiliation at the hands of two people who each thought they knew what was best for her.

Balu waited for a week to pass, coming home each evening with flowers for her stone Ganesha, one that she had had newly installed into a small dome-shaped niche in the wall of the front porch. He had handed her the flowers, wrapped in their cool casing of banana leaves, with great solemnity and she accepted them with humility, knowing this was part of his punishment, a gesture that was supposed to signify the magnanimous overlooking of her role in that evening's debacle.

When he finally did say something it was in triumph, flicking his fingers violently across the page of the evening paper that he was reading, his face lit up with the sort of pleasure that only a successful settling of scores can inspire.

'Janu, didn't I say this would happen?' He rapped the paper again, hitting out at a photograph tucked in a corner of a page of the Tamil tabloid. 'All her education couldn't stop her from having a big mouth.'

He read aloud the account of Mrs Bhaskaran's very quick rise and almost immediate fall out of favour with the Chief Minister and his newly established Task Force for the Betterment of Women. Within a week of having been appointed to the prestigious body, Mrs Bhaskaran had managed to create a very public stir, accusing the civil servants on the board of merely paying useless lip service to the aims of the Task Force, and pointing out the disproportionate ratio of male to female committee members. The final nail in her coffin was when she foolishly made the very pertinent but also the totally unforgivable query: she publicly questioned the Chief Minister's motive in establishing what she declared was in effect an impotent organisation. The reprisal was swift and her photograph in the paper showed her at the steps of the Secretariat, with her arms thrown up in the air in frustration, Mr Bhaskaran in the background fielding questions from a battery of mikes.

'So, you tell me, what good was her education? Look, her husband was her spokesman in the end! Huh, all those ideas above her station but no notion of how to make them work. Just proves what I have said about her all along.'

With that, Balu folded the paper with a great sense of achievement and flung it to the ground on the verandah, where it remained until they went in for dinner. The topic of her unfinished degree never came up again.

To Janaki's relief, Mrs Bhaskaran was so caught up in her own efforts to be reinstated and later, when that move was unsuccessful, to join a privately-funded American-based women's literacy organisation as an adviser, that she had no time for an individual case like Janaki's. The woman continued to call occasionally at the house, insinuating each time to Janaki, in a roundabout way, that she had very reluctantly given up on her cause, on advice from Mr Bhaskaran, who had taken note of Balu's attitude and pointed it out to his wife. Mrs Bhaskaran would then go on to fill Janaki in on the details of all her important contributions to 'my women' as she very proprietarily liked to call her illiterate flock.

Initially Mrs Bhaskaran's every visit left Janaki with conflicting emotions. She was genuinely relieved that Balu's displeasure had put Mrs Bhaskaran off and had thus eliminated any chance of another confrontation and yet another indefinite period of having to put up with the resulting peevishness on Balu's part. Yet, when Janaki heard of all her exploits first hand, including details of the evening when Mrs Bhaskaran had been introduced to the American Consul's wife who had remarked on her command of English, she was unable to contain her envy. She consoled herself by thinking about her sisters, who despite their completed degrees were no better off than Janaki herself. Later, as the months went by and the memory of that humiliating time had almost faded, she further comforted herself by remembering that her sisters in fact envied her for her failure in her examination.

Janaki always found it strange that it was Balu who bore the most visible and long-lasting after-effects of that evening's conflict. Despite frequent claims that he had no time for her type of busybody, he developed a nearly obsessive interest in all Mrs Bhaskaran's activities. He was unashamedly biased and vicious in his judgement of her, and soon his critical assailment of all she did and stood for spread to include the organisation she worked for, the missionary group that funded the organisation, America for spawning such missionaries, and the American President for being the person with whom the buck for all this stopped.

★ ★ ★

Right now, with the applause from her fellow travellers still ringing in her ears, Janaki was sure that had they witnessed her performance, both her father and Mrs Bhaskaran would have been very proud. She could feel the heat of her embarrassment beginning to fade from the tips of her ears but she was still in a bit of a daze at her own daring. From the corner of her eye she could see Inder giving Balu a congratulatory thump on his back.

Romi was leaning towards her and saying something about the *bhajan* but Janaki wasn't really paying attention. She was straining to hear what Balu was saying to Inder.

'Yes, in fact years ago, for that very reason, an American charity wanted her to work with them. They thought she would have been very good, you know — 'on the ground' as they call it, but she was devoted to the family. We always came first: I made sure she had her priorities right.'

Inder laughed as he thumped Balu on the back again. 'You have a well-trained wife. At least one man has had some success!'

Janaki just couldn't bear to see her small moment of triumph get pushed to the side with Balu's boastful and chauvinistic interpretation of the very events that had made her wish her father and Mrs Bhaskaran had been present this evening, at this hotel at St Goarhausen on the banks of the Rhine, in the company of all these people from around the world who had listened to her so attentively, who had thought she was great — for hadn't they applauded her twice, the first time even before she sang, just listening to her explanation of the words?

Janaki looked at Balu. 'Priorities can change.'

'My daughters keep telling me that every

time they date a new *bhakara*.' Inder was rolling his eyes heavenwards.

Balu was looking back at her, puzzled.

'I have decided that I'm going to complete my college degree.' Janaki felt a sense of elation as she made the declaration. Suddenly she had an urge to stand up once again, to unburden herself to everyone in the audience, to tell them all the story of her incomplete education. She was sure this time she would get a standing ovation, the kind Mrs Bhaskaran used to say she always got, when she addressed important gatherings. Janaki looked at Balu defiantly, willing him to say something and ready to answer him back, but he refused to take up her challenge, looking down into his glass instead, twirling his drink listlessly.

'Let's drink to that,' said Romi, topping up her glass with the house wine and pushing the carafe towards her husband who did the same before passing it on to Balu, who all of a sudden became very animated, a big smile on his face as he filled up his wine glass.

'Yes, of course. Education is a very noble aspiration that calls for us all to drink to it. Come on, Janu, you especially.' Saying that, he held out his hand for her glass.

Janaki was taken aback at Balu's sudden change of mood. However she had no doubt in her mind as to what was happening here. He was doing it again, trying to intimidate her with sarcasm disguised as solicitousness. Oh, he was a master at it, goading her into defying him even more, so that he could have the final moral high ground.

She gave him her wine glass with no further hesitation, determined to call his cruel bluff, though she balked at the way he filled it up to the brim. A minute later he had dragged his chair over to be closer to her and then to her complete surprise, put his arm around her shoulder and gave it a squeeze. Then, exuding a distinct aura of joviality, Balu raised his glass. Everyone else followed suit and though all Janaki's senses reeled from the unfamiliar taste and smell of the wine, she managed to smile at Inder and Romi and then pointedly at Balu, wondering if he would still pretend to be as irritatingly happy when, as she was planning in the heat and anger of the moment, she asked him for a second glass.

8

In the last hour, Balu had nudged Janaki every few minutes when he thought her snoring was getting too loud. He had tried to wake her earlier but she had barked at him, her viciousness uncharacteristic, asking to be left alone, saying she could not bear the light streaming in through the picture windows of the coach, asking him angrily why he could not understand how she was feeling.

'Thierry says we are driving through the famous Black Forest.'

'I don't care.'

'This is where Ram's favourite cake comes from — you know, the one that he always insists on ordering in five-star hotels. So, will I tell our son how you slept as we drove through the Black Forest?' Balu dug her gently in the ribs.

'My son will understand. He has always understood my problems.'

Balu was quiet for a while. There were others on the coach who were also fast asleep. The Chicago ladies had been complaining bitterly about the relentless pace of the tour and the dissent had begun to spread,

226

prompting Thierry on this, the morning of their fifth day, as they pulled out of the narrow car park of the small family-run hotel in St Goarhausen, to address the issue. Wielding the mike in one hand, the Tour Director gave them a loud lesson on the vast geography of Western Europe, the economics of travel and the speedy passage of time; he then juxtaposed all these factors against the value for money that a tour like European Kaleidoscope provided. The Chicago ladies muttered darkly and Balu wondered what it would take to satisfy these demanding Americans.

But barely an hour since Thierry made that defensive speech, now Balu himself was beginning to feel weary, and with Janaki sleeping so soundly beside him, he too began to question the logic of speeding around Europe in this fashion, attempting to get the flavour of eight countries in just a fortnight with barely a breather between meal stops and sightseeing.

He knew he had fallen asleep only when Janaki shook him awake, accusing him rather self-righteously, he thought, of snoring too loudly for her comfort and at the same time informing him that they had stopped for a break. He shook his head at her in annoyance and looked at his watch. He had slept soundly for forty minutes and now had no notion of where they were. Thierry clarified their precise position to him as he alighted from the coach, reminding Balu that they had a mere half an hour before they would be off again heading, he promised enthusiastically, for the Bavarian Alps.

The coach pulled out of the service area at Ellewangen precisely thirty minutes later. Balu had occupied the window seat, very pointedly declaring the aisle seat more suitable for Janaki since she had made it a habit to fall asleep as soon as the coach began to move. He wasn't sure if his peeved remark had found its target or whether Janaki was also trying to prove a point, but she stayed awake for the remainder of the morning, leaning heavily on his shoulder as she looked out.

The Schwaben Plains that they were traversing on the way to the Bavarian Alps were the very epitome of German orderliness. The rolling fields were so manicured in their appearance, either ripe for harvest or neatly tilled, every farm so incredibly tidy, with clean, disciplined cows that looked well fed and content, their implausibly large udders full to bursting. The sight of such pristine tidiness and fecundity on this grand scale made them both gradually forget their irritation and soon they were pointing out sights of interest to each other.

Balu shared Janaki's fascination with the hints of autumnal colour apparent in the woods and large coppices that dotted the farmlands and bordered sections of the motorway. She had never before seen such delicate tints, the foliage still green but rimmed in countless shades of bright red and varying hues of golden yellow. Dotted amongst all that colour were more spectacular combinations, with rich shades of plum and burgundy tipping leaves that had turned orange.

Balu sensed a semblance of normality return between himself and Janaki as he good-naturedly put up with her increasingly animated exclamations when she began to spot in the trees the colour combinations of her favourite, traditional Kanjeevaram silk saris.

'That mustard with the brick red, that is the exact colour of the saris we gave your two aunts at the time of Ram's wedding. And remember my green silk with the maroon border, which Amma and Appa bought for me when Ram was born? You do know it. The one that had gold *buttas* and you thought it was too grand — how could you forget? Look, there it is — the same two shades on those trees!'

She carried on in that vein for a while, reminiscing about her various saris and urging Balu to jog his memory and recollect, as she was doing, the occasions for which they had been bought. Every new colour that caught her attention made her recall a particular sari, the manner in which her sisters had coveted it, fingering the fabric jealously and admiring the beautiful shades. She remembered her painstaking search for the matching blouse fabric, the anger at the tailor for ruining the cut, making the neck too deep or the sleeves too short. A copse of bright yellow trees they had just passed she said reminded her of a Benares silk that Balu had bought for her on his first trip to Delhi. Having mentioned that sari, she immediately went quiet for a while before looking at Balu with a nervous smile on her face. Did he, she asked, reading his thoughts correctly, recollect what had happened to that sari?

'I have always told you that Muthu needs supervision at all times. Janu, if the servant class were so intelligent, would they remain servants? If you had kept closer control on her, the way I had always advised you to do, the stupid girl wouldn't have left the sari soaking in a bucket all morning long. You would still have that sari to wear today.'

Balu took a deep breath. He wished Janaki

hadn't brought up the topic of her saris and particularly the yellow Benares. He was curious that she had actually mentioned it though, for it was out of character for her to court trouble — but then on the other hand, it was a failing of hers that had frustrated him many a time. It was something that he had come to accept as one of the very few things about her that he would never be able to change — this ability that she had to speak without thinking, even when it was obvious that the consequences would be to her detriment. However, he decided not to say anything more about servants or saris, for it was pleasant to have Janaki awake and animated for a change.

So he pointed instead to the tiny little airfield they were driving past, drawing her attention to the several precise rows of small red, blue and yellow planes.

'I'm telling you, Janu, it is no wonder they are world leaders. These Germans even park their aeroplanes neatly.'

'I never liked red and blue together,' Janaki said thoughtfully. 'It is a good thing Viji's parents sent me three saris to choose from at the time of the wedding. Can you imagine? One was red and blue, and another blue and yellow! Even Ram was surprised. Thank God the third one was more to my taste. How people talked about that sari, even months after the wedding! No one had seen such a deep bottle green with a rusty orange border combination before. When we get back I must remember to take it out and refold it; sometimes these saris can begin to come apart, tear along the crease. Do you know, I often wonder about the quality of the things they bought for us. Not that Ram allowed Viji's people to buy more than the token items, of course.'

'He is his father's son, after all,' replied Balu with no hesitation. He had heard this thread of conversation before.

'Everyone wanted to know what the girl's side had given. As if we would have accepted a dowry!' Janaki sniffed as she firmly pushed a couple of her hairpins deeper into her bun. 'Yet I sometimes feel it is better for the girl's parents to give as much as they can. Why be beholden to the boy's side for ever?'

Balu was taken aback by her last remark. Had she realised what she had said? He bristled with indignation and tried hard to give her the benefit of the doubt. Maybe the snide implication of her words hadn't struck her. To insinuate that he had expected or wanted her family to be grateful to him for the rest of his life was, he thought, a grossly unfair accusation. Is that what she was trying to say after all these years? What had come over her? At the very first formal meeting that had taken place with her family and several times since then, he had made it very clear that he was no hero for not wanting a dowry — he was merely doing what he thought was the right thing. Was he to blame if her parents had chosen to ignore his modest protests and make much of him? What could he do if Janaki's sisters constantly compared their husbands to him? And as far as that brother of hers was concerned, how was Balu to have known that the dowry that he had refused to take would be immediately earmarked to further that arrogant fellow's education?

In fact, Balu had made a conscious effort never to rub in the fact that he had refused a dowry. He had never told Janaki of the incredulous reaction of his uncles and the disappointment of his aunts when he had informed them of his decision, though he would readily admit that Janaki had, very soon after their marriage, found out how cheated they had felt. But at that time, on hearing how they had slighted her, he had shrugged off their sly remarks, declaring very logically that he had no control over their small-minded attitudes or for that matter their tongues.

Of course, it was quite acceptable for them,

given Balu's family circumstances, to have had a vested interest in the dowry that the bride's side would provide. The customary silk *veshti* and shirt that would have been given to Balu's father, had he been alive, would now be rightfully claimed by Balu's elder uncle, along with a set of fine trousers and shirt for more regular use, while the younger uncle might have benefited from a wrist watch or even a gold ring. Balu's mother, being a widow, would have forfeited to her brothers' wives the silk saris with matching blouses and petticoats that she would have most certainly been given, along with a gold chain of decent weight, or if she had preferred, perhaps a stainless steel Godrej cupboard.

It took Balu a couple of years of marriage to get used to the fawning attention that he was paid by Janaki's parents and to come to terms with what he considered the unreasonable resentment that his brother-in-law held against him. Balu had astutely diagnosed that it was just false pride, an offshoot of a ridiculous inferiority complex that prevented Janaki's brother from being gracious about the stroke of good fortune that Balu had sent his way. Balu had seen him single out Janaki for more than her fair share of ill-disguised cruel teasing, and it was clear that his brother-in-law was merely expressing his frustration at being obliged to Balu, albeit in a very roundabout fashion, for his education and his subsequent career.

Matters between the two men had worsened after Janaki's brother got married. Balu was highly disapproving of his actions, for he had not hesitated when it came to a dowry, taking everything that was offered and, given that the bride so carefully chosen for him had turned out to have an extra toe — a fact that had been discovered only after the wedding had taken place — he had continued to make demands on her parents well into the first decade of his marriage, easing the pressure on them somewhat only after their daughter had produced two sons for him, both with the normal number of digits. In Balu's estimation, the whole affair of his wife's right foot and his subsequent avaricious behaviour should have made it difficult for Janaki's brother to ever look Balu in the eye, or to hold his head up with any dignity.

But none of that was any of Balu's doing. He had not demanded that Janaki or anyone else feel beholden to him for not accepting a dowry, and moreover — how was he to blame for her brother's insecurity or her parents' eternal gratefulness? He shook his head unhappily. Was this the reward he got for the decision he took thirty-three years ago? He straightened himself in his coach seat and at the same time urged himself to let the matter pass, for if he did confront Janaki about the insinuation she had just made, she would only deny it totally and retreat behind another headache.

'Ram did what was right. Nobody needs to feel obliged to him or to us,' said Balu firmly. 'And if they do feel that way, we are not to blame. No, that sort of nonsense is their problem,' he added sharply.

'Of course it is their problem. We don't have to put up with it.'

Janaki's swift reply confused Balu, muddying his thoughts. His irritation with her inconsistency was now complete and he deliberately concentrated on looking out of the window, straining to catch the first sighting of the Danube. Thierry had just minutes ago stood up at the front of the coach to announce dramatically that they would soon be crossing the famous river.

When they did, with cameras all at the ready, Balu was very disappointed. The series of locks and small dams on the Danube, very close to the point at which they crossed it, had robbed the river of any majesty, and the dirty greenish-grey waters had none of the awe-inspiring qualities of the Rhine. As they drove across the Danube, Janaki fretted that the windows of the coach could not be opened. She had managed to throw coins into the Rhine at various places when they were on the cruiser and then once more, very solemnly, at the little jetty opposite the hotel at St Goarhausen, while she along with a group of others waited for the coach to be manoeuvred into position in order that the bags could be loaded.

After flinging the coins into the Rhine at the jetty with her eyes closed and a silent prayer on her lips, she had turned to explain to the curious onlookers who included the Chicago ladies, the Australians Don and Pat as well as a sceptical Sister Bernadette, that the act of throwing money into major rivers was as much in gratitude as it was a plea, and a sure-fire method of invoking various useful blessings from the river goddesses. After her explanatory introduction to her *bhajan* the previous night, she had become a minor celebrity in the Allsights group and the Chicago ladies were convinced of her mysticism and near enlightenment. Janaki was herself surprised at the ease with which she was able to explain the Hindu belief in the implicit holiness of rivers. She answered many probing questions put to her by the

Australians and politely countered the doubts of Sister Bernadette with confidence. Having never before come across any occasion to explain her beliefs she had not realised how sound her knowledge of her religion was. She held court for a short while, her self-assurance growing with every new query. Her audience lapped up all that she had to say and promptly began to dig in their bags for coins.

'Does it matter what currency it is?' someone had asked. 'Should we use the local currency or the currency of our own countries?'

Janaki had been stupefied by this very specific question and had promptly turned to Balu. He could see Inder and Romi with large smiles on their faces, trying hard to control their laughter, and he was embarrassed at the way the Americans had hung on sincerely, waiting for a reply.

'Whichever is of greater value,' he had mumbled, unable to think of any other answer. A barrage of coins hit the surface and sank instantly and Janaki once again closed her eyes briefly, much to the satisfaction of the Chicago ladies who were sure that with her wise intervention, they would have a brief but direct line to a Higher Being.

Balu's reply was coloured by that memory.

'Enough is enough. Have you even thought of how much money you have already wasted? If you convert it, it is well over two hundred *rupees'* worth that you have so happily thrown away.'

'Happily, yes.'

She was smiling at him earnestly and Balu remained quiet for a while after that exchange, commending himself mutely for his tactful silence. The road began to rise steadily and the scenery grew more magnificent with each passing mile. Everywhere they looked they could see verdant meadows dotted with farmhouses that had identical window boxes overflowing with geraniums, and one neat little village after the other, all with identical whitewashed churches topped with red tiled roofs.

Balu was not at all prepared for his first glimpse of the Alps. He clutched Janaki's arm at the sight of the majestic peaks — snow-capped, jagged pinnacles whose crazily serrated outline stretched across the width of the horizon. Ten minutes later he was still holding her arm as she leant on him, craning to get a good view; they were both awestruck by the sheer scale of the mighty range and the way it had presented itself so suddenly.

Balu was the first to speak, squeezing her arm as he did so. 'One day we will have to make a trip to see our own Himalayas. Their grandeur will be unsurpassed even by this, I am sure of that.'

Janaki just nodded and they continued to look out together, all the while listening, like the others on the coach, with rapt attention as Thierry regaled them with every sort of Alpine information, from geological data to the conquering of individual peaks. He gave them drama too, touching on avalanche stories and rescue missions, occasionally throwing in titbits about the favourite ski destinations of the British Royals.

It had been an exhilarating drive and as they approached Neuschwanstein, Balu, if asked, would have described himself as tired. The visual spectacle had been unending and in some inexplicable way had drained him of energy, as if all of it had been spent in the surge of excitement, in the constant drawing in of his breath at every new and wondrous view that presented itself as they headed deeper into the Bavarian Alps. Then, almost as if nature's canvas was not enough, the sky was filled with graceful hang gliders, dozens of them soaring, circling and dropping only to catch the wind and rise again. As they climbed daringly higher, the fluorescent colours on their wings caught the sun now and again, sending out brilliant explosions of blinding light. Thierry soon spotted and pointed out the distant and very high mountain meadow from which the hang gliders where launching themselves. What pastimes these Westerners invented for themselves, thought Balu, as they drove past a large field where the hang gliders were making their rather clumsy landings.

It was at lunch that Inder accosted Balu, sliding up closer on the bench next to him, as soon as their wives had ordered and disappeared in the direction of the toilets. They were seated outside an inn at the little village at the very foot of Neuschwanstein Castle. All four of them had ordered the potato and bacon soup that Thierry had recommended as they pulled into Neusch-wanstein in time for lunch.

'Your Janaki has set the cat amongst the pigeons for me!' Inder wiped his brow with a paper napkin, dropping the cutlery that was rolled up in it as he spoke.

Balu was not sure he had heard right and he waited for Inder to continue, to explain the curious thing of which he had just accused Janaki.

Inder realised that Balu was waiting. 'For some time, Romi has been talking of doing an Open University course. Now she wants to go ahead with it. You know, after you raised a toast to your wife's decision, my wife decided to get after me last night. You called it a 'noble aspiration' but tell me, what use is it at Romi's age?'

It was the last thing Balu wanted to be reminded of. Last night his own aspirations had been far from noble; his appetite for more sexual adventure with his slumbering, intoxicated wife seemed not to have diminished and even now he knew that he could not guarantee that he would let another opportunity to have her similarly and conveniently inebriated slip by. Janaki had woken him in the middle of the night talking loudly in her sleep about Mrs Bhaskaran, tossing her head on her pillow as she called out to her, pleading for one extra day to fill out application forms. Balu had propped himself up on one elbow and watched his wife writhe with the anxiety that the dream was causing, and his own arousal at seeing her toss and turn was quelled only when she turned and flung out her arm, catching him painfully with her ring on the bridge of his nose.

Balu stroked the sore spot on his nose as he tried to fob off Inder. 'No education is ever wasted.'

'But see what it did to my daughters! Nowadays they are even dating, white fellows

at that, too. They have become so independent, with good jobs and salaries of their
own, that we have no control, no say in their
lives.'

'It's the environment they grew up in, not
their education.'

'I tell Romi sometimes that we sealed their
fates and ours when we educated them. My
daughters went to grammar school, you
know. They are very clever girls — too clever,
in fact. They want their mother to have an
education now.'

'What does she want to study?'

'Oh, her daughters will choose something
for her.' Inder looked resigned.

Balu thought about Janaki's outburst, her
declaration about completing her degree. It
was a strange thing for her to have said out of
the blue, never having expressed such a desire
even when Mrs Bhaskaran had tried long ago
to influence her into joining evening classes
for mature students at the university.

'Everything has to have a purpose, even
education,' said Balu, speaking his thoughts
out aloud.

'So your wife is planning to work after she
completes her degree?'

'No. I mean no she wasn't really being
serious. You know how women are. I think
she just has a bit of a complex sometimes. You

see, her father married her off before she could complete her degree.'

'My Romi has no education really, you know. Just schooling — up to the eighth class. She was content enough for a long while. I think my daughters are secretly ashamed of her. Not of their mother herself, but the fact that she has no education. It would make them feel so much better if she had. But how could I ever tell her that? All three of them, mother and daughters, would be at my throat.' Inder laughed.

Balu felt sorry for this man with his difficult daughters. Thank God for Ram. He would never dream of creating trouble between his father and mother. Moreover, he had been taught to respect his mother for what she was, *as* she was. Balu would not have expected anything less from him.

'It is a difficult situation,' said Balu, his sympathy genuine.

'So what will you do?'

'If I were you?'

'No, I meant your situation — you just said it was difficult.'

Balu was about to correct the misinterpretation, keen to put right the impression that he had a problem with Janaki, but the two wives had come back, deep in conversation which they ended very pointedly as they arrived at the table, exchanging a laugh and a look as they sat down.

'What have you been saying about me, Romi, eh?'

'Oh, this and that. The same sort of things that you have been saying about me.'

'Made for each other we are — right, love?'

'I was telling Janaki that we should share a horse carriage to take us to the top.'

Inder shook his head. 'I've had enough of sitting. I want to walk around and stretch my legs. Don't forget Romi, once we get back into that coach, we won't be stopping till we get to Innsbruck.'

Balu looked at Janaki, but she spoke before he could say anything.

'I want to see the inside of this fairytale castle.'

Balu made up his mind quickly. He felt that he had unfinished business with Inder, matters that he needed to clarify. The last thing he wanted was to appear to be like Inder, confused by his wife, unable to take firm charge of his own domestic situation.

'Why don't you ladies go together?' he suggested.

It was not until a good while later that Balu was able to steer the conversation with Inder back to where he wanted.

'Are these Open University courses expensive?' They were back at the inn where they had lunched, for it had taken them a mere twenty minutes to walk around the tiny village that was really a cluster of a few small souvenir shops, cafés and extensive public toilets for the numerous tourist coaches that seemed to keep pulling up. They had managed to carry on walking for a further half an hour by strolling a short distance up the path leading to the castle.

'There are grants available for women like my Romi. It is not only my daughters, you see. Nowadays the Home Office also wants us immigrants to integrate.'

'At least that is some sort of reason. Janaki has no need to be bothered with education at this stage of our lives. Moreover things are different in India. She has a busy household to run, servants to supervise. It is not like the old days any more. The servant class are not what they used to be, not at all. Janaki is always saying they sap her of all her time and energy. Of course, supervision is the key.'

'Sounds like personnel management is what she should be studying.'

Balu laughed aloud. 'It will be enough if she just takes a few vital tips from me. Run the house like I run my branch office. Keep them all busy is what I say. Idleness is the root of all problems.'

'Just think, in my line of work I supervise

idleness! Sometimes I think that's what the Drop-in Centre is about.'

'Oh, but it is different when one is old. The aged have earned their time off.'

'I have to say, your Janaki sounded very serious last night. Romi was full of admiration for her.'

'Even if she was contemplating it, Janaki will soon realise it is not practical. So many other tasks need her attention.' Then a thought struck Balu and he brightened up considerably. 'What if we have grandchildren soon? Not that Ram and Viji have decided to start a family, of course, but Janaki must be available to give a hand with the child if needed. They both work, my son and daughter-in-law. Highly educated, both of them, with good jobs. You see, Janaki has to think of the future. Of what use will her degree be to Ram and his wife?' Balu gave a satisfied sigh. If it were so obvious to him, there wouldn't need to be any arguments. Even Inder was nodding quietly and Balu was sure it was because he had absorbed the logic of it all.

★   ★   ★

The approach to Innsbruck, heading into the Austrian Alps via a most spectacular high mountain pass, surpassed anything the Allsights group had seen earlier, and all thoughts that Balu had at Neuschwanstein of teasing out the issue, if there was any in Janaki's mind to start with, was forgotten till they arrived at their hotel. Balu waited for her to make him some tea and then sipped it slowly, trying not to watch her too closely as she unravelled her sari and then draped the towel that she had fetched for herself from the bathroom across her chest and one shoulder, before sitting down in front of the mirror to undo her hair and begin the ritual of freshening up.

He looked on impassively as she combed out the switch of false hair that she used to give her bun more volume. Years ago, when Janaki had first realised that her long hair was slowly beginning to thin, she had begun the painstaking task of collecting the dropping strands every single time she combed her hair. She would pull out the hairs that had fallen and become entangled in the teeth of her comb, placing them in a drawstring bag that she had made for that very purpose and which she had hung on a small nail on the wall beside her dressing table.

A couple of years later when she had collected roughly four or five well-stuffed bags of hair, she had told the old man Patta to remember to send the false hair man to the house next time he came selling his wares in the locality. A few weeks later, the man called at the house and at first, tried his very best to just buy the hair off Janaki. He weighed the bags and offered her a good rate but she was adamant that she did not want to sell it, but instead wanted him to fashion a long switch for her. He agreed finally, telling her that it would take a day or two. She had laughed knowingly, informed him that she was no fool and told him if he wanted her business he would have to sit on the verandah and make it while she watched, ensuring that he did not substitute some other hair of inferior quality for her own.

The false hair man knew he had met his match and that he was not going to make a sizeable profit out of the collected hair as he had hoped, for he could tell at a glance that it would make a lovely long switch. He had sighed dramatically and immediately begun negotiating for a free meal to be included in his fee. It would take the better part of the day to comb out so many bags, he said as he set out his equipment on the verandah on a clean bedsheet provided by Janaki.

Balu remembered the incident well for he had been inside the house, listening to snatches of the conversation as he read the

Sunday papers, glad that his wife was no fool and satisfied that all the prudence that he had encouraged in her had been worth the effort. He had turned a blind eye, difficult though it had been, when she had not only given the man tea and bread to eat but also plied the fellow with a cup of coffee to finish off with when he had completed his handiwork.

That switch of hair had been lovingly cared for all these years. It had been washed, dried and combed like she would the hair on her head. Now, having put the switch away, she massaged her scalp with her fingers for a few minutes and then began to comb out her hair.

'You should start collecting hair again,' Balu remarked. 'That false piece is so old.'

Janaki laughed. 'Is that what you have been thinking about? You looked so serious, I thought you might have had something important on your mind.'

'Will you?'

'Huh, I won't have to collect for as long this time. Look at my hair, the way it falls out nowadays is shocking. It is beginning to go grey here and there too. Ram was saying that I needed to have more vitamins. Take supplements is what he said.'

'That will not stop the greying. We are

growing old. Just accept the changes gracefully is what I say.'

'He meant for my falling hair.'

'There is an age for everything.'

'Yes, yes.'

'Some things are beyond us now. We just
have to accept it. Some opportunities passed
us by long ago.'

'And some are still waiting to be taken.'

She had stood up as she retorted this and
was heading for the bathroom, a wooden look
on her face. So she had realised what he was
trying to say! Did that mean she really was
hankering to complete her degree? Balu had
been so glad when the Bhaskarans had gone
to live with their son in America. But it
looked as if the seed that that interfering
woman had sown had come to bear fruit after
all.

If they had been back in Madras, he would
have brought a swift end to this unnecessary
drama, these grand public declarations that
Janaki had made without even the courtesy of
discussing it with him. But he wanted a
peaceful holiday, a pleasant few days more to
enjoy without having to put up with her
peeved silence and her cunning headaches,
which he knew would surely follow if he
pursued the matter. It would be awkward as
well, with the Singhs now so friendly with

251

them, if Janaki were to retreat into a bad mood.

He followed her into the bathroom intending to rinse his tea cup, and found that she was at the sink, her face lathered, groping for the taps. She had hung away the towel that had covered her so modestly, and as she bent over the sink to wash off the soap, he had an urge to hold her by the hips and press himself hard against her, into her.

When she came back into the room washed and refreshed, he had already changed into his *lungi* and was in bed.

'Lie down for a while, it will be too late after dinner,' he said in explanation. Once under the sheets, she shuffled up her petticoat and waited dutifully, closing her eyes serenely the way she always did if it happened to be daylight.

9

Janaki woke refreshed, the first time she had done so in the last few days. She was immediately glad that she had decided the previous night at the optional Tyrolean Folklore evening that Balu had booked them into, to stay away from any sort of liquor, refusing point blank to even try the free drink in shot glasses that was being handed around by two very large women dressed in traditional ensemble. It was also a pleasant relief to know that their suitcases did not have to be packed and ready outside their room doors by dawn for collection by the porters, and that they did not have to have a rushed breakfast. It had been difficult, she had found, to summon up an appetite at that early hour and the splitting headaches from which she had suffered for the last few mornings had not helped at all. It was nice to know that the routine would be relaxed for the next three days while the tour halted in Innsbruck.

She turned, almost contentedly, on to her side and looked out of the large picture window at the mountains. They had been fortunate to get a room with such an incredible view. Not everyone had been as lucky and Balu had been smug at dinner when the Chicago ladies had compared notes and expressed their disappointment to Thierry. Janaki had taken a strange liking to the four women who had revealed themselves, on a shared carriage-ride up to the castle at Neuschwanstein as rich divorcees, holding up in proud unison the small lapel pins on their jackets. These, on closer inspection, had turned out to be a very firm fistful of dollars.

Janaki had been taken aback by this the brazen declaration of their status while Romi found their attitude hilarious.

'Hush money,' they said, explaining the significance of the little badges. 'We went quietly.'

'You were lucky you had rich husbands.' Romi was itching for the details, digging Janaki in the ribs very discreetly, as if warning her to prepare for scandalous revelations.

But the Chicago ladies dealt with the comment with just a single-worded acknowledgement.

'Very,' they said.

Then it was their turn and they got to the point very quickly, firing questions at Romi and Janaki, curious to know if the two had

had arranged marriages, wanting to know all the terrifying details about having to marry a man chosen for them, rather than by them.

Romi shrugged. 'I didn't know any different. You see, I was only seventeen and I was told England was a beautiful country with a television in every house. I had just sixteen days to dream about it before I was married. Of course, when I arrived I only noticed the cold. I used to make Inder warm his hands over the radiant heater before I would let him touch me!'

Janaki was embarrassed. Perhaps they would expect her to make a similar very personal and funny revelation. She felt a sense of déjà vu, as if she was back with her sisters, listening to their coarse stories and unable to contribute anything interesting to the discussion. In her mind's eye she could also picture women she had met on other journeys, in trains and on coaches, who had unburdened their secrets, entrusting her with them so confidently, knowing they would never meet again. What if I told this lot here that, while my husband was consummating the marriage, I was praying fervently with my eyes shut?

She hadn't expected them to laugh so loudly when she did.

'Actually my dear, I never ever *did* stop

doing that,' said one.

'I didn't get this halo for nothing!' added the oldest-looking of them.

By now Romi had her hands to her mouth, stifling her laughter, signalling urgently to them that the carriage driver appeared to be concentrating hard on their conversation.

'What the hell! If he understands English, let's give him something to think about,' said one of the Chicago ladies, after which there was a free-for-all, with wild revelations exchanged loudly amidst much giggling and tomfoolery. Though Janaki had nothing personal to contribute, she enjoyed the harmless ribaldry and forgot herself in the moment. Thinking back on it now, she could only envisage Balu's horror if he knew how she had behaved, abandoning all her normal decorum to recount tales that her sisters had once shocked her with. It had seemed just the thing to do then, but now lying in bed in Innsbruck a day later, Janaki was amazed at herself. Laughing as she had in the company of those four divorcees!

'Can you imagine, their husbands have left them and they have that attitude?' she had said to Romi later as the two of them stood admiring King Ludwig's amazing bedroom in Neuschwanstein Castle.

'You mean being happy?'

'Yes. We would be ashamed to even admit it. Divorce is a terrible thing.'

'They don't think like us Indians. We put up with so much, sometimes too much, before admitting that our marriages are failures. And after all that we still stay together.'

'I am sure being divorced must be harder than being unhappy,' countered Janaki.

'Money makes it easier. My daughters are always talking about it.'

'Oh? I thought you said they weren't even married.'

Romi laughed, clutching Janaki's arm. 'No, not about divorce, but about money. They have a word for it — 'empowering' or something. Inder can't stand that kind of talk. However he has no option but to put up with it. At one time no school was good enough for his girls and look how it has backfired on him. Now, would you believe it, my girls are after me to get an education. I never finished school, you see — marriage came in the way.'

'What do they want you to do?'

'You mean education-wise? Oh, they want me to train to be a translator. Conversational, you know — Punjabi to English, English to Punjabi. My daughter Rupinder, the Immigration Officer, she says there is a great need for Asian language translators, particularly at

Heathrow Airport.'

'Have you decided?'

'Can you imagine me translating for these poor unsuspecting fools arriving from Punjab? Do you know what I'd do? I'd tell them to go back! I'd tell them quietly, in Punjabi, that there are no servants here and that it pisses with rain all the time! That's what gets me, you know, the bloody rain and all the bloody weather talk all the time.'

Janaki winced at the crude language but Romi carried on earnestly' 'I admire your husband. I think men in India are in actual fact more progressive than our men here. Your Balu toasted your decision and yet just look at my Inder — so very unenthusiastic about his daughters' plans for me. If he at least showed some small interest, it would be an encouragement for me.'

Janaki just nodded. How wrong Romi was. She had been fooled by Balu's behaviour, which was a cruel mockery, his punishment for her speaking out so boldly and singing publicly, couched in a way that only Janaki would interpret correctly.

'That night you said you wanted to complete your degree.'

'Yes, I did say it but when you think of it carefully, it will be a waste of time I am sure,' answered Janaki, suddenly sensing the futility of it all.

Balu would demand a reason before he would agree to it. For him everything had to have a logical motive, and what was she going to be able to dig up in her favour? That she wanted distant, now-migrated Mrs Bhaskaran to be proud of her? That would go down well with Balu! That she wanted the American missionaries to shake hands with her and compliment her on her speeches? Balu hated them with a vengeance. Janaki thought sadly, I am not even clever enough to think up valid grounds for wanting to finish my degree in History. And imagine if I failed again. Balu, being Branch Manager now, would not be able to bear the shame.

Romi interrupted her dejected thoughts. 'Why do you say waste?'

'Oh, it is not like what your daughters want you to do. Their idea for you has a definite purpose, mine has none really.'

'If it is irrelevant, then don't finish it. You could do something new. Otherwise can you imagine me, I will literally have to go back to school — I'm only an eighth-class pass, you know. I can tell you that in confidence, but most of my friends and neighbours think I finished school.'

'Something new, at my age?'

'There must be things that you enjoy doing.'

They had wandered out onto the ramparts, and now it was obvious why the views from the castle were so beloved of the Mad King Ludwig, who had commissioned the building of this multi-turreted, enchanting palace which was the inspiration for Disney's fairytale trademark.

Janaki thought hard as they took in the vista. My house and my home is all I know about, she acknowledged to herself. Anything I like to do is domestic by nature. She began to despair, convinced that all her determined resolutions of the previous night must have been fuelled by the drink she had so foolishly indulged in.

'I enjoy movies,' she said. It was the only thing she could think of.

Romi looked at her and they both laughed at the picture that her declaration conjured up.

'I wouldn't even get work as an extra.'

'Why an extra? Think big is what my daughters keep saying to each other and to me. Character actresses are in demand these days.'

Both women laughed again and as they headed off to rendezvous with the carriage for the return journey, they had an animated discussion about the latest cinema releases and the outrageous innuendo-laced song and dance sequences which had become the mainstay of the latest Indian blockbusters.

Yes, it had been an up and down sort of day yesterday, thought Janaki as she propped herself up on her elbow to look at the time on the travel clock that Balu had placed so precisely on his bedside table, positioning and repositioning it several times before he was satisfied. Six thirty! She wished she hadn't woken so early; she just did not have that weekend ability that her son and daughter-in-law seemed to have perfected, to rise early out of habit and then to doze off again after having had a cup of coffee. How all that would come to an end when their first child arrived! She looked out of the window and pondered on that exciting prospect. Ram and Viji would surely start a family soon; after all, they had been married long enough. Viji would have to give up her job for a while, but which mother wouldn't when it was a question of being there for your own child?

She shifted restlessly, smoothing her nightdress down under the sheets, her thoughts drifting to the last bits of conversation that she and Romi had had with the Chicago ladies on the return leg down from the castle. Janaki had been quiet for most of the carriage ride, her mood swinging downwards once again, all the cinema talk with Romi forgotten, once more regretting her foolish outburst after her song at the hotel in St Goarhausen.

She had consoled herself, trying hard not to let the disappointment ruin her day and attempting to look on the positive side. There was no point in pursuing that incomplete degree and in History, too. Anyway, hadn't she hated History with all those dates and names for which she had no aptitude or interest at all? Even Balu often told her she had no sense of history

But her father had insisted, she remembered it well. It fitted in with his grandiose plans of having each daughter study for a different subject, the subject and the daughter matched up by him according to what he thought were their most outstanding personal capabilities. Thus Janaki's older sister was landed with English because she had beautiful handwriting, Janaki was matched up with History because she was hardworking and one needed that ability to memorise details. The third sister was forced to do Sociology as its scientific-sounding 'ology' appealed to her father, and the youngest was made to do Fine Arts for it was obvious that she was the neatest of the four sisters.

Nobody had dared point out to Janaki's father that his notion of having a medley of degrees hung in the front room of the house was a ridiculous, meaningless fancy. Janaki felt again a twinge of the same frustration they had felt as sisters all those years ago. What was all that supposed to have achieved? He had married them all off immediately and they never had the chance of doing what he had assured them that they would do — be an accomplished group of sisters. He died basking in admiration that he was so confident he deserved and yet, thought Janaki, all that fuss about educating them had finally amounted to nothing. Haven't I managed well enough without it, she asked herself. Are my sisters any better off with their degrees? It just wasn't ever in my fate to have a useful education, she decided, and forcing it to happen will only bring unhappiness. Even just thinking about it has made me feel bitter, so why pursue the matter?

Balu stirred beside her and Janaki became alert again ready to shut her eyes if he did wake. She had never fully got rid of her inhibitions regarding sex in the daytime and though it was, thankfully, a rare enough experience, the way Balu had behaved last night, there was a chance she might be expected to oblige him now in the morning. He had acted oddly last night, trying to roll on top of her and attempting to lift her night-clothes himself. She had flinched in surprise and he seemed momentarily put off and a few brief minutes later had fallen asleep, snoring deeply.

I was not to blame though, she thought as she watched him now to see if he was merely stirring or if he would indeed wake. He normally was a patient man, waiting for her to ready herself before he began, but he had drunk a considerable amount at the Folklore evening, urging her all along to at least sample the free drink that was being handed out, and then to compound matters, she was sure that he was annoyed with her for having refused.

When he did wake up a quarter of an hour or so later, he caught her off guard as she was looking out of the window thinking about the four divorcees from Chicago.

'What is this Romi like?' he said, startling her out of her reverie.

Janaki got out of bed to make him his tea and he propped himself up against the headboard and waited, asking her the same thing once again.

'Why?' said Janaki, curious that he had used the word 'this' in referring to Romi.

What had she done to annoy him?

'Inder was telling me about the dilemma she has put him in. Give me two tablets for my head and make sure the tea is quite strong, Janu. I tell you, keeping that poor fellow company while he drank was too much for me.'

'Why, what did he say? What has she done to him?' Janaki felt strangely protective of her new friend, whom she liked for her cheerful disposition and the way she spoke her mind so plainly.

'The daughters are part of the problem as well, I believe. They are after him to let their mother do some Open University course or the other. You see, he educated them so highly, they are ashamed of their mother now.'

'And of their father? Does Inder know what they think of him?'

'The kettle has boiled, Janu. How is it possible for me to know all that? I am only telling you what he said to me. Poor man just doesn't know how to handle the situation.'

Janaki stirred the tea briskly. 'There is no 'situation' from what I gathered. They, her daughters that is, want her to become a Punjabi translator at Heathrow Airport. You know, to help the people who arrive in London. So many of them can't speak a word of English apparently.'

'If they can't speak English, why do they come? These uneducated types are the ones that give us Indians a bad name. They should be discouraged is what I say.'

Janaki remained quiet. There was obviously something bothering him and she knew from experience that she did not have to say anything more, that he would do all the talking from now on. But he remained quiet as well, sipping his tea noisily as he liked to do when he was not in company.

'I am glad we got this room. You must spend some time looking at the view. You know, Romi may have given you the impression that it is nothing, but at the end of the day, Inder, like all of us, is just looking for some peace. After so many difficult years, bringing up a family and providing for each of them, that is all one wants. To be fair, who would want more trials and tribulations with exams and studies and jobs? Hasn't he done it all himself and then been through it again with his children? All he wants now is just some peace and relaxation with his wife.'

Janaki walked to the window and pushed the curtains further apart. The town of Innsbruck lay nestled snugly at the foot of an Alpine amphitheatre, with the tallest peaks, some over ten thousand feet, literally piercing the day's clear blue canopy above. They inspire respect, thought Janaki melodramatically, but they are cold and distant, not unlike the men we are married to. I never really stood a chance, she reflected, cracking her knuckles as she stood leaning against the curtain, taking in the view as Balu had suggested. I never stood a chance, not then, all those years ago, when Mrs Bhaskaran was after me, and not now when, for one crazy night, I was so full of bravado.

'Don't you agree?' Balu sounded impatient.

Not to answer him when spoken to was something Janaki had never dared contemplate in the early years of her marriage, and even now it was something that she reserved for occasions when he was very obviously in the wrong. Am I getting worked up on behalf of Romi or am I doing this for myself? She wondered now. Wasn't it only yesterday on the way back from that fairytale castle that I decided to forget all about it? 'Do something you enjoy,' Romi told me and I can't even think of anything. Even *that* I will have to ask him! The ignominy of it was too much and she blurted out her reply.

'Leave Romi out of it, please. I myself want to do something, but what is the use?'

'Yes, what is the use? And why, when you are so fully occupied already?'

'With what?' she said, clutching the edge of the curtain to steady hands that had begun to tremble slightly. It was just as she thought. He had pronounced it a useless idea, dismissed it the minute he heard it. Over the dull thudding in her head she heard his unfaltering reply.

'The house, the servants. What about me? And Ram and Viji? And what if they have children?'

'Ram will never object to anything I want to do.'

'Don't drag my son into this notion of completing your degree. What has come over you, Janu? What good will it do? Why unnecessarily call attention to the fact that you failed all those years ago? And even if you pass it this time, the reality is you won't get a job. Is that what you want in the end, a job? People will think I can't provide for you. And anyway, who will keep the house ticking over? Doesn't make sense on any count. Completely illogical is what I say.'

Janaki put her hands up to her ears. She was sure in the background she could hear her father and mother too, cajoling her, insisting, in fact, that she should consider marriage, the practical solution to her failure in the examinations. She also remembered Romi's suggestion.

Her voice remained steady despite the over-powering sense of being crushed. 'So many cruel words, so much said, and all I want is to do something that *I* enjoy.'

'Like what?'

She saw Balu's incredulous look and the satisfaction that followed when he realised that she was stumped for an answer. He was waiting to move in for the kill, to quash her ideas once and for all, confident in the knowledge that she wouldn't be able to think of anything at all. How right he was! She was so uselessly proficient in every domestic art. After thirty-three years what use was her cooking or tailoring to anyone except her husband, whose meals she made and whose clothes she fashioned?

'If I had some support from you, perhaps I could think of something,' she replied, and with nowhere else to go to hide her humiliation, she headed blindly for the bathroom.

'I am tired of everything and of everybody. Even you,' she added as she stumbled in and locked the door. Once inside, faced with her recklessness and the seriousness of the confrontation she had had with Balu, she was unable to control her horrified nerves. The futility of her altercation was apparent to her even before she started, so why had she gone against her better judgement? How did I manage to turn this holiday into such an unhappy time, she wondered, beside herself with misery.

She sat on the edge of the bathtub, putting her fingertips to her mouth, trying to calm the trembling at the corners of her lips, but like her hands themselves the rest of her body seemed to be convulsed with dread. It was the knowledge that she had irreversibly crossed a line in her marriage, challenging her husband, expressing her dissatisfaction outright without turning to the safer recourses, her normal weapons of silence and headaches.

She did not know what would follow an outburst like that, though one thing was certain — peace would be a long time returning. She sat still, straining to hear to any movements coming from the room. Balu must still be on the bed, shocked and angry, she supposed. How long would it be before he demanded that she come out, if only for him to use the toilet? Would they go out at all today? Balu had arranged to meet up with Inder and Romi for lunch and then to do a walking tour of Innsbruck. She felt tired and wished she hadn't picked the bathroom to run away to. I should have just got back into bed again and turned my back to him, she decided.

She wrung her hands feebly, feeling sorry for herself. The sharp emotional eruption, so hasty on her part, had now left her with an awful reality to face. She would have to put up with a relentless barrage from him, all very familiar. There would be his long patient sermons to listen to as they ate, interspersed with pointed kindnesses all throughout the day, which would all in all be too difficult for her to bear. She stiffened suddenly; she could hear him moving around, unzipping his suitcase. Should she open the door if he knocked? Or should she dig herself deeper into this pointless hole? She shrank, as shortly afterwards she heard his footsteps approach the bathroom, and then listened in astonishment as he walked on past and opened the door to their room instead. A few seconds later she heard the scrape of the keycard being taken out of its slot and finally the closing of the door behind him.

Where could he have gone at this hour? Maybe he was looking to see if a newspaper had been left outside their door, or maybe he hadn't really stepped out, and was still in the room. She was listening carefully, her ear to the door, when the lights went out abruptly. So, he had indeed gone, taking the room keycard with him, automatically turning off the electricity by doing that.

The windowless bathroom was pitch dark and she felt her way back to the bathtub, sitting on the edge as she had done earlier. She could open the door and step out into the room, but she was weary and wanted to postpone for as long as possible the inevitable confrontation that would follow when he returned. I wish I could sleep, she thought. She longed for a deep dreamless sleep, the kind she managed to have with satisfying frequency in Madras. She didn't know what made her grope for the stack of thick fluffy towels that she knew were on a shelf just above the tub. She shook one out and laid it inside the tub. Placing the remaining towels at one end of the tub, she climbed in; lying down with her feet drawn up, so that she would fit, and adjusting the towels into a pillow-shaped pile under her head, she closed her eyes. The bathtub wasn't the quietest of places to try to get some sleep; the darkness and subsequent loss of one sense seemed to make the others far more acute, and she was aware of every single whoosh, rattle and rumble of water as showers, taps and flushes in other rooms nearby, on floors above and below, came to life as the occupants woke with what seemed to be a gathering momentum for, after a while, the sound of plumbing in operation was non-stop.

Perhaps that was what finally lulled her into a short sleep, and when she woke her heart skipped a beat, for the lights had come back on again. Balu was back in the room and here she was, still lying in the tub. She listened again, trying very hard over all the sounds emanating from the bowels of the hotel, to see if she could guess what he was up to. She rubbed her cheeks against the soft towel-pillows as she shifted her position, stretching herself out and letting one leg hang over the edge of the tub. She had once heard Mrs Bhaskaran boast about staying in a conference hotel where even the bathrooms had telephones. She wished this one had. She could have spoken to Romi or maybe rung room service for some coffee. Janaki remembered with a thirsty longing that she had been about to make some for herself, when instead, all of this had happened. Of course Mrs Bhaskaran would never have shut herself in the bathroom and gone to sleep in the tub.

Janaki turned her head away from the bathroom door. Though she had at times wished she were more like Mrs Bhaskaran, she couldn't bear to think of Balu being anything like Mr Bhaskaran. The latter was a man better known because of his wife's exploits, rather than for anything that he ever did. Most people did not even know what he did, that he worked diligently as an insurance agent, regularly exceeding his targets, once coming only three life policies away from winning the Agent of the Year title in his branch. However happy the Bhaskarans seemed, the neighbours were convinced they knew better and consequently Mr Bhaskaran commanded everyone's pity and nobody's respect. And yet, thought Janaki, Mrs Bhaskaran managed to hold her head up so high.

The knock on the door took her by surprise, she had been so absorbed in her analysis of the Bhaskarans. Her heart began to beat wildly again.

'Have you finished your shower, Janu?'

Janaki coughed, taken aback by Balu's mild enquiring tone. Did he think she had gone in for a shower? She stayed in the bathtub, lying very still, not wanting him to know what she was doing.

'Breakfast is in an hour's time and then we can go and look for the cuckoo clock as planned.'

Janaki stayed as she was, curled up in the bathtub not sure of what she wanted to do. As horrible a situation as it was, it was also a novel one. She wondered why bathtubs were such a rarity in India. A bucket of water and a mug was all that an Indian needed to have a bath. Of course some homes had showers, but Balu felt they added to the wasteful consumption of precious water.

Janaki found the bathtub a snug, comfortable cocoon, a secure place in which to contemplate her next course of action. Perhaps I should have my shower, she thought, let him believe that I am as calm about what took place earlier as he is. The minute she thought about it she knew exactly what she was going to do — and it was a course of action that would ensure she wouldn't have to leave the safety of the tub for another little while longer. Having made up her mind pretty fast, she proceeded systematically, shaking out and folding away the towels and putting them back on their rack. She washed out the bathtub, swirling water around all sides of it, and then put in the plug and turned on the taps, leaving the tub to fill while she carefully read the little sachets arranged on a plastic tray next to the sink. She picked up the one that said Bubble Bath and gratefully read the one-line instruction — *Shake granules out under running water.*

Janaki had never before had a soak in a bathtub; her only experience of it was visual, having seen her favourite heroes being seduced, in the main unsuccessfully, by sud-covered vamps. There was one difference however, she consoled herself, for those celluloid tubs of ill-repute were nearly always heart-shaped or circular in the very least. This was an ordinary bathtub and very respectable, one that she could safely stay in for a little while longer.

She tore open the sachet and shook out the powdery contents under the gushing hot water tap, watching in delight as masses of fragrant pink bubbles began to carpet the surface of the water. When the tub was three-quarters full she turned off the taps and then prepared to get in. Divested of her clothes, she placed her arms across her chest and shivered nervously, overcome with last-minute doubts, unsure of what all those bubbles would do to her. She wondered briefly about the morbid possibility that she might drown; after all, she had seen that happen in the movies as well. People slipped and hit their heads against the taps, or some fell asleep and went under. So she crept the few steps towards the door and pushed the bolt open silently. Just in case she thought, just in case. At least he will be able to get to me in time.

She stepped into the tub awkwardly, standing in it before squatting on her haunches for a few seconds and then, grabbing hold of the handles on either side, she sat down and stretched first one leg out and then the other, and finally let her head rest against the edge of the tub. Submerged neck-deep in the suds, she felt her body relax, and a few deep breaths later even her tense muscles slowly began to loosen up in the warm water. With that, she gathered enough courage to close her eyes like she had seen a woman doing in a picture in the hotel's guest magazine.

If only my sisters could see me now, they would be amazed at my boldness, she thought as she scooped up a handful of suds in the palms of her hands and squashed them. Janaki, like her sisters, did not know how to swim, their immersions in water having been confined to religious rites and ceremonial dips in the stagnant but holy waters of a temple tank or on the bathing *ghats* of a sacred river. Those immersions invariably took place in the early hours of the morning, fully clothed, in water that was cold and in full view of hundreds of other devotees each taking their dip before performing their own particular ritual.

Sitting confidently now in the comforting warm water, she was able to laugh at her silly fears about stepping into the bathtub, for this was tame compared to the many other immersions that she had experienced, each of which were fraught with various anxieties. The depth of the water had to be considered, while the obvious lack of cleanliness sometimes just had to be ignored. More often than not, she had found that she had to be mindful of being ogled lecherously by hangers-on, while her wet sari clung to her like a second skin. Then there was the very real possibility of encountering water snakes, and how could she ever forget the sheer terror she and her sisters had experienced when, years ago on a pilgrimage with their parents, a languid buffalo, lolling in the River Krishna, suddenly turned aggressive, charging across the fifty or so metres of muddy water that separated them from the placid-looking herd, with a speed that belied its ungainly size.

Two of her sisters, restricted by their wet saris and the drenched petticoats that clung to their ankles, had tripped and had fallen into the water screaming for their mother. Had it not been for the efforts of a party of people nearby who were in the process of immersing the ashes of their loved one, the angry buffalo might have succeeded in goring one or both of them, for the sisters lay thrashing in the shallow water, unable to get up, paralysed with fear. The mourners had reacted with astonishing presence of mind, blowing the conch shells that would have marked the passing of the departed soul to the other side, at the animal instead, waving their fists and twirling their funereal garlands of marigold and their long saffron scarves in the air. This, as intended, distracted the buffalo, stopping it in its tracks long enough for the girls to be helped up and practically dragged up the steps of the *ghats* to where they were reunited with the rest of their traumatised family.

Janaki remembered the incident very well, for it was the only time she had seen her mother stand up to her father, defending her daughters and openly berating him for losing his temper with them. The family had returned to their lodging house immediately knowing that they would have to face their father's fury, for he had already shown as much of his impatience as he could in front of the crowd that had collected around them. As expected, no sooner had they entered the room than he had set upon the two sisters, telling them they should be ashamed of the ruckus they had created.

'What will people think? That I can't look after my own family?'

The girls had been unable to comprehend his attitude and all four had immediately dissolved into more tears. It was at this point that their mother had intervened, first shooing her four cowering daughters away into a corner of the room. Then in one short burst of temper, releasing all her own pent-up emotions caused by the few minutes of terror, she shut her husband up totally, her outburst so cutting that in a few minutes he had left the room. Then she had started to tremble, shaking like a leaf while her daughters sat silent and fearful, too scared to approach her and not knowing what would follow on their father's reappearance.

Her father had returned in half an hour and brusquely informed them that he had just ordered lunch for them all in the Udipi lunchroom across the road. As they shuffled out of the room, it was as if nothing had happened at all. Over lunch, he alone spoke, none of the women daring to say anything, not being able to gauge what his real feelings were behind the charade of normality. He told his daughters that they should be thankful that it was not a river crocodile that had attacked them. In a large river like the Krishna, he said, pushing the plate of steaming hot tomato rice towards his wife, it was not uncommon for pilgrims to be dragged under, grabbed by the ankles by fearsome creatures who had got a taste for human flesh on account of the number of bodies that were immersed uncremated in the holy waters. Not all families could afford the cremation, he explained. As he spoke to his daughters, he was watching his wife from the corner of his eye, to see if she would partake of the face-saving peace offering that he had pushed towards her

'Your father is right,' said Janaki's mother, serving herself. 'We have much to be thankful for.'

With that conciliatory statement, the rest of the pilgrimage continued as if nothing had transpired between her parents.

Janaki sighed loudly, sending bubbles skittering across the bathtub. Perhaps this immersion in warm water was a ritual in its own right. Maybe when she was finished, she would have an indication of how she should proceed. Should she placate Balu like her mother had done to her father? Janaki felt she had nothing to gain from doing otherwise. Right now she just wanted to stay in the bathtub for a while longer, loving the novel sensation of being suspended in water so safely. The bubbles had begun to diminish in size and the layer of froth had thinned out, when she heard Balu outside the door again.

'Are you finished, Janu?'

Janaki shut her eyes, not knowing what to

say. What would he do if he realised how she had wasted away so much time, while he had been harping on about being late for breakfast?

'Janu?' He was knocking impatiently now.

She could hear him try the door and she kept her eyes shut, her pulse racing in trepidation. She heard him step in and he must have stood there, barely a few feet away, for a good half a minute before edging closer. She could hear him exhaling heavily and then sensed him right beside her, for she could smell the tea that he had drunk earlier. She was sure he was kneeling beside the tub. Could he possibly see her eyelids twitch, she wondered, trying to keep her breathing as natural as possible. She tried to concentrate on what he was mumbling; he sounded upset. The water rippled and she knew that he had put his hands in, and it was when he reached out for her under the surface of the water, his fingers touching her breasts that she sat bolt upright, her eyes opening just in time to see him jump back in shock and then quickly get up and leave the bathroom, visibly upset and trembling.

He must have feared the worst — that I was dead, she thought to herself.

'I am okay,' she called out to him. 'I was

just about to get out.'

She began to feel remorseful as she pulled out the plug, standing up in the bath and hurriedly turning on the shower. Janaki had no doubts that Balu was genuinely upset at seeing what he thought was her lifeless form; it was obvious from the way he had staggered out of the bathroom, choking with relief. Having analysed his reaction to her satisfaction, a warm glow of contentment began to spread over her. As she briskly towelled herself dry, she tried again to picture the look on his face. She had never thought he would be as distraught at losing her as she would have been if Balu had died. It was a pleasant surprise to know that her despair at such an unfortunate fate would be matched by his, if it should befall him.

By the time she came out, he seemed to have composed himself and hurried past her in his normal matter-of-fact manner, fussing with the stiff zip on his new leather pouch as he headed for the bathroom.

'We must leave in the next twenty minutes,' he ordered as he shut the door behind him.

She nodded her head, glad that the transition to normality had been so smooth. It was only much later, as she was finishing her breakfast and thinking about the events of the morning, that she recalled her sudcovered nudity and found herself feeling sorry for Balu. She knew what her husband thought about women who indulged in *that* sort of thing.

10

Irritated though he was, by the notion of having to buy a present for his detestable brother-in-law, it was definitely the cuckoo clocks that had kept Balu going for the last few days. His natural fascination with their mechanisms, some of them simple, others with ingenious and complicated inner workings, and the sheer variety of them, not all with cuckoos, provided a welcome diversion from the prevalent confusion in his own troubled mind. It was in Innsbruck, four days ago, that Janaki had begun her search for a clock that would be good enough for her brother and yet come within the budget that Balu had set aside. For though Janaki's brother had insisted in his detailed letter, that arrived in Madras from Jamshedpur by Registered Post a few days before they had left for London, that he would of course pay for it, Balu knew that no money would ever change hands.

Janaki had immediately sprung to her brother's defence. 'At least he didn't overlook his duty as an uncle. Didn't he come for Ram's wedding with his whole family?'

How could Balu forget his brother-in-law's loud presence at the wedding? But at least the man's sons had turned out well, impressing many an elderly person attending the ceremonies, their details being mentally filed away by several interested parties on account of their handsome looks and quiet demeanour, their engineering degrees, their steady but transferable jobs in Calcutta and their obvious eligibility. Balu himself would have rated them very close to Ram.

But when the latest letter arrived, Balu had been deprecating. At this stage in his life, why would the silly fellow want a cuckoo clock? Did he not realise how awkward it would be to carry something like that back?

'I tell you, Janu, has he any knowledge of aircrafts, of international travel? It is nothing like him arriving in Madras by train, with his bundles of bedding, water carriers and huge steel trunks. We had to hire three coolies the last time we went to pick him up from the station.'

Fretting at Balu's comments, Janaki who had managed to fold and refold the letter into a tiny square by then, unfolded it painstakingly. 'He does say here 'if it is not too much trouble'.'

Now, standing outside Lucerne's famous department store Bucherer, Balu felt his

286

irritation with his brother in-law return again.

'We have three days in Switzerland,' Janaki had replied confidently to Balu's warning earlier that day as they left Innsbruck, that she had no choice but to make up her mind and pick up something in Lucerne before they left for Paris.

'Just choose something suitable quickly,' he had snapped. 'Haven't we seen enough of them?'

She had looked at him in surprise almost, shaking her head in disagreement. 'Suitable is what is difficult. The one we saw the first day, that beautiful one with the double windows, you didn't like. One cuckoo is enough, is what you said. Yesterday, I liked the small one with the blue and pink cuckoo and you said it was not natural. Is it my fault that I am unable to find something that you and my brother will like? Anyway, he wanted a Swiss cuckoo clock so I am glad that despite all that looking, we did not find anything in Innsbruck.'

Balu was annoyed that she should even think that her brother's tastes would match his. When he had thrown in that reminder about the clock to her from the other side of the bathroom door in the hotel in Innsbruck, he had intended it to be a sort of a lifeline, a face-saving way for his wife to emerge from the bathroom. It had been difficult, but when at first she had shut herself in the bathroom, he had chosen to ignore her outburst. Over the years Balu had realised that it was the best course of action, for to give her irrational bouts of unhappiness any attention would have made her think they were really worthy of consideration.

He had left her in the bathroom, having decided not to force her to come out and thus give her an excuse for further grievance. Instead, he had hurriedly pulled on his trousers and shirt from the previous day and flicked a comb through his hair, for a flash of inspiration occasioned by his urgent need had directed him to go down one flight of stairs where he had used the toilet in the hotel lobby instead. He was not surprised that Janu was still in the bathroom when he returned — in fact he was glad. He could ignore her for a little while longer and then, when he deemed it time enough, he had gone on to mention the wretched clock to her. Much later, when she had still had not responded, Balu had lost patience and when he finally tried to force open the door he was surprised to find it had not been locked after all.

That was four days ago and Balu had still not got over the shock of seeing her lying so unexpectedly in the bathtub, her breasts floating like water lilies on the surface of the water. He had knelt beside the tub, gazed on her with his mouth dry, his breath getting shorter as he reached into the water, a man possessed, wanting to brush her nipples with his fingertips and watch them stiffen, before sucking them deeply into his mouth. But she had spoilt his moment by waking up, splashing his face as she sat upright so suddenly and saying something about being okay. The spell broken, he had fled the bathroom horrified that he had been so close to being discovered lusting after her in that manner.

But it hadn't been easy to just shake off what he had seen. He had stood by the picture window in the room, trying to overcome the crazed urge to ask her to stay where she was so that he could do as he pleased with her breasts. Maybe I could even join her in the bath, he thought, desperately trying to work out some way of catching the opportunity before it passed by. The gurgling of the water as it emptied out of the bathtub brought him back to reality. But ever since that morning he had grown obsessed with that sudsy image of her, and nothing they had done or seen in Innsbruck was able to divert his mind from the unattainable yearnings that it stirred in him.

His face masked by apparent interest in all that the optional excursions had to offer, he was part of the Allsights group only in body as they ventured beyond Innsbruck exploring Austria, for his mind was pleasurably occupied with his fantasies; in his mind's eye the bathtub had become more spacious — a heart-shaped one even, like he had seen in so many Indian movies. He imagined Janaki in watery repose, oblivious as always to what was going on, her eyes shut like on those first two nights when she had had too much to drink. Time and again, he wondered if he could get her to drink once more, but despite his best efforts, Janaki stuck to her decision and would not let herself be persuaded.

It was a cause of even greater irritation to him, that when Janaki had eventually emerged from the bathroom that day, she had, as predicted by him, seamlessly reverted to her normal self, and it was as if nothing had troubled her at all. All that melodrama was for nothing. The next time I will not be so tolerant, he thought, for look where it has got me.

Right now, as he recollected the frustration of the last few days, he was standing waiting for Janaki to come out of Bucherer, the famous Swiss store that had enticed them all with discount coupons and free maps of

Lucerne, which Thierry had obligingly handed out as their coach had driven into the city. Standing outside the impressive old building, looking up at the many floors that it boasted, Balu was sure that in here his wife would find the clock that she wanted.

They had wandered around the store with Balu clutching onto the discount coupons, but he had soon grown exasperated with Janaki's inability to make up her mind in the vast clock section. Once there, she had presented him with option after option, pointing to various sizes and models, boldly lifting the heavier models and examining them closely, unnecessarily reading the guarantee cards and operating instructions but never accepting his opinion or making up her own mind. He had had enough of it, and handing her the wad of coupons he had told her brusquely that he would wait outside.

Balu was well aware that to put up with her indecision was a self-imposed punishment, for he normally would never have tolerated such dithering from her. But allowing her to pick the clock had kept her occupied for the last few days, leaving him in peace to mull over his own turmoil. As each day passed since Innsbruck, he had found it more and more difficult to cope with the gap between his fantasies and the depressing reality. He would have continued in the same vein, his erotic thoughts mingling with self-pity for his predicament as he stood outside the grand façade of the Bucherer store in Lucerne, if it hadn't been for a hearty slap on his shoulder.

It was Inder. 'You will be pleased to know that she has paid for the clock. She picked the Heidi one, with the double cuckoos. She and Romi are now selecting watches for our daughters.'

Balu was both relieved at the news and annoyed that Janaki's saga with the clock and his own exasperation regarding it had somehow registered with the Singhs.

'Come on, it is no use standing here. I told them when they finish to walk along the lake till they see us. I'm sure you need a drink.'

Balu readily agreed, for it was more pleasant to listen to Inder grumble about Romi and his two daughters than to dwell on his own unfulfilled desires. Within minutes they were seated on a bench, can of beer in hand, facing the many splendid yachts and boats moored at the marina on Lake Lucerne.

'Much hazier on the lake today isn't it? Did you enjoy the tour to Stanzerhorn yesterday? Romi was terrified on the cable car, you know.'

Balu laughed. 'So was Janaki. She was

afraid even on the funicular railway. The gradient was so acute, she thought the little cog railway train would never make it up to the cable car station. Then once we were in the cable car, every time it lurched at those mid-air junctions, she thought we would plunge to our deaths! I kept telling her we are in Switzerland, the home of precision machinery, never mind your fears, just look at the spectacular panorama. But she was shaking by the time we reached the summit.'

'Romi had to rush to the toilets when we got up to the top.'

'Did you wonder how they managed to build that visitor centre on the summit of Stanzerhorn? All that sheet glass!'

'Yes, it was incredible. But they rushed us around a bit yesterday, don't you think?'

'The lake cruise was relaxing though.'

'Good thing it wasn't as hazy as it is today.'

Balu nodded and both men took long sips from their cans.

'Have you spoken to your son since you left London?'

'He rings us every other day. Very responsible boy, you know. Photocopied the itinerary before we left.'

'Good solid upbringing and like-minded people with the same values around you, that is the advantage of living in India. I don't know what lies ahead for mine. They're not Punjabi enough for the Punjabis and not white enough for the whites.'

Balu tut-tutted in sympathy. 'There are problem children in India as well, you know.'

'Oh no, mine are not problems. It is just that they do what they want and don't see anything wrong in that.'

'Does their mother encourage them?'

'They encourage *her* so she in turn feels she must encourage them. In our house, mother and daughters, they feed off each others' sympathy. I have to fight alone for my corner. Don't mistake me, we get on well but when it comes to gratitude — zero. I am the one who allowed them to be different, now I am part of that establishment they are making a stand against.'

Inder took a small sip from his can and Balu, not knowing what to say, followed suit. The setting sun was warm and there was something satisfying about being able to just sit around with no real purpose even if it were only for a short while. They stayed that way, looking out across the water in silence, each immersed in thoughts of what could have been, if only they had had the foresight to have moulded the women in their lives differently.

★ ★ ★

On the excursion to the Rhine Falls the next day, it fell upon Balu and Janaki to escort Sister Bernadette to the viewing points. Balu was certain that the nun had picked them for the task, waiting for them to get ready to alight from the coach before whipping out of her seat, following right behind and then talking to them constantly as she negotiated the steps of the coach. Janaki had held out her hand helpfully before Balu could say a word, but the nun chose him instead and once they had begun to walk slowly towards the thunderous falls, there was no denying the fact that Balu would be the support that Sister Bernadette would be leaning on for the rest of the morning.

'Your husband is a strong man, my dear,' she said as she weighed Balu down with each step that she took.

'Would you like me to help you too?' Janaki was beaming back at her.

'No, no, a pair of good hands is all I need and I have them right here,' she said, stopping in her tracks to pat Balu's forearm. 'You go ahead and keep my sister company. She could do with the change.'

Balu laughed feebly at Sister Bernadette's joke, his arm already beginning to feel her weight. As they got within sight of the falls, the throng of tourists was almost impassable and their own slow progress made people jostle them. The impatient ones flashed remorseful smiles when they realised that it was an elderly nun who was causing the delay, but all Balu got was curious second looks. He and the Irish nun made an incongruous pair. By the time they reached the viewing areas on the north side of the Rhine, many in the Allsights group had begun to double back. Inder and Romi were also walking back with Janaki right behind them.

'The view is better from the south side apparently,' said Inder, pointing to a castle on the cliff. 'We'll have to pay but the crowds are less and you can actually see something.'

Now Balu led the group as they turned around and just as slowly as earlier, made their way across to the Schloss Laufen. The steps down from the souvenir shop to the viewing platforms were damp with the spray from the falls, but the sight of the full might of the Rhine roaring past them, barely a few inches from their noses, was electrifying. It wasn't the height of the falls that was so impressive but the width — one hundred and fifty thundering metres wide according to Balu. The Rhine with its rising halo of misty spray was a magnificent sight. Incredibly, there were boats on the river bringing tourists frighteningly close to the falls for a view that

Balu imagined would, if one actually had the courage to look, be doubly inspiring. Sister Bernadette had let go of him and was clinging to the rail of the platform. Balu shook out his arm as discreetly as possible, flexing it above his shoulder and then down again before looking around for Janaki. He wanted Inder to take a photograph of the two of them against the backdrop of the falls.

From the far end of the platform Janaki had caught his eye and she shouldered her way towards him, her hair catching the sunlight, fine droplets of water glistening like dewdrops on the curly strands that framed her face. He had seen her look like that before. Was it ten, fifteen years ago? Ram had been left alone in Madras, so it must have been fifteen years ago. Janaki had been reluctant to come, but he had insisted that she accompany him on the Branch Office's annual employees' picnic to Kottithur Falls.

The brief monsoon had swollen the falls and yet it was a mere trickle compared to the spectacle they were standing beside today. Towards the end of the hot and humid day, the water at Kottithur, which fell from a considerable height in three distinct columns onto a rocky platform, was too tempting, and abandoning the relatively tame stream that they had picnicked alongside the whole day long, Perumal and a few others stripped to their loose *jhatis* and ventured under the waterfall, clambering across large boulders to get there. Soon, more were persuaded to walk gingerly onto the very slippery rocks, where the force of the cool water immediately took their breath away. Balu, fully clothed, his only concession to the day being his trousers rolled up to his knees, kept his distance despite repeated calls and friendly taunts from Perumal. Many of the ladies in the group, wives in the main, approached closer, laughing and ducking, turning their faces away as the force of the spray reached them, even where they stood in relative security.

For a while, there was much banter and joking back and forth and Perumal managed to persuade his wife to join him under the water. She had squealed loudly when the water hit her; her nylon sari was drenched in seconds, clinging to her every curve, her white blouse leaving nothing to the imagination. All the while she had continued to let escape small giggly screams of terror, clinging to Perumal, her arms around his neck. Later, when she had calmed down, she held her arms up near her head, constantly pushing her hair and the water away from her eyes. The effect on Perumal was obvious: the sudden and massive bulge in his wet *jhatis* was plain to see. Not many of the men that day had been able to keep their eyes off her, none daring to stare for too long in case she had the same effect on them. As for Balu, he had felt nothing but disgust at the immodest display. He had looked away towards Janaki who, embarrassed for all those around, was walking away from the edge of the Kottithur Falls, her hair covered in droplets of water that glistened in the sun, just as it was now.

Perumal had been unrepentant and unmindful of what anyone thought of him and his wife, and they had stayed on under the water, canoodling shamefully in the tiny rocky space behind the opaque curtains of water. Balu had not been surprised at the vulgarity of what he had seen, for Perumal had once boasted to him about his wife's capacity for sex. Anytime, anywhere, he had said to Balu. 'And anyhow,' he had added with a satisfied wink. Balu had been appalled at the divulgence of such personal information and had not even wanted to think about the content of what was said. But at the end of the day, it was an old friendship going back to their apprenticeship days and Balu had come to accept Perumal for what he was. Moreover, Perumal had never expected Balu to reveal anything in reciprocation. That day at Kottithur, Balu had been grateful that he did not have a wife like Perumal's who could not help oozing her sexuality so overtly.

I was so smug then, he thought, turning back to look once again at the Rhine, with my wife who was the epitome of modesty, who embodied the mythological virtuous and chaste Sati Savitri herself. Janaki would have put any celluloid version of the much-venerated legend to shame. If only I had chosen for her to be otherwise, he thought, his regrets now overcoming him rapidly, for who ever heard of a Sati Savitri who enjoyed sex? Janaki was talking to him now about getting Inder to take a photograph, trying to make herself heard over the roar of the Rhine, but all he could hear were the echoing squeals of Perumal's wife as she cavorted with her lucky husband.

★　★　★

On their last evening in Lucerne, the air of anticipation and excitement in the Allsights group was palpable. Even Thierry was in ebullient form, promising all sorts of sights and wonders to an enthralled audience gathered in the hotel bar, for the talk was of France and their much-awaited arrival in Paris the next day. Balu was finding the going tough, keeping up a semblance of good cheer

300

when he was in company, but lapsing into quiet and agonising fantasy when alone with Janaki. He had made love to her twice a day, as soon as he woke and then again before they slept, but her predictable and matter-of-fact response which he had not faulted and had considered so normal all these years, now seemed to take away from his climax.

She had sensed his moroseness and was on the edge herself, quick to take offence and not hesitating to tell the Singhs how glad she would be when they were back in Madras. Balu was a bit more animated this evening, having booked many optional excursions from the sheet that Thierry had given each of them on their arrival in Lucerne. At the start of the tour, Balu had budgeted for only two of the optionals in Paris, the trip up the Eiffel Tower and the day excursion to Versailles. The Singhs had persuaded him that the Gala dinner and cabaret show on their last night in Paris would be a fitting finale to their European tour.

'Everybody will be going,' said Romi. 'You can't miss it.'

Then, in a moment of weakness, brought on by the memory of a Tamil movie of the same name, he also ticked the 'Paris By Night' option. He told a thrilled Janaki, rather sternly, that they were well over budget so she would have to curb her spending when they got back to Norwich. When he finally handed the sheet to Thierry, he found himself being persuaded to sign up for the tour of the Louvre as well.

'The Louvre optional is the best way to be economical with your time. Less queuing, see just the highlights in the company of a knowledgeable guide,' said Thierry and everybody around nodded sagely. Balu took the sheet back and ticked the box for the Louvre.

Thoughts of being in Paris the next day cheered him up considerably and that evening he and Janaki joined a few of the others and headed for the Jewel of the East Tandoori, in Lucerne's town centre. Having lunched there the previous day, Inder and Romi had rated it high enough for a return visit, this time with Balu and Janaki and the Malaysian nurses, all of whom were longing for their first spicy meal in ten days. After a heated debate amongst themselves about the cancer-preventing capabilities of the green chilli, the Chicago ladies had decided to join them.

As they strolled towards the town centre restaurant, not far from their hotel, Balu's mood did indeed lift. It had struck him that, given the company and the high spirits everyone was in, he might actually be able to get Janaki to have a glass of wine. If I get her to sit between these Americans and at the same time opposite Romi, he plotted hurriedly, they may well persuade her. I could raise a toast to her new friends. His mind raced wildly ahead, thinking of what he would do that night in bed, confident that after she had one drink it would be easier to ply her with another.

But Janaki thwarted his every effort, choosing to drink a *lassi* instead, asking particularly if it could be sweetened with honey.

'I have this every day in India,' she explained to the Chicago ladies, taking small delicate sips from her straw. 'Yoghurt and honey, it is excellent for, you know, your morning movements.'

Upon hearing this, the Chicago ladies immediately ordered four more *lassi* with honey and the conversation stayed on the subject of constipation for a good part of the evening. Balu's attempt at raising a toast halfway through the meal was a resounding success, with much hearty and sentimental talk about breaking the boundaries of race and religion, but Janaki, encouraged by the attention she had attracted with her drink order, stuck to her *lassi*.

It was a listless Balu who walked back to the hotel along with the others. He had been unsuccessful with his plans for Janaki and he was uncomfortably full, having eaten greedily of the familiar foods, indulging in two *rossagullas* after the meal and finally agreeing to share half of Inder's *gajjar halwa* as well. Several souvenir shops were still open, and Romi and Janaki lingered outside nearly every shop, window-shopping and constantly falling behind.

'Save some money for Paris,' Inder called out to Romi.

'Now that we are here, what is the harm? We aren't buying anything,' she replied, as they disappeared into the shop they were currently looking into.

Balu knew they were looking at more cuckoo clocks, for now Janaki was obsessed with making sure that the one she had picked up in the Bucherer store had not been over-priced.

'Of course one has to pay for quality as well,' she said to Romi, countering in advance any disappointment she might feel if she discovered she had been fleeced.

Inder wandered in after them, pottering around the shop and then heading into the clock section at the back of the store. Balu stood under the awning and looked down the pedestrianised avenue, where he could see the Chicago ladies walking slowly towards the hotel. He suddenly thought of his mother and her infallible faith, recollecting the way she would look for signs and decipher them suitably when faced with a dilemma. He closed his eyes wearily and found himself praying silently, asking for release from this vortex into which he was getting irretrievably sucked. When he opened his eyes he found the neighbouring shopkeeper beckoning him.

'I have very special clocks inside,' he said. 'Come in to see. No obligation at all to purchase.'

Balu hesitated, about to just look away as if he didn't understand English, but the man persisted. 'Works of art each one. No obligation, seeing is believing.'

Intrigued, Balu followed the man into his shop and past a curtain that was pushed aside for him briefly, into a small but plush section. The shopkeeper busied himself, turning on spotlights and taking out several boxes from under the counters. These he arranged neatly to one side before he turned to Balu.

'You Arab?'

Balu shook his head silently. He wondered if Janaki and the Singhs were looking for him.

'Oh.' The shopkeeper seemed immediately deflated. He sighed. 'No extra charge for credit card, okay?'

He picked out the first clock from its box and placed it in front of Balu. He wound the arms to six o'clock and the double windows flew open. A bed emerged and to Balu's amazement the tiny naked wooden figures on the bed began a slow copulation, their cries of ecstasy ringing out six times. Balu stared hypnotised as the bed rolled back and the windows shut precisely behind them. All was silent for a few seconds and then the shopkeeper rubbed his hands.

'I have more positions, many more,' he said, aware that he had got Balu's total attention.

One after the other, every open clock window revealed a couple in a different sexual pose, performing their special act on the stroke of the hour. When all the boxes had been emptied, the shopkeeper just went back to the first and got them each going again. Within minutes the little room was resounding with joyful grunts and happy, drawn-out moans.

'Which position is your favourite? I will discount it for you,' offered the shopkeeper, raising his voice so as to be heard over the din of the fornicating couples.

'They all make the same sounds,' said Balu standing up, though his eyes remained on the last clock that was still going, the wooden man with his eyes turning heavenwards the six times his lady friend took him in her mouth.

The shopkeeper shrugged helplessly. 'I know. I have often raised that point with the supplier.'

Balu had backed his way out of the room. The shopkeeper followed him. 'Take one and I will give you the second one at half price.'

Balu stumbled out of the shop, his hands to his ears, unable to block out from his memory the sounds of uninhibited coupling going on inside the cuckoo clocks. Janaki spotted him straight away and walked towards him from the bench she and the Singhs had been sitting on.

'We had just sat down, wondering where you were. What is the matter?'

Before he could answer, there was a small commotion close to where Inder and Romi were, and a small crowd gathered around a dazed tourist, distraught at having had her pocket picked. The throng of curious onlookers peered over each others' shoulders, and watched as a couple of people gave chase in the direction of the assailant. When the drama had died down, Balu was grateful for the diversion that the incident had provided. All the way back to the hotel and as he climbed into bed beside his wife, he tried to think of how his mother would have interpreted the sign that he had received from the cuckoo clocks.

It was only the next morning, in the lobby of the hotel as they were checking out, that Balu realised it was he who was the real victim of the crime they had witnessed the previous night. His passport had gone, along with his wallet and his little steel comb that he had placed for safety in its fold. The inner pocket of his jacket had been cleverly picked as he stood gawking. He and Janaki had had their breakfast and were about to check out, with half an hour to spare before the coach left for Paris when Balu made the discovery, panic gripping his chest so tightly he thought he wouldn't be able to breathe.

Janaki noted his distress immediately. 'What is the matter? Are you okay?'

'I would be okay, we would be okay, if it wasn't for you,' he spluttered in Tamil. 'My passport is gone — stolen last night, I am sure.'

Once he had launched into it, Balu was unable to stop the hurtful tirade. 'None of this would have happened if you weren't the way you are. I wouldn't have been distracted. I would have been alert as always. Cuckoo clocks! Hadn't you already bought one for that brother of yours? What was the need to stop again? This is all your fault!' He stopped to take a breath, his eyes bulging and the vein in his temple clearly visible.

Janaki let out a small wail and sat down on a nearby sofa with her head in her hand. The Malaysian nurses who were waiting to check out behind them crowded around, asking if she was okay. Thierry was found and Balu was shaky as he explained what had happened.

Soon Inder came hurrying from the buffet area, brushing crumbs of toast off his shirt. He hovered around supportively, while Romi joined the group that had gathered sympathetically around Janaki.

Thierry was looking at his watch as he spoke. 'Your wife has her passport and half the money?'

'Yes, thank god.'

'That's something at least. There is no reason she can't carry on to Paris then. You will now have to make a police complaint first and then get your Embassy to issue you with a temporary passport. Don't worry, we have an Allsights office in Lucerne. Our local representative will look after you, sort out the police formalities and paperwork. I will let them know right away.'

Thierry rushed off to make the promised arrangements, calling over his shoulder as he went, 'Oh and also, check with your wife. Does she want to carry on to Paris?'

★　★　★

A cheerful picture of a smiling Mahatma Gandhi had been staring down at Balu for the last hour. This was the second visit in three days that he had made to the Indian Embassy in Berne. It may have been situated on an elegant avenue that housed many other grand embassies, but once past the doors, the ambience in the consular section was distinctly ordinary, and he immediately felt as if he was back in India, in one of the thousands of central government offices that kept the cogs of the administrative machinery from moving too fast. Old Air India posters and stern notices about the consular timings and lunch hours dominated the walls. Lists of fees and services were outlined in detail, with many of the printed figures for fees having been crossed out firmly and the increases penned in beside them in a flowery hand. Every notice had an authoritarian *By Order* printed at the bottom right-hand corner. Two unhealthy-looking plants that stood in wooden pot holders had umbrellas stuck into their soil, and woven into the large well-worn coir mat inside the door, Balu could just make out the large, faded motif of a woman's palms pressed together in a welcoming *namaste*.

He had taken in most of the detail on his first visit to the Embassy, arriving in Berne via train after finishing the formalities with the police in Lucerne. This had turned out to be a straightforward affair. They had been efficient, sympathetic even, but it was obvious that they considered him a fool.

He had walked into the Indian Embassy in Berne just as the window in the wooden partition wall inside the room was being bolted shut. It was the lunch hour, *By Order*. He knocked urgently on the window.

'Can I just have the forms, sir? Lost passport applications?'

'Window will open in one hour,' said an expressionless voice with a cussed finality that any Indian would know not to question. Balu settled into the worn leather sofa, clutching the envelope with copies of the police documents. Within minutes the tantalising smell of Indian food wafted through the small gaps in the partition. He could hear people, three or four of them, all talking with their mouths full, discussing the latest South Indian film crew that had arrived from Hyderabad to film in the Alps.

That first day Balu had done nothing but

311

wait around impatiently in various offices both in Lucerne and in Berne, and today was no different. He started where he had left off, continuing his detailed appraisal of the interior of the consular section as he waited for the window to open and for someone to tell him that his temporary passport was ready, as had been promised to him the day before yesterday.

Well-locked, old-fashioned bookcases lined the walls, containing the collected speeches of politicians past and present. Bound volumes of economic data, censuses and statistics packed the shelves. Copies of the Constitution, Indian civil and criminal law journals and hard cover copies of import and export regulations lay stacked against each other. There were no other callers to the consular section and Balu felt he had been singled out by fate to be the only one who needed help. Everything was so quiet, and nothing seemed to move anywhere else in the large building, and he despaired that there were any staff in attendance at all. To compound his feelings, on the other side of the partition the phone rang in vain and Balu found himself uselessly counting the number of rings. He remembered the two phone calls that had been put through to his room early this morning but which he had stubbornly refused to pick up.

Balu hadn't wanted to talk to either his son or his wife. He had found it difficult to control his irritation with Ram, who admittedly had been very concerned and had called Balu more often than necessary, all the while assuring him that under the circumstances, his father had done the right thing.

'So glad you persuaded Amma to carry on. Of course I'm surprised that she did. No, no it's a good thing. What I meant really was, she normally would be hesitant to leave you and go off on her own. The Singhs? Oh yes, she did mention the Singhs. Apparently they have been very good to her and that sort of thing. She's made some American friends as well. Yes, she was telling Viji about them. By all accounts she's having a great time in Paris, Appa. Don't worry.'

And it continued in that vein: every phone call from Ram reassured Balu that he wasn't to worry, Janaki was having a good time. 'I told Amma she was great to go on without you. She said she didn't want to waste the opportunity. By the way, don't call her today, Appa. They have probably left for Versailles and when they return to Paris, they head almost directly for a cabaret show and dinner.'

When Ram had called last night, Balu had been watching television in his room. He had been brusque with his son, not wanting to hear anything more about Janaki. 'The police have nothing to do with it any more. Haven't I told you that already? If the fellows at our Embassy give me the passport in time tomorrow, I can travel to Paris by train, otherwise I will just have to come directly to London.'

'Are you okay for money, Appa?'

'Yes, yes, I still have travellers' cheques.'

'You sound tired.'

'I am.'

Ram laughed. 'I told Viji you'd be lost without Amma and I was right!'

Balu stopped midtrack in his angry reminiscing about phone calls, for there was activity behind the window. He could hear someone typing. He went up to the window and pressed his ear against it. It had been over an hour now. Were they making the paper with which to fashion his passport he wondered. He walked back slowly to the sofa.

Thirty years ago, this was how he had waited for Janaki in an office not dissimilar to this Embassy. Waited so anxiously in the Assistant Collector's office in Allahabad. He hadn't abandoned her like she had abandoned him — going off to Paris without any remorse, her decision emboldened by the gathering support of all and sundry, who had

314

good intentions but no idea of the way he felt. It was ironic, he thought, the way the Allsights group had gathered around, promising him faithfully to mind her, look after her, she who was the cause of all his problems. Sister Bernadette was the only one who had given him any thought, pledging to say the rosary every fifty miles for the safe return of his passport.

The freshly-raked up memory of his long worrisome wait at the Assistant Collector's office peeved him even further. No, it is on the record that I did not abandon her, he told himself. She who had so stupidly got herself lost, prostrating in the dust churned up by hundreds of naked *sadhus*. What would she have done, penniless in that city teeming with many millions of pilgrims, and rife with the normal quota of tricksters that such a congregation automatically attracted? It had been a sobering experience, searching for Janaki in Allahabad.

They had arrived in the holy city early in the morning by train, carrying Balu's mother's ashes in a pot. Mrs Shankar had made the expected death-bed wish of someone so devout, asking for her ashes to be immersed in Prayag at Allahabad, the holiest of the *tirthams*, the Divine confluence of the three rivers, the Ganga, the Yamuna and the subterranean Saraswati. For over seven months his mother's ashes remained in a pot, hanging from a tree outside their house in Madras. Custom dictated that the ashes could not be brought into the house and Janaki fretted for months while Balu made the arrangements for his leave and for their three-day journey by train via Delhi to Allahabad.

Balu had wanted to head for the *ghats* to perform the immersion straight away, before they located their lodgings, so that they did not have to bring the ashes into their room. Leaving their luggage at the station they walked towards the *ghats*, Balu clutching the pot. The township around the confluence of the three holiest of Hindu rivers was teeming with hundreds of thousands of devotees, and as they walked through the narrow congested streets, the noise of nearby drums and conch shells split the air; people were held back by *lathi*-wielding stewards and pushed aside to allow a procession of over seven hundred or so *nagas*, the naked Shaiva *sadhus*, to pass unhindered. Their long, matted locks, their ash-smeared bodies and the resplendence of their total and proud nakedness was an awe-inspiring sight, and as the procession made its way towards the *ghats*, people were overcome with the emotion of having

316

witnessed these holy men at such close quarters.

The devout vied with each other to prostrate themselves fully in front of the *sadhus*. They scooped the dust from the ground and placed pinches of it on small pieces of torn paper, fashioning it into little packets to give to family and friends who did not have the good fortune to make the pilgrimage. Separated in a matter of a few minutes from Janaki in the sudden melee, Balu watched her where she stood on the other side of the road, his exasperation growing as he saw her trying to lay her hand on as many of the naked *sadhus* as she could, even bending low to try and touch a few of them on their feet as they passed by. As the procession went by a particular section of the crowd, the stewards removed their restraining *lathis* and allowed people to carry on with their business as before.

Some devotees rushed behind the *sadhus*, following them to the *ghats* to watch them take their holy dip. Many others rolled on the ground in the dust trodden on by the holy men. To think that that was what Janaki was doing when she disappeared from his line of sight, rolling on the ground, dangerously close to being trampled on by the mini-stampede in the wake of the *sadhus*!

Balu had immediately begun to search the street, looking up and down, walking briskly in and out of shops, and asking people if they had seen her. He scoured the *ghats* urgently trying to see if she had followed the naked *sadhus;* he sought her out in the winding streets, the railway station and the *ashrams* for at least four hours, running practically everywhere. Then with his mother's ashes still held to his chest he headed for the police station where he was told that the Collector's office had a special division dealing with lost people. If it had not been for a Tamilian clerk in the office, who had for some unknown reason befriended Balu, he would not have sat waiting in the anteroom of the Assistant Collector's office, waiting for news of his wife to be announced through a window in a partition wall that looked just like this one in Berne. Come to think of it, reflected Balu, a smiling Gandhi had cast his cheerful gaze on him even then.

I waited for her, he thought bitterly. She who had temporarily abandoned all her prudishness in a stroke, grovelling on the ground those seven hundred naked men had walked on. And look at her today! She had just gone, carried on to Paris, without so much as an offer to stay on with him.

Balu looked up from where he had his head

in his hand. The window was being slowly unbolted. His temporary passport was ready and was pushed towards him.

'Check it, please. Why no smile in the photograph?'

'It's not my fault, none of it is,' snapped Balu as he turned and walked away, clutching at the passport in his hand.

Epilogue

Madras, 2 October, 1999

My dear Romi,

I have wanted to write to you ever since Rupinder and John left Madras last week. Where do I begin? Let me first ask, how are you, my dear friend? I hope Inder has recovered from his daughter's wedding. Rupinder told us how his blood pressure had shot up so terribly, but what has he to worry about? Tell him both Balu and I think that John is such a nice boy. He was far more polite than most Indian son-in-laws anyway. Just imagine, he offered to cook us curry and rice! So what if he likes to cook, I told Balu. But you know Balu, he is old-fashioned in his ways.

We went with them to Madurai as planned. After that we left the honeymooners alone. Despite all the shopping your daughter did, she was quite happy to take some small things back for Ram and Viji. I really hope John likes Kerala. I was telling them four days is not enough time to see all those many miles of beautiful backwaters and the

320

lovely beaches but you know, it is the same with Ram. Never enough holidays, the poor fellow. Talking about time — can you believe, dear Romi, that it is over a year since our Europe tour? I will never forget the way you and Inder looked after me in Paris.

In your last letter you asked about my tailoring school, so let me tell you that four months on and it is still doing fine. I feel shy, calling it a school — as I charge nothing and it is just something I enjoy doing. At the moment, I have five girls, four of them are from a home for the disabled and one is my servant's daughter. They come together for their lessons, every alternate day, in the afternoons. I look forward to all their chat and girlish talk. An American charity provided the machines but I had to use some influence though — one Mrs Bhaskaran, who used to be my neighbour many years ago, pulled some strings for me from America. Can you imagine! Balu grumbles a lot if he finds my girls still in the house in the evenings, so nowadays I make sure that they have finished and everything has been tidied away before he comes back from work. Not that he is disapproving or anything like that — in fact he feels that I am making *good use of my time.*

Thank you for the photographs you sent. With all those traditional Hindu arrangements, who would believe that the wedding did not take place in India? Rupinder looked beautiful and as I was telling Balu, the main thing is that she looked happy. Now that all the fuss is over, what are you planning to do? Have your daffodils bloomed? Rupinder said you spent two days planting the bulbs at the time of her engagement. Your house and garden must have looked lovely for the wedding. Ram was saying if we ever come to England in spring he would take us to Amsterdam to see the flowers. But Balu is not at all keen on travelling abroad any more. India is good enough, he says.

To tell you the truth, things were a little difficult for him when we first got back. Not at work, of course — in fact it was his work that kept him going. He was very moody, came home very tired and had no time for anything or anyone at all. It was very confusing for me as he was quite changed and even now I don't know what was really on his mind for all those months. You know how men are — they won't say what is bothering them and still expect us to understand! But you will be glad to know Romi, that recently he has been very much better. I have been urging him to get back to walking early morning, just to keep fit at least. I read that in one of these new women's magazines. I tell you, we never had articles of this sort to read when I was newly married. You should see the things some women write and ask! Balu doesn't approve of some of the features they print. Anyway, it was in one of these magazines that I read about how to cope with men's moods and their changing needs. I cut out the pages and refer to them again and again. I hope Romi that you will not mind me telling you this, for it is quite personal. Apparently they can get dissatisfied for no reason, lose interest in many things including, you know, the intimate side of marriage. Unfortunately, that was how it was with us when we returned from Europe.

What did Balu have to be unhappy about? I will never know, and though it has taken me a long time, I think I am slowly drawing him out of his needless depression. I buy a lot of women's magazines these days. They are very good as a source for simple tailoring projects for my girls. But apart from that Romi, in the privacy of my own home, I can search for advice on many very personal topics. Of course a lot of the matters discussed are only meant for the younger ones, still there is so much to be learnt. To think that we were married off with no words of counsel except 'Be happy'!

Coming back to what I was saying at the start of this letter, I must say again that we enjoyed the company of the newly-weds. John's interest in India and his many questions did Balu a world of good and now we are looking forward to Ram's visit in three months' time.

Please write and let me know the news from your side. Rupinder said she and her sister are still trying to persuade you to pursue the idea of English-Punjabi translation. Hope you are able to decide on that matter soon. I tell you, it is so nice, there is such satisfaction in having something of your own to do. Look how long this letter is, Romi! I must end now, it is late and Balu will be home soon.

With my best regards to Inder,
Your friend,
Janaki

Janaki reached for the roll of Sellotape that she kept locked in a little steel box in the drawer of the desk. Balu insisted she kept the stationery under lock and key for the servants, he felt, had no value for things like that. She used Sellotape only on the letters that she sent abroad — to Ram and to Romi, and when she wrote the occasional courtesy letter to Viji's parents in Delhi. All her other correspondence was sealed with a few grains of cooked rice that was mashed to a paste between her fingertips and then applied expertly to the edge of the envelope. Having sealed the letter to Romi with two economically small pieces of Sellotape, she called out to Muthu. The servant maid was sent with the letter in hand to the post box at the corner of their road and Janaki headed into the bathroom to bathe.

She picked out a tiny glass bottle from the shelf in the bathroom and tapping it gently with one finger, carefully shook out just a couple of drops of sandalwood oil into a mug of warm water. How lovely it would have been to have a bathtub she thought, and to immerse oneself fully in the delicately perfumed water. Balu had been talking about renovating the house next year and maybe she could persuade him to consider installing one. She hummed softly to herself as she swirled the mug around several times before dividing the fragrant contents between two buckets of water that Muthu had filled up for her. The September issue of the *Women's Era* had recommended this particular traditional bathing routine before bedtime, and to Janaki's satisfaction the fragrance had had the desired effect on Balu, first drawing him closer to her and then like the old times she had felt his feet reach out for hers. She found herself keeping her eyes open, watching his face and rather surprised to see the pleasure she was giving him.

Tonight, before she bathed, she was first going to gently rub her body with a paste of ground rice and oatmeal — the magazine had promised it would leave her skin velvety to the touch. She knew it would be a while before she was finished, but it didn't matter if her long hair hadn't fully dried by the time Balu returned from work. She would gather up the damp tresses and tie the ends into a loose knot, just the way he liked it.